THEY RULE HOME AND HEARTH . . .

They patrol castles and barnyards, ships that sail the seas and starways. They are masters of mystery, of the hunt, and of their humans' hearts. . . . They are cats and these are some of their stories:

"Under the Sign of the Fish"—  power- ful spell change th prey?

"Every Life Shou t out practitioners of m voc, would he condemn sne con- sorted with cats?

"Death Song"—How could he protect the humans from an evil they could neither see nor feel?

A Constellation of Cats

ALIEN PETS *Edited by Denise Little.* What if all our furred, feathered, or scaled companions aren't quite what they seem to be? What if some of them are really aliens in disguise? Or what if space travel requires us to genetically alter any animals we wish to bring along? Could we even find ourselves becoming the "pets" of some "superior" race of extraterrestrials? These are just a few of the ideas explored in original tales from some of science fiction's most inventive pet lovers, including Jack Williamson, Peter Crowther, Michelle West, Jane Lindskold, David Bischoff, and John DeChancie.

CATFANTASTIC I, II, III, IV and V *Edited by Andre Norton and Martin H. Greenberg.* With fur fluffed and claws unsheathed, they stalk their prey or stand fast against their foes . . . with tails raised and rumbling purrs, they name and welcome their friends . . . with instincts beyond those of mere humans, they ward off unseen dangers, working a magic beyond our ken. . . . They are cats and you can prowl with them here in stories by Mercedes Lackey, Andre Norton, C. S. Friedman, Elizabeth Ann Scarborough, Elizabeth Moon, Charles de Lint, and many more masterful tellers of tales.

CREATURE FANTASTIC *Edited by Denise Little.* If you've ever yearned to meet such legendary creatures as dragons, unicorns, the phoenix—or even cats and dogs gifted with talents of mythological proportions, here is your chance to befriend them all. In this all-original collection some of fantasy's finest tale-spinners have woven their own unique legends, breathing new life into those most ancient of mythological beasties.

A Constellation of Cats

Edited by

Denise Little

DAW BOOKS, INC.

DONALD A. WOLLHEIM, FOUNDER

375 Hudson Street, New York, NY 10014

ELIZABETH R. WOLLHEIM
SHEILA E. GILBERT
PUBLISHERS

www.dawbooks.com

First Printing, November 2001
1   2   3   4   5   6   7   8   9

ACKNOWLEDGMENTS

Introduction © 2001 by Denise Little.
The Stargazer's Familiar © 2001 by Mary Jo Putney.
Three-Inch Trouble © 2001 by Andre Norton.
Purr Power © 2001 by Jody Lynn Nye.
Star © 2001 by Kristine Kathryn Rusch.
Under the Sign of the Fish © 2001 by Karen Haber.
Every Life Should Have Nine Cats © 2001 by Mickey Zucker Reichert.
Once, We Were Worshiped © 2001 by Diane A. S. Stuckart.
Praxis © 2001 by Janet Pack.
Death Song © 2001 by Bill McCay.
A Light in the Darkness © 2001 by Pamela Luzier McCutcheon.
Mu Mao and the Court Oracle © 2001 by Elizabeth Ann Scarborough.
Star Song © 2001 by Nina Kiriki Hoffman.
Ecliptic © 2001 by Von Jocks.

CONTENTS

INTRODUCTION

by Denise Little

CATS are cosmic creatures. Any person who has ever been owned by a cat knows that the moon can make them crazy, and that they will dance under the stars at every opportunity. When a cat leaps up out of a sound sleep and goes tearing through the house at top speed for no apparent reason, it might very well be reacting to celestial influences that only cats can understand. Or something like that. . . .

Regardless, the concept of cats and constellations is an intriguing one, and one well rooted in the dawn of history. Both astrology and cats were central to the ancient Egyptian civilization, where their fates were joined and intertwined. Whether because of cosmic forces out of our control or for more prosaic reasons, from the first time they crept to our hearths until today, cats have been alternately worshiped and reviled by us, but have always been associated with mysticism, gods, and magic. From ancient statues of Bast to the arched black cats on today's Halloween bags, cats represent something more to us than simple house pets.

Even as simple house pets, cats give us much more than a warm and furry presence in our laps on a cold night. It can be said with some justice that mankind's fate has often hinged on the well-being of the cats in our keeping. During the thousands of years that cats have deigned to share our lives, their careful patrolling of food storage areas has made possible surpluses that free artists to create, inventors to invent, writers to write, and armies to march out on wars of conquests. Without cats, the terrible events portrayed in the tale of the Pied Piper of Hamlin—where rodents overrun civilization to the point of crisis—move all too swiftly from the world of myth to reality. In periods of human history when cats have been tortured and killed in large numbers, plagues have decimated human populations. On several levels, domestic cats have made our existence as a society possible.

These days, when cats have finally outpaced dogs as the pet of choice in America and Europe, would seem to be halcyon for our feline friends, but the sad fact is that millions of unwanted cats and kittens are put to death every year in animal shelters. If the world is indeed governed with an eye to cosmic balance, who knows what price we'll pay this time for our short-sightedness. I look forward to the time when all the world's creatures in human keeping, and especially cats, will finally be cherished.

There's certainly no denying that in this day and

age, cats are an essential part of everyday life for many people. Those of us who keep cats know the joy of a warm cat in our lap, the soft caress of a velvet paw on our face, the restful sound of a cat purring us to sleep, and the fun of watching a cat's amazing antics in pursuit of a catnip-scented toy. But no matter how familiar they are to us, cats always retain a certain mystery, a core of wild beauty in their soul that whispers to us of other places, other times, and distant and forgotten gods. In this collection of cat stories, each with a connection to some aspect of cosmic influence, several writers explore the essentially mysterious nature of cats, as well as their influence on the people who love them. Cats and people and the patterns of stars—it's a dance that is endlessly fascinating.

So here, for your entertainment, are stories by some of today's finest writers that celebrate the mystical bond between our cats and us, and our cats and the celestial influences that only they seem to understand. You are about to embark on a voyage into magic and mystery, one I hope you'll enjoy as much as I did. Happy reading!

THE STARGAZER'S FAMILIAR

by Mary Jo Putney

Mary Jo Putney is a prolific *New York Times* best-selling novelist with too many book credits to list. Her most recent releases—*The China Bride, The Wild Child,* and *The Burning Point*—are all superb reads published to broad commercial success and rave reviews from even the stodgiest of critics. Her rare ability to portray complex, flawed characters with deep emotions makes her one of genre fiction's strongest voices. She's been the recipient of many national awards for her work, including two RITAs, two *Romantic Times* Career Achievement awards, and four appearances on the *ALA Journal's* annual list of the year's top five romances. A lifelong cat addict and a student of astrology, she couldn't resist the opportunity to craft a story for this anthology.

IT was a dark and stormy night. I didn't mind the rattling wind because placing the celestial observation tower on the highest hill in the kingdom meant there was always wind, but rain was another matter. When the first gust struck, I dived inside through the window set in the angled roof.

Quite apart from a dislike of getting soaked, I knew from experience that the slate observatory roof was dangerously slippery when wet, even for someone as agile as I. A fall from this height would rob me of another of my nine lives, and already I was down to six. (Five if one counts that incident involving the wolfhound, but I'm sure my escape was entirely my own doing.)

The Stargazer glanced up when I leaped from the telescope to the floor. He was young for a royal astrologer, but he'd been raised in the trade by his father—as I had been raised to be an astrologer's guardian by mine. "I see from your fur that the rain has started, Leo. Remind me to close the window as soon as I finish this calculation."

I ignored him, since it is not my job to remind an absentminded astrologer to use common sense. Settling into my spot on the hearth, I carefully licked away the raindrops. The Stargazer might not mind untidiness, but I have higher standards. There isn't another coat of fur in the kingdom as sleek and black as mine.

Grooming done, I settled down to doze and contemplate the pleasures of the evening ahead. Life had been exceptionally comfortable since The Stargazer brought The Lady home. Soft and sweet, she knew the very best way to stroke a throat or scratch behind an ear. She adored me, of course. What human female wouldn't? It was The Lady who'd thought to place cozy blankets beside my favorite fireplaces. So much nicer than cold stone. She saw that both The Stargazer and I were fed properly as well. Just this morning, before seeing us off to work, she'd whispered a promise to find me a special bit of fish when she went to the market.

Best of all, she'd brought Melisande with her. Exquisite Melisande of the silky silver fur and insouciant tail. The mere thought of her made me purr.

Yes, life was good . . .

My slumber was disturbed when the door opened with such force it banged against the wall. I came awake instantly, my fur prickling with warning. The man who entered wore the rich court dress of a nobleman, but jewels could not disguise the miasma of evil that clung to him. I backed into the shadows, tail lashing.

Though he lacked my perception, The Stargazer appeared wary when he greeted the intruder. "Lord Klothe. What an honor. What brings you to my humble observatory on such an unpleasant night?"

Klothe closed the door behind him, then strolled across the circular room, his velvet mantle shedding water. "I've a commission for you."

"I'm honored, my lord, but I'm very busy at the moment with work for the king. If your need is urgent, you'd best take it to Sorvinus, who is one of the finest astrologers in the kingdom." Though The Stargazer's words were perfectly polite, I knew his real desire was to see Klothe leave, but even royal astrologers don't say that to lords.

"Sorvinus is an amateur compared to you, and I need the best. This won't take long. 'Tis said the heavens are about to align in a pattern that will generate enough power to change the fate of nations." Klothe's black eyes gleamed. "I need an electional chart that will enable me to harness that power to achieve my ends."

The Stargazer's expression became so blank that I knew his concern equaled mine. "A Grand Conjunction exceeding any other in our lifetimes is imminent, but I could not cast a proper electional chart for a great enterprise without also doing an accurate natal chart for you. There is simply not enough time for me to calculate that before the Grand Conjunction occurs tomorrow morning."

"I have my chart here." Klothe drew a scroll from inside his mantle. "Your father himself cast it on the day I was born, so you cannot doubt its accuracy."

Reluctantly, the Stargazer accepted the scroll and unrolled it, scanning to get a sense of his guest's natal potentials. Blood drained from his face. "You wish to assassinate King Rolande!"

"Your skill is equal to your reputation." Klothe's smile was colder than ice on a winter tree. "A soothsayer once prophesied that in this year I would reach the highest place in the kingdom. The time has come to make my move. Determine the moment when the powers of heaven will grant me success, and you will find your new king to be a grateful patron."

"No." Hand shaking, The Stargazer hurled the scroll toward the fire. It bounced off the mantel and almost struck me. His aim has always been atrocious. "King Rolande is a strong, just man who has brought peace and prosperity to everyone in the kingdom. I would die before helping a usurper murder my sovereign."

A hiss of steel against leather, and suddenly the tip of a blade was pressed above The Stargazer's heart. "That can be arranged. The choice is yours."

"How will killing me help you achieve your ends?" The Stargazer retorted. "You're right, Sorvinus is an amateur. Only I can give you the information you seek, and if you slay me, you will fail in your enterprise."

Stalemate. Klothe was evil, but no fool. Seeing the man's uncertainty, The Stargazer said persuasively, "Put aside your ambitions, and I swear your words will not go beyond this room. In return, I shall read your chart and counsel you on how to use your strength and will to the best advantage. The best *legal* advantage."

Klothe lowered the sword a few inches, and I thought The Stargazer had won. Then my keen ears detected soft footsteps starting up the winding tower stairs. The Lady was coming to learn when her husband would be down for dinner, and her presence would change the balance of power.

Klothe must be disarmed. I growled menacingly. The Stargazer heard and looked in my direction. Praying he'd have the brains to take advantage of my intervention, I charged from the shadows, screaming the threats of my kind, and hurled myself at Klothe. With one mighty leap, I landed on the shoulder of his sword arm. The weapon clanged to the floor as my razor claws drew blood and my fangs ripped into his tender ear.

Yet Klothe was a trained warrior and fast, almost as fast as I. He fell back with an oath, wrenching at me. Through pure luck, he managed to tear me loose from my hold on his shoulder. As I fell toward the floor, he kicked. His booted foot sent me sailing across the room to crash into the wall. "You shouldn't have sent your foul familiar!" he snarled. "Now I have reason to slay you even if no purpose is served."

"You've killed Leo!" The Stargazer ran to my side, tears in his eyes. "He's no familiar, and I am no sorcerer. He is simply a cat. The best of cats."

If I'd had the strength, I'd have slashed him with my claws. *Simply* a cat? How dare he! But the breath had been knocked from my body, and pain seared through every muscle. Worse than the pain was the knowledge that I had failed, because The Stargazer was too much of a dolt to seize Klothe's moment of distraction.

Now it was too late. The door opened and The Lady entered, a smile on her face. "Will you be down for dinner soon, dearest? The bread is just from the oven and smells delicious." Seeing Klothe, she halted, saying shyly, "I'm sorry. I didn't realize you had company."

To my horror, Melisande walked gracefully at her side. Both of the females were in kit, their bellies rounded with new life. The balance of power had shifted to disaster.

As clever as he was wicked, Klothe seized The Lady and yanked her against his chest, whipping out a dagger and laying the blade against her throat. "You might be willing to die for your king, but will you sacrifice your wife and unborn child?"

"Dear God, don't hurt Serena!" The Stargazer gasped. "I . . . I'll do anything you wish."

"Then we have an agreement. Calculate the hour for my triumph, and you shall become my valued adviser. Defy me, and you all die. Try to fool me by offering the wrong time . . ." his smile was wicked beyond imagining. "Your little wife will leave with me today. If my attempt to kill the king fails, my servants will slay her even if I can't."

"You mean to assassinate King Rolande?" The Lady struggled against her captor, but in vain. "You monster!"

Melisande sank her claws into Klothe's calf. He kicked out wildly. "Another damned cat! Why can't you have hounds, like a normal man?"

Since he was encumbered by his grip on The Lady, his kick went awry. Hissing curses I didn't know she'd ever heard, Melisande darted away to hide amidst stacks of books. When she saw where I lay unmoving, she gave a wrenching cry of grief. I reached out to her with my mind. *Have faith, beloved. While I live, there is hope.*

She stilled, and her love gave me strength.

"I shall calculate the best time," The Stargazer said dully, "but I cannot swear you will achieve the success you crave. Only God can guarantee that."

"The soothsayer has already promised success. You need only provide the moment for me to act. Now do it!"

"This won't take long. I've already calculated the Grand Junction's period of greatest power since King Rolande wants to use the energy of the conjunction to send peace envoys to our neighbors." His voice became sardonic. "I need only find the exact moment for you to undertake such a different purpose."

The Stargazer set to work, consulting his texts and scribbling calculations. Keeping a wary eye on him, Klothe tied The Lady to a chair so that he needn't continue to hold her. And I watched with cold rage as pain slowly ebbed and my strength returned.

Something about the calculations puzzled The Stargazer, for he frowned at his charts. "You are in a period of great peril, Lord Klothe. The Mars aspects are most threatening. For your own sake, I advise you to drop this endeavor."

"Of course killing a king has potential risks," Klothe said impatiently. "But that doesn't matter since I will achieve the highest place in the kingdom."

The Stargazer shrugged. "I've done my best to warn you. Your chosen moment falls tomorrow morning at . . ."

Klothe cut him off again. "I want it in writing."

"As you wish." The Stargazer dipped his quill into the ink and wrote the time on a piece of foolscap. "Here is the precise moment for you to assault the royal castle. If you live long enough to do it."

Ignoring the warning, Klothe raised his dagger and struck The Stargazer on the back of his head with the hilt. As he collapsed, the paper fluttering down beside him, The Lady cried, "You *villain!* God rot your wicked soul!"

"Don't worry, I only hit your husband hard enough to put him to sleep for several hours," Klothe said as he tied The Stargazer's wrists together. "I didn't want him to succumb to foolish ideas of heroism."

It was now or never. With a prayer to Bast, goddess of my kind, I leaped to my feet, forcing myself to ignore the pain as I crossed the room with lightning swiftness.

This time I did not assault Klothe. Instead, I snatched up the fallen foolscap and sprang through

the angled window onto the roof, giving thanks
that The Stargazer hadn't bothered to close it.

Klothe bellowed with outrage. "You damnable
beast! I'll rip your limbs off one by one and throw
them into the fire."

Furiously he clambered up along the telescope,
then through the opening to the ledge of roof that
ran below the window. It was easily done, for the
first Stargazer who built this tower had designed it
so he could observe the glory of the heavens with
his own eyes as well as the telescope.

Though the rain had ceased, the slates were still
lethally slippery. Growling, my fur spiked all over
my body, I backed away from Klothe, staying just
out of his reach.

The lord assessed the seemingly flat roof, then
stepped onto the slates, thinking he could corner
me against the chimney that ran up the side of the
observatory. But the roof was not flat. A slight
downward incline caused Klothe to start slipping
toward the edge.

Swearing, he dropped to his knees. When he regained his balance, he locked one hand around the
edge of the roof and lunged at me with the other.

I dropped the foolscap and sank my fangs into
the fleshy part of his hand. He screamed and jerked
backward, dark blood spurting from his puncture
wounds.

The shock of assault made him release his grip
on the roof edge. He went from aggressor to pan-

icky prey in an instant, clawing like a trapped rodent in a vain effort to find a new grip.

He was still screaming when he pitched over the edge. It was a long way down, and he made a most satisfactory splat when he hit.

The soothsayer had said Lord Klothe would reach the highest place in the kingdom, and this observation tower was it. She hadn't said how long he'd stay there.

Limping and thanking Bast for Her help, I crossed the slates and returned through the window, landing more clumsily than was my custom. With a *mrrrrp* of joy, Melisande darted from her hiding place and pinned me to the floor with one sleek paw. Frantically she began licking my ears and ruff, all the time scolding me for taking such a risk. I gave a sigh of pleasure, content to surrender to her gentle female punishment.

Having managed to loosen her bonds, The Lady stood, swaying a little after the terrors she'd seen. Then she knelt by me, her touch as light as Melisande's. "Dearest Leo, you saved us all. You are the hero of heroes."

Naturally, I accepted the tribute as my due.

The Lady crossed to her husband, who was already coming awake. Apparently Klothe wasn't a good judge of how hard to hit, or perhaps The Stargazer has an exceptionally hard head. Cradling it in her lap, The Lady explained what had happened, finishing with, "I had no idea Leo was such a fierce warrior."

The Stargazer and I shared a glance, for we both knew the answer to that.

My name is Leo.

But my sun and soul are *Scorpio*.

THREE-INCH TROUBLE

by Andre Norton

Andre Norton has written and collaborated on over one hundred novels in her sixty years as a writer, working with such authors as Robert Bloch, Marion Zimmer Bradley, Mercedes Lackey, and Julian May. Her best-known creation is the Witch World, which has been the subject of several novels and anthologies. She has received the Nebula Grand Master Award, the Fritz Leiber Award, and the Daedalus Award. She lives in Murfreesboro, Tennessee, where she oversees a writers' library.

TAILED banners, bearing the codes of many trading companies, snapped in a brisk wind over the booths jammed together. A constant din of voices, raised in argument or in praise of this or that ware, assaulted the ears.

Raven tightened his claw-hold on the perch where he rode with the ease of long practice. As a crew member of the Free Trader *Horus,* he had experienced such gatherings before. Cargo Master Grospar was in no hurry. Once the main cargo was aboard, the star-sailors combed these fairs for personal gambles of their own, a tradition going far back to a time when ships were borne on planet-bound seas and men never dreamed that the next port could be another world. Fortunes had been gained from more than one lucky private deal.

"You choose, Raven. Or are you more eager for offerings to satisfy the innards?"

Raven butted his black-furred head against that of the man on whose shoulder he rode. Such a crude suggestion! He'd provide an answer to fit. Languidly, he drooped his tail to one side.

"Ros-rats? You're losing it, mate!" Grospar sneered, but, disdain notwithstanding, he pushed through the crowd in the direction the cat indicated.

Ros-rats were nasty vermin, but even they had value: they could clear alien wildlife out of a cargo hold in a very short time. As a result, every warehouse had cages of the creatures.

However, a booth to one side displayed distractingly exotic offerings. A pile of furs lay heaped there, with two other spacers arguing over prices. Cages of brilliant-hued flying things hung on display chains. Raven spat at a hand-sized dragon from Kartum as it flickered a forked tongue at him. Transporting live cargo was twice as hard as hauling nonliving wares, and only a few large ships could do it successfully; but even reduced to bundles of bright plumes, lengths of scaled skin, mounds of sensuous fur, outworld creatures would attract buyers.

A woman squeezed around a booth and stepped directly into Grospar's path. "Moon be clear for you, Cargo Master."

Martin Grospar laughed. "You here, Lasseea? I hope fortune favors you, as well, and I trust your moons are clear indeed."

The tall, thin female was not in space uniform but rather wore a colorful flowing robe. Her hair was hidden by a glitter-sewn scarf, and the breeze played with the fringes of twin shawls about her shoulders. Lasseea was a star-reader, and justly famous: several of her important predictions had been accurate.

The seeress leaned forward and tapped Raven between his golden eyes.

"Greeting to you, brother-in-fur." Feline eyes and green human ones locked in a deep gaze. "Sooo—" Now she spoke directly to Grospar again. "There will be work for this little one soon, and then he will prove the worth of all the cargo you have checked into your ship."

The cargo master's smile faded. Lasseea may have insisted, planet-years ago, that Raven shared an important birth star with her and was a bringer of good fortune, but Grospar prided himself on being free of the superstitions that spacefarers could collect. Star-voyaging brought much that was difficult to believe when experienced, and the unusual—even more so than for other adventurers—was the usual for Free Traders.

"He's already earned his rations several times over," the man answered gruffly. "What will we have to thank him for now?"

"One sees ahead but little." The star-reader pulled her top shawl closer about her. "Watch and wait."

Then she was gone.

Grospar and Raven continued on to the booth that had attracted the cargo master. As they arrived, the dealer was occupied with a sale, bargaining with two spacers who wanted the shining furs of Arcalic Night-Bats. The *Horus'* officer took advantage of the chance to survey the wares. He was attracted first by a string of small bone carvings hanging against a display rack. Then his eyes shifted to a box below them—a container that looked vaguely familiar. Grospar picked it up. The clasp proving loose, the box opened, and man and cat looked inside.

Within lay six slender bottles, or maybe "vials" was the word. Each was frosted down its length, except for a space at one tip, but those areas were so small that they afforded no glimpse of the tubes' contents. The cargo master caught sight of markings on the nearest and held the box closer. Raven nearly lost his shoulder-seat as he leaned down to sniff.

The Free Trader glanced at the dealer, who was now collecting credit slips. Grospar did not know him, but that was not to say he was a jack dealing in stolen goods. The fact that he had openly displayed this container meant he believed he had nothing to fear. On the other hand, both box and contents were stamped "SURVEY PROPERTY," and such artifacts were usually strictly guarded.

"You have an eye for a mystery, Cargo Master?"

The booth-keep, Grospar guessed, was a fellow Solarian—from Mars, to judge by the brown skin that nearly matched his thinning hair.

"Mystery?"

"That there—" the dealer jabbed a showman's finger at the vial-holder "—come in 'bout ten days ago. Ast'roid miner found it hooked on the belt of a floater who'd got caught in the rocks he'd been blastin'."

Grospar pointed in turn. "That's a Survey stamp," he said. "The law is—"

The hawker's laugh interrupted him. "Laws! They don't hold much, 'cept when a gov'ment man's there to back 'em up. Who's gonna make an extra flight to Jason or Silenea to turn in somethin' that little? Gimme ten credits, *you* can take it, and," his eyes narrowed shrewdly, "maybe get yourself a reward."

"Eight," the Trader countered, then automatically turned his head. "Worth that, Raven?"

The cat gave a small chirp of encouragement. There was something decidedly interesting about their find.

"Eight an' a half." The merchant fell into the natural rhythm of a sale.

The haggling went on for a few moments. When the cargo master left the booth, the box and some of the bone carvings were tucked into his shoulder-tote.

As the partners made their way back to the ship, Grospar stopped now and again to examine other offerings. Raven, however, paid no attention. He was keeping an eye on the bag that held his companion's selections and striving to pick up the thread of a very strange scent. Nor did he go off on his own when they were once again in the *Horus* but instead kept close to the cargo master's heels after he had leaped from his moving perch.

Grospar opened a chest built in under his bunk to stow away his most recent purchases, but before he closed the storage place, he opened the box again to view the six vials.

"*What—!*" The cargo master grabbed for a hand light and shone it into the interior, full on the transparent portions of the tubes. A—head? Some kind of carving?

There was no time now to make sure, for the liftoff alert had sounded, and that meant strapdown. He paused to boost Raven into the cat's hammock, then made his own preparations for ship-rise.

Raven wriggled until he could still see the box, which Grospar, for some reason had never placed in the chest. His lips shaped a soundless snarl. What was it? His feline senses were strained to the limit, but he was still frustrated. There had been no movement, no increase in that curious scent—nothing to sound the alarm, yet his inner warning system was clamoring ever more loudly.

The cargo master held the box with both hands, peering within. Carvings? No, he was seeing heads, with staring eyes—heads hardly bigger than his own thumbnails. Well, Survey often brought back samples of strange life—insects, plants—and this container bore their seal.

Found on a space-suited body . . . how long had its owner floated in the void, cast to a lingering and horrible death by some starship disaster? If the vials had once contained specimens living at that time, they were surely dead by now.

Once more Grospar inspected the tubes, tilting the chest to see their tiny clear windows. One of the half dozen had somehow worked loose. Before he could push it back into the padded crevice that had held it, the vial broke completely free and rose in the now-gravityless air of the cabin, moving upward with surprising speed.

The cargo master snapped the box shut and wedged it under his own body, lest another tube escape, then swept up a hand to snatch at the floater. It seemed to jerk, as though eluding his fingers.

But it did not escape Raven. Claws hooked, swung, and dragged the prize to the feline.

"Hold it, mate!" Grospar ordered. "Don't bite it through!"

As if Raven had any intention of doing *that*. Man's four-legged companions in space had been chosen because, among other traits, they possessed a well-developed sense of caution. The cat simply pressed the vial against the webbing in which he rested, summoning more strength to hold it there.

But the tube rolled, as though it had a will of its own and was fighting to escape. Raven stared into the unfrosted portion. Now he was sure he saw eyes—eyes that met his own. He blinked. They were—*no!* He would not—he would not!

Yet his warding paws moved against his wish, and the vial gained near-freedom even as the cabin was weighted once more with the partial gravity of ready-flight. As he fought to keep his trophy captive, his forelegs, insanely, did just the opposite of what he wanted: they opened. The tube spun lazily down to the floor—and met Grospar's metal-soled boot.

Raven snapped the safety catch of his hammock and leaped, only to pass through a puff of greenish vapor that burned his eyes and brought a squall of pain from him. He landed on the cabin floor and rebounded a little, dazed and limp. The cargo master caught him up, but seconds later the man began to cough with a force that made him drop the cat to gasp and clutch at his own throat.

The feline hit the floor again. Rubbing a paw at

his smarting eyes, he let out another cry as Grospar continued to hack, collapsing back onto his bunk. The Survey box joined Raven on the floor, and a second of the vials was jarred loose.

Out of that tube's green gas skidded a reddish blur, an occurrence of which the sickened cat was only half aware. Then the blur made a scuttling approach to the container and its remaining vials. Raven strove to raise a paw but found himself unable to do so. However, while his eyes still hurt, his vision had cleared, and he could see what was happening around the mysterious cache.

The cargo master lay flat on his bunk, coughing in deep, racking bursts. But the tubes were all out of the case now, pulled free by the thing—no, *two* things—that had got out first. The breaking of each vial released more of the breath-stealing vapor to torment the rightful occupants of the cabin.

Those . . . creatures. The cat squinted. They were as large as his human partner's longest finger, and they had four appendages, but they moved so fast it was hard to see more than that they used an upright position as well as scrambled on all fours. He sprang toward them and, to his utter astonishment, missed.

The cabin door signal sounded a note. Grospar's head turned, and he tried to call out, but a strangled cough was the only sound he was able to make. However, it was a sufficient summons, and the door opened.

Raven squalled again—not in pain, this time, but at the thwarting of his performance of duty. Those elusive beings, avoiding Captain Ricer's booted feet, vanished past him into the corridor. Determinedly the cat started after them, but his steps wavered, and he did not get far before the captain scooped him up.

Thus began a reign of, if not terror, at least fierce frustration for the crew of the *Horus*. The creatures from the Survey box seemed not only uncatchable but unseeable as well; but the wrack and ruin they appeared to deliberately cause was more evident every day.

Some cabins had their furnishings nearly wrecked, while smaller treasures were either bashed beyond repair or disappeared altogether. Across the bunks where off duty crew members were attempting to rest, the things began to scuttle—and worse. The medic treated several nasty bites as best he could.

Raven grew thin, apt to hiss warningly when approached by even his favorite shipmates, and always he hunted. At last, however, he managed to corner one of the enemy in Supply Storage, while it was busy tearing at some packets of the captain's treasured Larmonte tea.

The cat had gotten his paws—or rather one paw—on the entity, only to be leaped upon by two of its kindred who had been devising devilment on a higher shelf. The impudent brutes had no fear of him but bit and snatched at his fur, tweaking tufts of it out of his skin. His battle cry soared into a yowl of pain, but he fought to hold his prize.

"What the—!" Rasidan, the steward and cook, loomed suddenly above the fray. Raven's prisoner bit, hard, into its captor's right front paw, and he snapped back, his teeth closing about one of the creature's forelegs. Then a smothering cloth descended upon feline and foe as they fought, and the warring beings were lifted into the air. Tenaciously the cat held his grip, even when the knot formed of himself and his keening captive was dropped onto a hard surface, and the fabric loosened to fall free.

They were in the captain's cabin, with crew members crowded around the pulldown leaf of the desk. Raven's prey went abruptly limp, but still he did not release his hold. It was Grospar who reached down for the small body. His furred partner growled, body tensed to spring away. He was going to finish this catch! That's what he was there for: to make sure that the ship—*his* ship—was free of such intruders.

"It's all right, Raven," the cargo master assured him quickly. "Let me have it."

The cat held on, studying the situation. He mistrusted Grospar's ability to keep a grip on the thing. It was far from dead, and he was sure that if he released it, it would vanish again. These invaders had already proved that they were too swift, too small to be managed by men.

"Raven!" Captain Ricer spoke now, and he held up a square of cloth. "I'm going to wrap this around it—then you let go."

That was a definite order—a captain's order—and even he had to obey. He ducked his chin, relaxing his jaws. As he did so, the being came to furious life, but the captain had it bagged. The cat edged back. His numerous wounds burned, and an evil taste filled his mouth; however, he had set his own mark on the menace. He moved forward again to lend the weight of his forepaws to the control of the heaving bundle, though his superior continued to pin it also.

"In that lower cupboard." Ricer was giving Grospar directions. "Yes—that's it!"

The cargo master had stooped and risen. What he placed upon the desk was equipment from his commander's own private hobby. The captain, when the *Horus* had time in port on a lesser-known planet, hunted flying insects, then studied them in holding boxes of his own design. Since some of his captives had not only been large in size but equipped with menacing jaws, claws, stingers, and whatever other defenses nature had chosen to give them, the cages were indeed right and tight.

The one Grospar held at the ready was a cube of heavy netting with a thick metal floor. Into this the captain now transferred the frantically-wriggling contents of the improvised bag.

The cargo master instantly slammed down the top of the box with force enough to make it catch and lock—and just in time, for the creature sprang, only to be knocked back by the lowered flap.

"Now, then—" Ricer beckoned forward those who wished a closer look at one of their miniature nightmares of days past. Those of the crew who had gathered in his cabin closed in, staring at the cage and its inmate. For the first time, since the things moved with such speed, they could all view a specimen as it tugged and hurled itself against the wire-net walls that now enclosed it.

The body was covered with what seemed to be matted brownish-red fur, but the front paws, shaped not unlike human hands, were equipped with pointed talons that were now hooked into the screen barrier. An open mouth displayed similar armament in the form of a set of needlelike teeth, which were dripping a green liquid. The nose was flat and the face hairless about the jaw, cheeks, and eyes.

Its first battle rage was stilled, but the small nightmare still clung to the wire. Glittering blood-red eyes were fixed upon Ricer as he knelt down to bring himself closer to the surface of the flap-desk. Without looking, he groped along its top, brought out a magnifier, and swung that circle of view glass between himself and the now-quiet prisoner.

Raven approached the other side of the holding box. He snorted at the musky odor that was so strong, then stopped, growling, as though he had come up against an unseen barrier. He sensed from the being an intense malignancy. He could pick up no fear whatever—only a raging fury.

"I—don't—believe—it—" Captain Ricer accented each word he spoke, apparently wanting to deny the report given by his eyes.

"Don't believe what?" questioned Medic Lothers as he pushed Raven to one side to better view the cage and its occupant.

"That," Ricer declared slowly, "is a *monkey!*"

"A what?" Lothers asked the question for everyone.

"If that beast were about a hundred times larger—" The captain let his sentence trail off unfinished as he swung away from the table. He opened a cupboard and reached within, emerging with a reader-tape from his personal library. This tape he slapped into the viewer that shared the desktop with the cage and its captive.

The cat paid no attention to his commander's behavior, not even to the picture that appeared on the screen as Ricer triggered keys. He was intent on what was happening before him.

The entity had released its clutch on the wires and dropped to the floor of the box, where it curled itself into a ball. All at once, Raven shook his head vigorously, feeling as though both his ears had been invaded by loudly-buzzing insects. After a moment, he realized that the creature was mind-calling—and in a manner he had never encountered before.

The feline could not interpret the sense of the message being sent, but he was certain that it was either a warning to the being's own kind to take cover or a plea to them for help. The thing turned its head, staring at him. Again Raven could sense no fear—only a consuming rage.

In any grouping of wildlife there was always a leader. Even in an assembling of ships' cats, such as occurred at times when a starport's fields were crowded, one or two would take precedence, and the others would accord them room, as was required. This angry alien was not such a dominant one, but it seemed to believe that its mental broadcasts would reach its fellows. And perhaps that vast hatred had, indeed, reached a level of force in its projection to where it would bring aid. . . .

The men had moved away from the cage and were concentrating on the reader. Raven closed his ears to the argument that seemed to be rising among them—something about a comparison between the information on the tape and the size of the thing in the box. The cat was entirely intent on its broadcasting of near-insane anger.

Suddenly he made a move of his own. A sweep of paw struck the cage to the floor of the cabin, and an instant later he was beside it. A hand grabbed for the holding box; a second caught one of his own feet in a trap-tight clutch.

"What you trying to do, Cat?" It was Grospar who held and questioned him.

No time! Raven bit—hard. The cargo master yelled and loosed his grip. His furred partner offered no more aggression but rather jumped for the cage, sank teeth into its netting, and dragged it out into the passageway beyond.

The prisoner's kin-ones were coming—the cat could not see them, but he knew. He yowled, standing directly before the box, which he was using as bait to draw the rest of the creatures out of hiding. Then a pair of space boots grazed his tail as Grospar stopped just behind him.

"Stun him!" someone yelled.

"No!" shouted the cargo master. "He's got some sort of plan—I'll swear to it!"

The feline heard this exchange as though it were a rumble of distant thunder that had no meaning for him. He bobbed his head and gave the box another shove.

Within its enclosure there was no stir; the tiny intruder was still enwrapped upon itself, concentrating on its call. Not for the first time Raven wished he could communicate with his human crewmates. True, he could convey broad outlines of feelings or ideas to Grospar, but not detailed ones such as he needed to share now. He could only—

The cat crouched down between the men and the

cage. Should these invaders turn away from the summons and seek hiding places, it might be a long time before they would be found and routed out. Let them come into the open to free their fellow, however, and any member of the crew with a battle-stunner might take them.

"By the Last Ray of Corbus—look—they're coming!"

The cargo master had apparently sighted one of those scuttling shadows Raven had already sensed, though he was keeping most of his attention on the entity in its pen. The cat raised his still-bleeding forepaw and shook the box back and forth. The reaction was instantaneous—a fresh burst of defiance struck at him, revealing that the little brute was still both aware and angry.

The men had been exchanging a rapid-fire volley of suggestions, but a single word from the captain brought instant silence.

"Stunner—"

"*Here?*" challenged the medic immediately. Use of a stunner within the narrow confines of a corridor ran counter to all the never-questioned rules of ship safety.

The creatures were all in view now, though spread well apart. Once more Raven rattled the cage, then almost at once shook his head again. The original broadcast of wrath seemed a love pat compared to the silent waves of killing fury that now crashed into his mind, causing actual physical pain.

Through the red haze he forced himself to think: *Get behind the ones who would rescue their fellow—cut off any retreat.* But how could he achieve that position—and how would his own crewmates snare the things still loose? These were monkeys, with the intelligence of all their kind, but incredibly small in size and able to move at a speed too fast for eyes, human or feline, to follow—

Raven gave a last bat of his paw to the box, then turned around. As he had hoped, the cargo master was right behind him. With a swiftness rivaling that of the aliens, he leaped upward, hooking claws deep enough into Grospar's ship suit to pierce skin. The man gripped the cat and ripped him free.

For a second time, Raven bit the hand that held him, thus achieving part of his desperate plan. He was hurled away (a spluttered oath loud in his ears) to land some distance ahead, well past the pen.

Perhaps what the cargo master called "luck" was truly on his side, for the cat by his actions had now placed the invaders between himself and the crew. The creatures scrabbled frantically, but escape was impossible from the section of corridor into which the mind-call of the captive had brought them. One tried to dart in Raven's direction, and the feline responded with the hunter's reflexes of his kind: he did not try to pin this being down but swatted it, straight back at its companions.

The men of the *Horus* had spread themselves across the other end of the passage where they stood forming a barrier, space boot to space boot. Once more Captain Ricer spoke the word that told how he would deal with this situation, but this time, as he turned to exit the corridor, he was not inviting debate:

"*Stunner!*"

Raven uttered a yowl of agony. The free monkeys were not attacking, but the beat of rage inside his head from the confined one was almost enough to knock him down. Almost, yes—but not quite. A stunner, though—the cat knew what such a weapon might do if fired at close quarters.

Retreat? No—not for him. That was a very fleeting thought. This was his ship, his territory, *his*—!

The crew members on the other side of the cage drew back a fraction, and the creatures, who had seemed frozen in place by wariness, suddenly stirred. Raven felt a thrust of anger that was purely his own. Were Grospar and the rest going to give the enemy a chance to escape again?

But it was the captain for whom the men were making way. And he was carrying a tube that the cat had seen borne in action planetside only twice when lives had been threatened.

Instinctively he braced himself. There would be no sound, no visible shot fired—there would be—

Blackness swallowed him. The dark was painless, but it carried fear. He was in bonds, and he could not escape—not even open his mouth to cry out a protest! Panic had almost overwhelmed him when a familiar scent reached his nose, his brain. Grospar—? Yes, the cargo master had picked him up, was cradling him.

"Raven! Come on, li'l shadow—"

A quick sharp stab in his shoulder, and the helpless weakness began to fade.

"That ought to bring him around—"

Those words broke through the blind bondage that no longer held so tightly. Raven opened his eyes. Medic Lothers was watching him, and behind him stood the captain. Grospar gave his friend a last hug and laid him down on the softness of a bunk. His returning senses registered the odors of the captain's cabin.

"Got 'em—every one o' the buggers!"

Fortunately, because his head still felt too heavy to lift, Raven could see what was happening from where he lay. First the cage containing his "bait," then Ricer's insect-capturing net were being placed on the desk, and the bug-bag was bulging with inert bodies.

"Dead?" The cargo master, his hand still poised above the cat's head to touch him gently now and again, had asked that.

The captain gingerly inserted fingers into the

insect-net. Bringing forth one of the small bodies, he held it out to Lothers for a medical verdict.

"Well, it can evidently survive being stunned because it's still breathing," was the doctor's reply. "Can't tell whether it's damaged, though—too alien."

Ricer produced another collecting cage, then a third, and into these the creatures were placed. With the three miniature brigs lined up before him, the commander could finally perform a careful examination of the inmates.

"Survey can certainly have you," he at last declared to the entities who might or might not awaken from their enforced slumber. Then, his prison inspection concluded, the captain swung around to Raven. Standing at attention, he lifted his right hand and touched his temple in the formal salute offered only on state occasions to valiant beings in the Star Service.

"Ship's Guard," he said solemnly, "well done."

Grospar smiled, giving the cat a second, more intimate reward in the form of a rub behind the ears. "Lasseea was right, fur-friend," he said with a sigh of relief. "Your lucky star was our luck, too."

The weary feline lowered his head and closed his eyes. These attentions were very flattering, but right now he just wanted his shipmates to clear out and let him sleep. What nonsense humans talked, he thought. Suns in the heavens an influence on fate? Better the light-of-mind that was his kind's common sense. Were he to attempt such a farseeing as Lasseea's, though, he felt sure he could predict that Grospar would never go salvaging Survey-sealed material again. He, Raven, Ship's Guard of the Free Trader *Horus,* would personally make certain that there was no more such—what was the expression the men used for foolhardy activity?

Ah, yes (the cat wished he could smile)—*monkey business.*

PURR POWER

by Jody Lynn Nye

Jody Lynn Nye lists her main career activity as "spoiling cats." She lives northwest of Chicago with two of the above and her husband, author and packager Bill Fawcett. She has written twenty-three books, including five contemporary fantasies, three science fiction novels, four novels in collaboration with Anne McCaffrey, including *The Ship Who Won*, a humorous anthology about mothers, *Don't Forget Your Spacesuit, Dear!,* and over sixty short stories. Her latest books are *License Invoked,* co-written with Robert Asprin, and *Advanced Mythology,* fourth in the *Mythology 101* series.

HORUS-SEMNET picked his way distastefully through the temple environs, following one of the acolytes to the High Priest's personal garden. Cats! Everywhere he looked, lounging lazily on the immaculately swept flagstones, sitting in the dappled shade, skipping like dancers, trotting in a businesslike manner toward who knew where, stretching out with tails held high as if they did not care who could see their nether regions, were cats of every color and combination, long-haired, short-haired, big, small and in-between. They wound around his muscular legs, arching their backs luxuriously against his flesh. The big, black-haired man nudged them aside and strode onward. With mental apologies to the Mother Goddess Bastet, he did not much care for the form She had taken on Earth, nor her worshipers.

All the way from the dock where his elegant boat was moored, he had had to fight his way through the drunken crowds who were in Bubastis to celebrate the festival of Bast, on the first day of the month of Tybi. Revelers from all throughout Egypt had come, following the flotilla of priests and priestesses who moored opposite their villages and cities, playing the goddess's favorite sistrum, chanting and calling out abuse to attract their attention. When they had gathered a crowd on the shore, the women would reveal their bodies and dance to the music of the men piping.

The insanity did not end when they reached Bubastis. Instead, it spread out through the city and temple environs open to the public, and became a downright orgy of beer, song, and fornication. Horus-Semnet, a devotee of Ra, found this lack of dignity distressing. Not that Bast starved in his house, no! He had a proper votive statue that he made offerings to, of fish and beer. But he was annoyed. His gold-trimmed sandals were stained where a young man, of some rank by the jewelry he wore, threw up at his feet. He, prince and general in the army of Pharaoh, had to walk on the stink the rest of the way to the temple, with the nobleman apologizing at his heels all the way. Horus-Semnet's guards kept the man back, at the same time steadying him to keep him from falling on his face. Horus-Semnet was glad when the temple guards shut the man out in the street.

The acolyte took the stained sandals, providing butter-soft slippers of woven silk in their place. "Thy servants will receive hospitality in the guest hall, my lord," he whispered, and left Horus-Semnet alone in the cool shade.

Well, almost alone. Gleaming, slit-pupiled eyes like paired jewels regarded him from every corner. Horus-Semnet tried to stare down some of the cats, even moving suddenly to surprise them, but these animals never flinched. They were serene, beyond surprise. Horus-Semnet knew a hundred courtiers who could take a lesson in deportment from them. He lowered his large form gingerly onto a carved bench, and was pleased to see it held his weight without groaning. One of the cats, an orange one, came up to nose about him. Horus-Semnet offered a thick finger for inspection. The cat sniffed it, then rubbed a soft cheek against it. Its whiskers were as fine as the wiry hairs on the back of his hand.

After a short time the chief priest came to him. The lean man, not above middle height, wore a white cap and kilt of purest white trimmed with gold and malachite, like the eyes of the cats. His pectoral necklace was made of gold and malachite, too, its tiny beads all pointed ovals, arranged in the shape of a huge cat's eye. It seemed to look at him. Green-gold eyes shone, too, from the priest's elaborate belt, enameled gold bracelets and even his painted leather sandal straps. Disconcertingly, the shaven-headed priest himself had wide eyes of a pale color in between light brown, gold, and green. His lips were not full, but the bow in the center was rather pointed, giving him a wry look.

"Bastet's blessings be upon you, Prince Horus-Semnet," the high priest said, bowing his head slightly. "I am Ti-Bast. Forgive me for the delay in greeting you. I have many responsibilities and duties today. It is the goddess's festival."

"We have not met before," the prince said, frowning, "and I did not give my name at the gate."

"Forgive me," the high priest said again, with another inclination of his head. "The gracious goddess has vouchsafed a vision of your coming to one of the dreaming priests. Your name was revealed to us, and you were described to perfection, to the feet of your sandals." He smiled a little as the acolyte who had admitted Horus-Semnet returned, bearing the now-cleaned shoes upon a tray, and bowed before him. Following the pure one were servants bearing pitchers and bowls of fruit and rolls. "A little refreshment after your long journey? A sherbet, at least, before we get to the heart of your mission?"

Horus-Semnet was glad to accept the cold fruit juice, served in a graciously large gold cup chased with a pattern of kittens pursuing one another around the rim. The cup was a thing of beauty, its use a tribute to his mission, if a little lofty for his rank as a son of one of the previous pharaoh's minor wives. or perhaps Ti-Bast was only showing off the temple's wealth. The cult of Bastet was over two thousand years old. Ancient families had been endowing it with their finest treasures for all that time. Bastet was nurturer and protector, another avatar of the sun like Ra. For two thousand years, she and her war-sister Sekhmet Lion-Headed had guarded the Two Lands, but Bast was also associated with fertility and love. Mothers who had difficulty conceiving or delivering gave offerings to Bast in thanks for her aid. Hers was one of the richest sects in Egypt, a fact that was known across the civilized world.

Once the sweet juice had cleared the journey's dust from his throat, Horus-Semnet unrolled the papyrus he carried in the pouch at his side and began to read it aloud.

"From His Majesty Sheshonk I, Pharaoh and King, Lord of the Two Lands, servant of the gods and master of all Egypt, in his palace in his capital city of Thebes, to Ti-Bast, high priest of Bast in the beloved city of Bubastis, greetings."

"May all Bastet's blessings be upon him and his family," Ti-Bast said, nodding.

Horus-Semnet took his time over the long protocol, not wishing to stumble on any of the words of courtesy. Ti-Bast was a good listener, his wide, hazel eyes patient. The message that followed was more to the point.

Sheshonk I had enjoyed several years of relative peace since ascending to the throne, though he had kept his army sharp by patrolling the realm's borders. His spies and scouts had lately uncovered information that the Persians were planning to attack the northern reaches of Egypt. ". . . Therefore do we command and request that you shall make ready to defend our most beloved city and temple against our ancient enemy. This message do we send by the hand of Horus-Semnet, general of our army, in whom we have the greatest of trust." The scroll, written in the court scribe's perfect hieroglyphs, was signed with cartouches showing the Pharaoh's names, both birth and reigning, since he was addressing the priest of his favorite goddess. Horus-Semnet finished reading, rolled the scroll up, and, after a moment, handed it to the priest.

Ti-Bast noticed his hesitation. "Is there more?" he asked.

"I can give you more detail if you wish. The Persians will most likely attack from two quarters, coming up the Nile on ships and across the Sinai by chariot. Our scouts have brought back reports of foreign princes bringing enormous armies to join the Persian force. They are greedy to strip our cities and temples of their riches. We have been prosperous too long. Our navy is massing in the tributaries of the delta." Horus-Semnet leaned forward. "If the ports fall, Bubastis and all the cities close inland will be in danger. How many men do you have under arms to guard the temple?"

Ti-Bast smiled. "Seven hundred. They are all brave men, among the most puissant warriors in Egypt."

Horus-Semnet groaned. Too few. In order to protect the city he would have to split the forces he would bring with him from the south. "It is Pharaoh's wish that the city be fortified and the temple be evacuated. Such a small force will not be able to withstand the ferocity of the barbarian warriors, especially the hairy ones from the north."

"Now, now," Ti-Bast said, in a chiding, lazy voice, not at all what Horus-Semnet expected from a grown man, "we do not mind whiskers here, do we?" The priest reached out a hand to stroke a lean, tan cat who stretched up a pair of slender paws to his kilted lap. Ti-Bast caught Horus-Semnet's expression with an indulgent smile. "Here we serve Bastet and do homage to her. Our mission is to see to the well-being and happiness of her dearest creations on Earth." He looked down at the cat fondly. "Are they not beautiful?"

Ugh. Then the general reminded himself these were sacred animals, and the priest was only acceding to the will of Bastet. "Yes, of course. About the battle . . . if matters should go badly, we will send runners. Will you be prepared to evacuate southward? Do you have boats ready?"

"We will not need to go," Ti-Bast said, still in the singsongy voice. The cat was now in his lap, purring. "We will stay here."

"My lord," Horus-Semnet said, rising to his feet. "You must prepare! The barbarians could be upon you within twenty days!"

The priest's smooth tan brow wrinkled for a moment, then his face relaxed. "Then we have nothing to fear. It would be a terrible thing for them if they were to try," he said easily. "Bast will protect us, especially then. The twentieth day of Tybi is our celebration of her going forth, and the twenty-first is the day upon which she opened her great paws to guard the two lands. If they come in that time, they cannot succeed. Bastet will protect us."

"It is Pharaoh's will that you be ready to go," Horus-Semnet insisted firmly.

Ti-Bast was just as firm. "And it is the goddess's that we stay. Who else will sing her songs and fulfill her rituals if we empty the temple on her most sacred days?" The high priest lifted the cat to his shoulder where it hung limp as a pelt as he stroked it. Ti-Bast reached out his free hand to his visitor. "Come. Join our celebration. You have come on a most joyous day. You are our honored guest. There is much to see."

Grudgingly, Horus-Semnet followed his host.

*   *   *

He found himself marching in a procession through the packed streets of Bubastis behind a litter carrying a huge statue of the goddess. Ti-Bast went before it with his priests and pure ones, crying out praise.

"How beautiful are your eyes, O Bast! How lovely your ears and whiskers!

The priests were preceded by whirling dancing girls in translucent linen and musicians piping a lively air. Thousands of people lining the route held up small statues and real cats to be blessed by the sight of the great goddess. Solemn acolytes bore the great image and many other sacred objects, most of them veiled with white linen cloths. The one nearest him made him curious. A domed shape about the size of a man's head lay on a platform borne by two acolytes still wearing the sidelock of boyhood. He put his hand on his sword hilt. The goddess's cult demanded sacrifice, but he'd never heard of her requiring the death of a human being.

"What is that?" he asked the boys.

"The Eye of Bastet," said the one in front. He looked about ten years old, with large eyes and a very small nose. The one behind shoved the litter into his companion's back. "Oops. Forgive me, highness. I should not have said."

Horus-Semnet smiled. "I will not tell," he promised them. "What comes after this?"

"We return to the sanctuary," the second boy said. He was taller and thinner than his companion,

and was perhaps two years older. "Washing and
blessing. Then the feasting. That will be wonderful.
Bast provides well for us."

Following a ritual cleansing, Horus-Semnet and
his fellow nobles were admitted to the second holi-
est of holies. Ti-Bast was there to greet them as
thousands chanted praise outside. After the hot sun
and sky like blue glass the quiet dimness of the
inner temple inspired awe. Around him the incised
and painted walls depicted the legendary deeds of
Bast: casting forth Set and his minions, killing
snakes, her traditional enemy; enfolding Pharaoh
in her grace, and accepting the supplication of the
priests. Horus-Semnet thought that the priest's
image near the door was that of Ti-Bast.

He followed the procession through the forest of
pillars shaped like lotus and papyrus reeds. They
stopped before a high, gold-leafed plinth. Horus-
Semnet looked up in awe. Upon it stood a gold
statue of Bast so beautiful that Horus-Semnet re-
gretted many of the things he had said or thought.
Bast's arms were crossed on her chest. In one hand
she held a flail. In the other, a sistrum. Over her
head was a sunlike halo incised with the head of a
lion, her sister-goddess. At the feet of the statue
was another pedestal, this one about breast-high to
a man, topped with cool, white marble. From it, a
pair of green eyes blinked at him, winking in the
torchlight. Horus-Semnet jumped as its tail

switched. It was a black cat, a real one. It squeezed its eyes shut, then opened them wide.

"That is Kasi," Ti-Bast's voice said softly in his ear. "Be thankful. She shows you favor. You will have good luck this day." The high priest bowed low, and the general followed suit.

"She is the Goddess-on-Earth?"

"She is today," Ti-Bast said, straightening up. "The female cats of the temple occupy this station in turn every month. Kasi is the second-day avatar."

At the conclusion of the ceremonies the acolyte came to bring Horus-Semnet to the feast. Indeed, the boy in the parade had been correct. Bast's worshipers were generous with their bounty. Servers came to kneel beside him with platters of fish, meat, roast fowl, wild game, fruit, and sweetmeats enough to fill a warehouse, and poured pitchers of wine and beer enough to flood a river. Dancing girls and musicians entertained the visiting nobles. Cats walked freely around, under, and on the tables. Horus-Semnet longed to push them off, but knew it would be frowned upon by his hosts. He didn't permit animals on the table at home.

The revelry went on long into the night. Horus-Semnet enjoyed himself greatly, but he had not forgotten his mission. In the hour just before dawn he finally located Ti-Bast again. The priest was sitting at ease on the cool flagstones in his small garden with a few of the visiting nobles in court robes and braided wigs, and higher ranking priests in white robes. They were listening to a poet recite his work to music played by a female harpist. The temple cats lounged in laps and arms with an air of entitlement, knowing they were the focus of the festivities. Everyone fed them tidbits or petted them. Their purring was almost as loud as the music. Horus-Semnet was irritated by the spectacle, seeing human beings acting as servants to animals, rather than the other way around. He made his way to the priest's side and stood gazing down at him.

Ti-Bast was tickling the ribs of a dappled cat that stretched blissfully out to its full length and rumbled its pleasure. "Ah, Prince Horus-Semnet! Listen to that. It is music, is it not?"

"It is pleasant," the general said, "though it serves no purpose."

"You are wrong, my friend," Ti-Bast said, smiling. "That is the most important thing they do. Sit down. Have a sweetmeat."

"No, thank you," Horus-Semnet said stiffly. "You said that I would have good fortune this day. May I return to Pharaoh and tell him you will prepare for war?"

"I will order the soldiers to arms," Ti-Bast said offhandedly. "We are prepared. This you may tell Pharaoh."

Horus-Semnet frowned. Why wouldn't the man take the threat of invasion seriously? He and all his kind would die! "He won't like it. Holy one, you do not understand. These barbarians are not like us. They will torture and kill anyone who resists them. They will kill women and children. And they will kill the cats! To you they are Bastet's beloved, but to them they are only animals. Nuisances."

Even that did not stir Ti-Bast's ire. The high priest looked up at him, the curious pale eyes reflecting the firelight like the cat's. "I understand. I will do what is necessary here to keep all of us safe: women, children, and especially the cats. I assure you, it will be enough. Good fortune and success go with you, Your Highness. I will see you on the other side of victory."

The Persians were expected to make landfall any day. Scouts, running back and forth between Thebes and the outposts, reported that the gigantic force was advancing across the sea. Horus-Semnet and his commanders made a final survey of the cities and towns of Lower Egypt, seeing to their readiness. Pharaoh's navy, numbering over a thousand ships, massed just south of the many mouths of the Nile. The enemy would be hard pressed to come in by water. Pharaoh himself would lead the naval defense, on a great warship propelled by two hundred rowers.

The land battle was in the care of Horus-Semnet, and was more difficult to coordinate. The army could not cover the entire frontier. All they could do was to guard the most likely passes and stretches of open desert, and leave scouts on watch in the others. In the meantime, the army prepared for battle. Soldiers trained and drilled until they could do their maneuvers in their sleep. Storesmasters stockpiled armor, food, arrows, spare axles, and wheels for the chariots. Trainers readied the horses, dogs, and fighting leopards. Metalsmiths and tanners burned torches night after night seeing to the armor and weapons. His scribes kept lists. The general vowed all would be as ready as could be.

A messenger stumbled into the room, kneeling exhausted at Horus-Semnet's feet.

"General, I have word from General Het-heret. A force is coming over the desert from the east. It is three times greater than that coming by sea. The Hittites have joined the battle."

Horus-Semnet sprang up. "Carrion eaters," he snarled. "Haret, what is the condition of the eastern cities?"

"Kantir is prepared, my lord," the scribe said. "They have plenty of food and water, unless the battle goes on too long. Tanis is withdrawing all its women and children upstream. Bubastis . . ."

Horus-Semnet looked up at the nervous tone of the scribe's voice. "What about Bubastis?"

"The messenger from the temple said they are gathering cats, lord," the little man said.

*   *   *

"General, we are honored by your presence!" Ti-Bast said, greeting him at the temple pylon gate. "What fine armor! What glorious weapons! You look quite splendid."

Horus-Semnet stepped down from his chariot. He took the messenger's report from his belt pouch. "What good is this? I told you to fortify the city! The enemy is less than a day away!"

"And we are fortifying it, my lord," Ti-Bast assured him. "Look around you."

And Horus-Semnet did. The city was certainly in motion. Men, women, and children hurried toward the temple bringing baskets and bags, all squirming, writhing and squealing. "Hurry, hurry!" priests and acolytes chided them. "Get them inside. We must gather ten thousand as quickly as possible!"

Ti-Bast steered him into the courtyard. "Do you see?" he asked.

Every space within the temple environs was covered with cloths or cushions. On each, a man, woman, or child had between one and five cats arrayed about his or her lap, in their arms or on their shoulders. The humans offered them bits of food, but mostly they stroked, caressed, and praised their feline companions, over and over again, trying to calm them down. The animals cried, hissed, and protested.

"What is this nonsense?" Horus-Semnet

shouted. "Cats? Where are your soldiers, your weapons?"

"Hush!" Ti-Bast said hastily. "Do not upset the sacred ones. They must be willing to aid in our defense, and they can only do it if they are happy."

"What are you talking about? They cannot make arrows or sharpen swords!"

Ti-Bast's face became very severe. "Not all parts of the battle are fought with weapons, Prince Horus-Semnet."

The general was aggravated. The enemy was within a day's ride, and he was wasting his time.

Two shaved-headed attendants carried a litter into the center of the courtyard and set it down. On it Horus-Semnet recognized the swathed shape of the Eye of Bastet.

"I must take care of this, my prince," Ti-Bast said. "May the goddess be with you on the battlefield. May she guard your back and be as another spear in your hand."

As Horus-Semnet watched, the high priest approached the litter. He pulled off the cloth, revealing a pyramidal pedestal of purest alabaster. Set into this base was a glittering, translucent beryl sphere. It was the largest single gemstone Horus-Semnet had ever seen. Draped across the-top of the orb was a band of gold cut into the shape of a Pointed oval, the pupil of the eye of Bastet. As it was revealed, a palpable sense of peace began to steal outward. Cats fighting with their neighbors stopped hissing and allowed themselves to be calmed. They began to purr.

This was suicide. Horus-Semnet strode out of the temple. He must lead Pharaoh's army to battle.

The charging chariots of the Egyptian army engaged their Hittite and Persian foes on the open desert less than half a day's ride from the eastern edge of the city. The messenger had been right about their numbers. The enemy was like a tide surging toward them, gleaming weapons whitecaps on the waves. Horus-Semnet could tell immediately that even with the temple guards added to his number he had too few men behind him. They had been fooled by the early reports. Most of the fighting force was with Sheshonk on the Nile. He dispatched runners, but it was unlikely that reinforcements would come in time to help.

"No matter!" he cried to his captains. "We are the chosen of the gods! We will just have to kill six men each before we are evenly matched!" They cheered, rallying their men.

The enemy thundered toward them across the flat gray-yellow scree. Horus-Semnet hefted his first spear and flung it. There was a cry from the Persian chariots as the man it struck fell down among the threshing hooves of the horses. First blood! It was a good omen. He could use many such.

Wheeling, turning, stabbing. Flanking, slashing,

chopping. Horus-Semnet ordered his forces into positions where they could do the most damage. His men fought doggedly. They were all trained to the highest degree, but they were badly outnumbered. As each of his soldiers fell, the gap was too quickly filled by enemy soldiers, forcing those nearby to withdraw a step to protect their exposed right sides. The Egyptians found themselves being pushed ever backward. To the southwest lay Bubastis, defenseless but for their thinning line. Its riches called to the enemy. Pharaoh would be angry if his favorite temple fell to the hated Persians. There was nothing that Horus-Semnet could do but fight on and on. The ground under their feet gradually changed from sand to rock to plowed fields. They were being forced onto the fertile fields around the delta city.

"What's that?" one of his captains shouted to him.

Horus-Semnet paused, hefting a spear in his hand. He heard a loud buzzing behind him. A sandstorm must be brewing. They were rare in the eastern desert, but devastating in their ferocity. His army would be lucky to live out the day, pinched between the enemy in front and a scouring, raging wind behind.

A glimpse behind him showed that he was within sight of Bubastis. Two chariots came up to flank him, engaging his bodyguards as a Persian general galloped up to do battle with him. Horus-

Semnet recognized the gray-tan skin stretched over spare bones, the leopard skin slung over his left shoulder. It was Tamilosheren, of the royal house. Horus-Semnet grimly drew his bronze sword. The foreigner was known as a fearless fighter and a worthy foe. He was honored by the battle offered, but it would be hard to win.

Their chariots circled one another as their swords clashed. Horus-Semnet could almost feel the walls of the city drawing ever closer to his back. Tamilosheren was a focused swordsman, his weapon darting toward every opening. Horus-Semnet gasped as the enemy slashed his arm. Blood ran down into his hand, making his sword hilt slip.

Suddenly, unexpectedly, the Persian general froze, his mouth dropping open as he stared forward. Horus-Semnet took the opportunity of his enemy's distraction to hack off his head. The body dropped, and Horus-Semnet looked back over his shoulder at what had taken his enemy's attention off their fight. His own mouth fell open.

Rising from the temple was a pillar of amber light five hundred feet high. In it was the figure of a beautiful woman. But not any woman. She had the head and paws of a great cat. It was Bastet come to life! She was translucent as glass, but he did not doubt that she was there. She *was*, by his hope of an afterlife, she *was*! He wanted to drop to his knees and pray.

Some of the enemy screamed and fled at the appearance of the gigantic cat goddess, but not enough. The Persians pressed on ever more grimly, killing and maiming, though with one eye on the huge figure looming over them.

The Egyptian army had lost more than half its number. Horus-Semnet mustered his diminishing force, fighting for every inch of ground. Just when he feared the Persians would break through at last, the goddess reached out to help them. Her gleaming gold-and-amber eyes fixed on the enemy. Like spears, her claws reached out to hook men out of their chariots and cast them down. The very ground swirled up around them, consuming the enemy, swallowing up soldiers, chariots, horses, and all. The screaming in the air was more than the wind. It bore the sounds of dying men to Horus-Semnet's ears. He squinted through the blasting sand as the golden figure of the goddess leaned over them, blotting out the sky. She reached out her great paws, raking and raking toward her, purposefully digging into the desert to the east of the delta. She dragged sand over her enemy, scraping it over them, burying them deep with disdainful paws. Horus-Semnet was blinded and deafened by the storm.

"Bast, save us!" he gasped.

An eternity later the wind died down. Above the general's head the figure of the goddess slimmed into a pillar of fire and shrank down behind the temple walls. Horus-Semnet clutched the shoulder of his charioteer. The man's face was pale under its covering of dust. Horus-Semnet knew he must have looked the same. The general glanced around. His soldiers and those of the temple stood alone on plowed earth that bore furrows the same shape as scratches from Her giant claws. Every trace of the enemy was gone, and so was the sand.

By sunset, the general and the remnants of his troops limped exhaustedly into the temple environs. A deafening roaring met them. Horus-Semnet recoiled. Was it the sandstorm? No, it was the sound of ten thousand cats purring! The animals blinked up lazily at him, and their human attendants stared in wonder. It seemed as though no time had passed here at all.

Priests and lay people alike leaped up, calling the soldiers heroes, bringing them water, oil, bandages, and food. The cats wound around them, bidding them welcome. Ti-Bast and his priests saw to Horus-Semnet's wound with their own hands. The soldiers could talk of nothing but the miracle that had occurred.

"Every single man, gone!" a captain said, flicking his hands. "It was a miracle!"

A well-orchestrated miracle, Horus-Semnet thought, glancing toward the Eye of Bastet. It was glowing golden-orange, the color of the giant Bastet's aegis.

By the time he was well enough to join the celebrants at a ritual of thanksgiving, the Eye had faded until it was a pale gold, the color of sand. With much ceremony the priests gathered it up, veiled it, and carried it into the inner temple.

"If I hadn't seen it with my own eyes, I would not have believed it possible," Horus-Semnet said, marveling as he followed. He knelt before the jeweled figure of the cat goddess, and offered his sword as a sacrifice. "I give thanks to great Bast for the blessing of a successful battle."

Ti-Bast held it and bowed toward the altar, but turned and handed it back to the general. "She thanks you but returns it that you may use this claw in her service."

"I shall." The black cat lounging on the plinth below the statue blinked its green eyes at him. She purred luxuriously. "My thanks to you, great goddess, and to you, for the miracle of your purring, O Kasi."

"That is Laila," Ti-Bast said severely. "She is the twenty-first-day cat. Can you not tell the difference?"

"Forgive me," Horus-Semnet said, bowing low. "Forgive one who is not versed in the subtleties of the chosen ones, but who is a convert from this day forward."

Ti-Bast opened his large, unblinking eyes so much like the cats'. "The goddess is pleased to hear you say so, Prince Horus-Semnet. But, of course, she is not surprised. All humans fall into the service of the She-Cat sooner or later. There are simply those who recognize it from the first, and those who do not."

Horus-Semnet knew divine truth when he heard it. He sheathed his sword and bowed deeply before the altar of the Goddess, surrounded by the glory and power of ten thousand cats purring.

STAR

by Kristine Kathryn Rusch

Kristine Kathryn Rusch is an award-winning fiction writer. Her novella, *The Gallery of His Dreams,* won the *Locus* Award for best short fiction. Her body of fiction work won her the John W. Campbell Award, given in 1991 in Europe. She has been nominated for several dozen fiction awards, and her short work has been reprinted in six *Year's Best* collections. She has published twenty novels under her own name. She has sold forty-one, including pseudonymous books. Her novels have been published in seven languages, and have spent several weeks on the *USA Today* bestseller list and *The Wall Street Journal* bestseller list. She has written a number of *Star Trek* novels with her husband, Dean Wesley Smith, including a book in this summer's crossover series called *New Earth.* She is the former editor of the prestigious *The Magazine of Fantasy and Science Fiction,* winning a Hugo for her work there. Before that, she and Dean Wesley Smith started and ran Pulphouse Publishing, a science fiction and mystery press in Eugene. She lives and works on the Oregon coast.

HE sat on the front steps of his house as if he were waiting for her. Anna Jarrett parked her dirty white Taurus against the curb and ducked her head as she got out. Maybe if she avoided eye contact, he would leave her alone.

But, just as she expected, he got up and strode across the lawn. She hunched even farther forward and hurried toward her house. It had a fence on all four sides and a gate she always left closed. Private, small, and hers. Wasn't the fence enough? Couldn't he understand that she wanted to be left alone?

"Um, Miss?" His voice was deep and resonant.

Anna clutched her purse against her side and fumbled with the latch on the gate. She could hear his approach, the slight crunching sound of his feet on the dry grass.

"Miss?"

His shadow fell across her, and she was trapped. She couldn't pretend she didn't see him.

Her breath was coming in short, nervous gasps. It was all she could do to keep from hyperventilating. She kept her head down, her fingers still struggling with the latch.

"I'm not going to hurt you," he said, and this time his voice was soft. "I'm your neighbor. I just have a question."

She closed her eyes for the briefest of moments, steeling herself, then she stood straight and faced him.

He was younger than she expected—in his mid-thirties—tall and broad-shouldered. His hair was golden and curly, the kind of hair usually found on pictures of cherubs, not on grown men. His eyes were a dark brown. They seemed warm. But she had been fooled by warmth before.

"Hi." He smiled. "I'm Pete."

She remembered. The house next door had originally been his parents'. She'd played with him a few times when she had been a child, but she didn't expect him to remember her. That had been a very long time ago.

"I was wondering if you owned a cat."

Warmth flooded her face, and she had to turn away so that he wouldn't see the tears which stung her eyes. She reached for the latch again, and he caught her fingers.

His touch was gentle. "I didn't mean to upset you."

She pulled her fingers from his grasp. "I don't have a cat."

"I was just asking because there's been a scruffy-looking white cat hanging around your house. If it's not yours, maybe I'll see if I can find it a home. I've been feeding it."

"White?" she asked in spite of herself.

He nodded. "All white except for a black star just above its eyes and black paws. I've never seen markings like that."

She had. Her stomach twisted. "He asked you to say that, didn't he?"

"What?" Pete frowned. "Who asked me what?"

"To say that you'd seen a white cat with a star on her face." Anna squared her shoulders. She was backed against the fence with nowhere to go. He was bigger than she was and stronger. Her only option was to run back to the car, and he blocked her way. Still, she'd get around him if she could. "This is just cruel. You bother me again and I'm calling the police."

"Wait." Pete held up his hands like a man who'd just touched something hot. "I didn't talk to anyone. I really am your neighbor, and I really have been feeding a white cat. If you wait here, I can prove it."

He backed away from her, then sprinted for his house. She waited until he let himself inside before reaching for the latch again. This time, she had no trouble opening the gate. She went through, shut it, and latched it again, wishing the front fence were tall enough to hide her yard.

She ran up her porch steps and was unlocking her front door when she heard his door close.

"Wait!" he said.

She slipped inside, shut the door behind herself, and locked all three dead bolts, then secured the chain for good measure. She double-checked her window locks, then went to the back door to make sure it was locked, too. She kept her curtains closed and sank onto one of her kitchen chairs until she was sure he had gone away.

The next morning Anna rose at dawn. She had gotten four hours of sleep, which was better than she could have expected under the circumstances. She had spent half the night worrying about the encounter, wondering what it meant. Pete had lived in that house all his life. She had just moved in six months before. Still, she couldn't get past the feeling that Neil had somehow contacted him.

Neil. The very thought of him made her shake. Even though he was safely locked up in Attica, not even eligible for parole for another thirty years, she still looked over her shoulder expecting to see him. And his obsession with her—his deep anger at her—hadn't ended. He'd sent threatening letters to her mother, which had taken more legal action to stop, and then he had started a subtler campaign to terrorize her sister—a campaign Anna's lawyer argued had really been aimed at Anna.

Finally, a judge had ordered all communication with Anna's friends and family off-limits to Neil, and the prison destroyed any letters he wrote to people on her list. But her new neighbor Pete wasn't on that list, nor were new friends here in Wisconsin. She would have to update the list immediately. And even that felt as though she were giving away too much of herself to her past.

Of course, using Star would be the quickest and most painful way to reach her. She had no idea why Pete would even ask her that question, what he hoped to gain from it. Perhaps Neil had told him it would be a joke. Even though she didn't know why anyone would listen to a man who wrote letters in pencil on lined paper, a man whose return address included the numbers of his cellblock in Attica.

She had resisted the temptation to go online and find out as much as she could about her neighbor, to see if she could find his motivation for seeking her out. She could only hope that he would take her anger the day before as the warning it was, and leave her alone.

After she showered, she made herself a light breakfast of cereal and tea, turning on a jazz CD instead of the morning news, and grabbing a romance novel instead of the newspaper. She knew better than to hear about violence at the start of her day. If she wasn't careful, violent news stories brought on panic attacks or worse. Her therapist said the post-traumatic stress symptoms would eventually go away, but it was always best not to trigger them. Anna had a two-page list of things to avoid just to keep herself somewhat calm.

Routines helped. So did her photography. When she finished eating, she grabbed her camera and went out the back door to see if she could catch the early morning light in her garden.

What she saw made her freeze.

A white cat sat on the dew-covered grass, haloed in a ray of sunlight. The cat had black feet and a star on its forehead.

Anna gasped.

The cat heard her, turned toward her and

meowed—a husky, raspy, unique sound that Anna thought she'd never hear again.

Anna screamed and stumbled back into the house.

She'd seen a ghost, and its presence in her sanctuary nearly broke her heart.

"All you do is fondle that damn cat." Neil snatched Star out of her arms. Star squirmed, hissing and spitting. *"Maybe you should pay attention to me sometime."*

He slammed Star against the wall. Anna launched herself across the room, grabbing for Star. The cat had stopped fighting. She looked woozy. Neil dropped her. Star landed on her back, and didn't move.

But Anna did. All the months of fear and terror rose up inside her. She clawed at his eyes, throwing herself against him, until he grabbed her by the neck and shoved her backward.

Her head hit the wall with a loud smack. Pain shuddered through her and she lost her grip on him. His thumbs pressed against her windpipe, and suddenly the fear was back.

She was going to lose this time. She was going to lose. . . .

And then she realized she was in her own kitchen. Arms were wrapped around her, a strong body holding her down, her head aching and her throat raw.

"It's all right. It's all right."

The voice was male and only vaguely familiar.

The faint scent of sandalwood surrounded her, and the touch, even though it restrained her, was gentle.

"Calm down. Please. It's all right."

She was in her own kitchen, Neil was in jail, and she had had a flashback. She went limp, and the arms released her. A hand stroked her forehead.

"You gonna be all right? Do I need to call someone?"

That was when she recognized the voice. Pete, from next door. She moved away from him, her skin flushing hot.

He was sitting on the floor, wearing gym shorts and a T-shirt depicting a wheel with the signs of the Zodiac. Sunlight coming in the open door illuminated the fine golden hairs on his arms and the unshaved frizz on his face.

"The door was open," he said. "I didn't mean to barge in, but I heard you scream, and then all that pounding."

She touched her head. She'd slammed it against the wall again. Flashbacks. She would have to call her therapist, see if he could squeeze her in this afternoon.

"Sorry," she said.

"Sorry?" He raised his eyebrows. "You don't have to apologize to me. I just want to know if I should call someone."

She shook her head. "I'll be all right."

He stood slowly, keeping his hands where she could see them. She realized that he was doing so out of concern for her, afraid that a sudden movement would startle her.

"I don't mean to butt in, but it looked like you were having some kind of fit. Medical attention might be in order."

"I'm fine," she said again.

He bit his lower lip, then shrugged. "Is there anything else I can do?"

"No. Thanks." She didn't sound grateful. She wasn't sure she was. She would have stopped eventually. The flashback would have ended, and she would have found herself in a heap on the floor, aching, bruised, and shaken. He hadn't made a difference.

Except that she'd had a momentary feeling of security, a feeling she hadn't had for nearly two years.

"I'm, um, a little hesitant to leave you alone." He hadn't moved.

"Oh, for God's sake." Her hands were shaking. The flashback was over, but the reaction wasn't. "I have post-traumatic stress syndrome. Thanks to your little prank last night, I saw a white cat in the yard and it triggered me."

"You think the cat was a product of your imagination?"

"You know it was," she said. "For some reason, you decided to do what Neil asked and tell me you saw a white cat with a star on its forehead, and that had the desired result. You can write to him and tell him that. It'll please him that he's still having an effect."

Pete rested his hands on the kitchen chair before him. The posture made him look relaxed, even though his expression was haunted.

"I don't know anyone named Neil," he said. "And I don't write to anyone, not even my mother. I have been feeding a white cat, and I can prove it."

"Oh, you can?" Her lips were trembling now, but with repressed rage. How dare he torment her after he realized how vulnerable she was? The moment he left, she would call the police.

"Yes." He was using that calm voice again, the one he had used to get her out of her flashback. "The cat's been sitting on your back porch during your entire fit. She's there now."

Even though Anna knew this was a prank, she couldn't help herself. She looked.

A white cat was sitting just outside the door, staring inside hesitantly. When it saw Anna, it mewed.

Anna shivered. The cat sounded like Star. But it couldn't be. Just before she'd passed out, she'd seen Star immobile on the floor. When she had gotten out of the hospital, almost a week later, treated for broken bones and internal injuries as well as the damage to her throat, Star's body was gone. No one would tell her what happened to her cat. All her friends had said was that she was lucky to have survived.

And she had been lucky. A neighbor had heard the pounding on the walls and the shouting and had called 911. By the time the police arrived, Anna was nearly dead. They had to pull Neil—still kicking and hitting her—away from her unconscious body, and it had taken three men to restrain him.

She knew what she had looked like for months afterward. She had no idea how Star had looked at the end, only that it couldn't have been pretty.

"It's all right," Pete said again. Only this time, he wasn't talking to her. He was talking to the cat. He had crouched, extending his hands.

The cat didn't look at him. It looked at Anna.

The cat's eyes were green, like Star's had been. The black mark was a five-pointed Christmas star, perfectly shaped, also like Star's had been. And her dainty feet were pure black, just like Star's.

But her coat wasn't soft or shiny like Star's. Her fur was coarse and dull, and she was so thin that Anna could see her ribs.

"Star?" Anna asked.

The cat made a small, hesitant chirrup. Anna crouched, too, knowing the wrong kind of movement could startle the animal.

"Come here, baby," she said in a voice she hadn't used in almost a year.

The cat chirruped again, stood and rubbed against the doorway. Anna kept her hands out, watching as the cat wound her way into the house.

Slowly she made her way past Pete, and then she came to Anna.

Anna hesitantly petted her back, felt a real live if scrawny and malnourished cat, and blinked back tears.

"Star?" she asked again. The cat bumped its head against her hand and purred so loudly that Anna's heart ached.

"See?" he said. "Is she yours?"

Anna shook her head. "She's probably just hungry."

"I think there's no doubt about that. I've been feeding her, but I've been doing it outside, where she has to share her food with every squirrel and raccoon who comes along."

"Who do you think she belongs to?" Anna asked.

"I thought you knew. You know her name."

Anna rubbed the cat's nose and the purring got louder. "That's just a logical name, considering her markings."

"No," he said. "You recognize her. And she knows you."

Anna swallowed. She started to stand, but Star shoved herself against Anna's hand again. Anna picked her up, and the cat nestled against her neck—just like the real Star used to.

"I had a cat named Star once," Anna said. "She looked just like this."

"How do you know this isn't the same cat?"

"Because she's dead," Anna said.

Pete stood. "Are you sure?"

Star landed on her back, and didn't move.

"Yeah," Anna whispered. "I'm sure."

He studied her for a moment. The cat's paws were kneading her neck, sharp claws making pinpricks in her skin.

"Well, then," he said, "what do you want to do about her? I can keep feeding her outside, but I have three cats indoors and two are elderly. I can't bring another in right now without upsetting the balance."

"That's okay," Anna said, surprising herself. "I'll keep her."

He was still looking at her. It felt as if he could see through her. For a moment, she thought he was going to say that she didn't dare take care of a cat, not in her precarious mental state. But he didn't.

"Let me know if you need anything," he said.

"I will." Then she smiled at him. It might have been her first smile since she got out of the hospital. She wasn't sure. It felt like her first smile.

He smiled back. "Take care of Star," he said and let himself out the back door.

Anna held the cat for a long time. The cat clung to her and then fell asleep against her chest—a deep, noncatlike sleep of relief and exhaustion. She wished she could believe this was the real Star. The odds against finding a second cat with the same markings were remote. But Star was long gone, the only good part of a world that Anna didn't want to remember, and Anna wondered at the wisdom of taking this cat in. Would it make the flashbacks worse? Would it hurt her recovery?

She carried the cat around like a baby while she filled a small bowl with water, prepared a bed near the dryer, and tore up newspaper in a cardboard box that would act as a litter box until she was able to get one. She didn't feel as shaky as she had after her attack. In fact, she felt calmer than she had for days. She wondered if it was the effect of a warm body against hers, a heart beating in concert with hers, or if she was just wrung out.

It felt good to have something useful to do, to have someone depend on her. Or so she told herself. She'd been living on disability and attending classes at the local university, thinking of doing some sort of computer work when her doctors— particularly her therapists—gave her a clean bill of health.

Neil's final attack had left her weak and thin. The bones in her left arm had been so badly broken that the physical therapists weren't sure she'd ever have full use of it again. But it was her therapists who urged her to leave New York. The city, which she had once loved, had seemed threatening. The constant noise had terrified her, and she spent most of her time crouched on her floor or hidden beneath her covers. They recommended somewhere small and safe, and so she had come back to the Midwest, where she had grown up.

The house had been her grandmother's. Her mother had rented it with only partial success for ten years. When Anna needed a place to go, her mother offered it to her. But the house hadn't had the healing effect Anna thought it would. Its largeness, after a decade in apartments, seemed excessive, and the nightly silence was almost as unnerving as Manhattan's noise.

She was beginning to think she wouldn't be happy anywhere. She had even written an e-mail to her sister, wondering if happiness should be a goal in life.

The cat purred against her shoulder. She rubbed her cheek against the cat's fur and felt, for the first time in years, as if she could purr, too.

A nearby vet managed to squeeze her in that afternoon. Anna made a cardboard box into a makeshift cat carrier, and drove Star to the vet's office.

She had asked the staff to give Star a flea bath. They did so before the cat saw the vet. While she waited, Anna bought cat food, a small litter pan and new crystal litter, and flea spray for the parts of the house Star had already been in.

Anna was concerned about Star's health. She was too thin by far and had clearly been starving. The pads of her paws were scuffed and raw, and her back was covered with poorly healed sores. The vet techs promised to be very careful with her as they bathed her, and even then Anna could hear the cat's plaintive mews echoing from the back room.

Finally, she was called into an examination room. Star started to purr the moment she saw Anna. The vet, a solid middle-aged woman with steel-gray hair and a manner of calm, entered a moment later, introducing herself as Dr. Twohy.

"So this little one is a stray," she said as she examined Star's ears, took her temperature, and took some blood.

"Yes," Anna said.

"You know she has an ID chip in her shoulder."

Anna stiffened. She was going to lose this little cat to its real owners, and she didn't want to. She hadn't realized how close she had grown to the animal in just a few hours.

"Have you read it?" she asked.

The vet nodded. "Strangely enough, she belongs to an Anna Jarrett. Only this one's from New York City."

Anna felt her breath catch in her throat. "On Eighty-First Street?"

The vet nodded. "We tried to call, but the phone number has been disconnected."

Anna nodded. Her hands were shaking.

"I was wondering," Dr. Twohy said. "Is she your cat?"

"No," Anna said. "I mean, she is now, but I just

found her this morning. Actually, my neighbor found her. She can't be my cat from New York."

The vet rested a hand on Star's back, as if she were guarding the cat. "Why not?"

Anna took a deep breath. "I—my—I—she was—my boyfriend hurt her. He nearly killed me that night, and when I got home from the hospital, she was gone. I thought—my friends said—that she was gone. They meant she'd died."

She had never voluntarily told anyone about Neil before. It felt strange to speak the words aloud.

"Well, it looks like she didn't. And she followed you here."

Anna shook her head. "That's not possible. I've been here six months, and she'd never been here before. There's no way—"

"You ever hear of the *Incredible Journey*?" Dr. Twohy asked.

"That's fiction," Anna said.

"Actually, it's not. There've been cases of animals trailing their owners across the country."

"No," Anna said. "There's no way it can happen."

"It does happen," the vet said. "There've been a number of documented cases."

"How?"

Dr. Twohy shrugged. "I have no idea. There are a number of theories. Cats have an inordinately good sense of direction. Studies have shown time and time again that if you take a cat far from its home and set it down, it will always turn in the direction of home."

"But that's a place it knows. This is thousands of miles away."

"I know." Dr. Twohy smiled. "Maybe cats were on ships not just to eat rats but because they could always find the North Star."

"That still doesn't explain how she would have found me."

"Some say that cats have a psychic ability. That's why this is called psi-trailing. People believe the link with cat and owner is stronger than anything else."

Anna was silent for a moment. "There's no way to know that the cat is the same animal."

"There are a number of ways to tell. This chip is a prime example. It's obviously been in there a long time. It hasn't been placed there recently. And this cat has done a lot of walking. You can tell by the pads on her feet." Anna winced and petted Star. Poor thing.

"Even if the chip weren't there, I've never seen a cat with a perfect star on her forehead." Dr. Twohy leaned forward. Her expression was sympathetic. "Maybe you should call your friends and find out what they did with your cat when you went to the hospital."

"The body was on the floor," Anna said. "I remember seeing her there."

"So someone had to dispose of it." The vet's

voice was soft. "I'd love to hear what your friends say. I've always been fascinated by a cat's ability to trail her owners like this. I'd love to have a documentable case right here."

Anna swallowed. She didn't want to think about the strangeness before her. "What about her health?"

Dr. Twohy scratched Star under the chin. "Considering the fact that she's been eating poorly and has obviously been on the street for some time, she's doing pretty well. Still, you'll need some salve for those paws and some antibacterial ointment for the sores. She's had a rough trip."

"All right," Anna said.

"I'd also like to see her in a week or so. Once she's put on some weight, we can give her shots and make certain everything else is functioning well. We took some blood just before the bath, and we'll call you with those results."

Anna let out a shaky sigh. "Why would a cat put herself through all this? Her life wasn't that great. My ex-boyfriend didn't hurt her until that last night, but he wasn't nice to her either."

The vet smiled at her. "I don't think she traveled all this way for him. She came here to find you."

Anna spent the evening on the phone, Star curled on her lap. The cat never stopped purring, even after she had fallen asleep. She smelled of perfume from the flea bath and she was so thin that she felt fragile.

Anna kept a hand on her, half afraid that Star would vanish if she stopped touching her. Anna didn't believe in miracles, and now she was being confronted with this one. Even if Star had survived, Anna wasn't sure that her cat would be able to handle the wilds of nature and such a long journey.

Yet somehow she had.

The phone calls confirmed the vet's suspicions. When Anna's friends and family finally arrived at the apartment two days after the attack, they didn't find Star. There was a lot of blood on the floor and along the wall—"Probably your blood, honey," her mother said as gently as possible—and tiny feline footprints smeared on the carpet.

The family had asked the neighbors about Star and were told that no one saw her but that the apartment door had stood open for nearly an hour after the police and paramedics left, until a kindly neighbor had pulled the door closed, fearing robbers.

"We figured Star had crawled out of the apartment to die," her sister said.

"Some of us looked for her for days," said Collette, one of her closer friends, "but she never came to us when you were around. If she was still alive, she wouldn't have come to us. To be honest, by the third day, we were looking for her body. We didn't find that either."

"No one told me," Anna said to her mother.

"Oh, sweetie," her mother said, "we didn't want to tell you. We figured you'd suffered enough already."

The next morning, the vet called with the results of the blood tests. Star hadn't picked up any unusual diseases on her journey.

"How's our traveler?" Dr. Twohy asked at the end of the conversation.

"Tired," Anna said. She was tired, too. She had spent all night wondering what Star had been through, how she had survived it, and made her way thousands of miles alone when she hadn't even been outside before.

"I've always thought cats are amazing," Dr. Twohy said. "Listen, with your permission, I'd like to write a paper about her. There aren't many cases of psi-trailing this easy to document. I'd love to see what I can find out about Star's journey."

Anna looked at her cat, asleep in a ray of sunshine on the kitchen floor. "I guess it wouldn't hurt. But Star's not going to tell you anything."

"Oh, you'd be surprised," Dr. Twohy said. "I'm sure she can tell me a lot."

Psi-trailing. Anna looked it up on the web. There were a number of crackpot websites, most of them devoted to old-wives tales and silliness. But a few seemed legitimate.

The one she found most convincing recounted studies done at various universities. The groundbreaking study had been done at Duke University in the early 1960s. That study had examined 500 documented cases of psi-trailing and applied four questions to the cases: Was the report honest? Was the animal accurately identified by some physical or behavioral trait? Was there evidence of travel? Were there supporting witnesses?

When the screening was done, Duke came up with legitimate cases involving twenty-eight dogs, twenty-two cats, and four birds. Subsequent studies, completed all over the world in the intervening years had similar results. At least ten percent of domesticated animals had the ability to psi-trail.

Anna wouldn't have believed any of it if it weren't for Star's presence. She brought the cat to her next therapy session, and her therapist seemed quite entranced by the entire story.

"Isn't it nice to know," her therapist said, "that you're worthy of such love?"

Anna hadn't thought of it in that way. She certainly didn't feel worthy of any kind of love. But her nervousness decreased around Star, and her home seemed more welcoming.

And best of all, Star seemed to have no desire to leave, not even to go outside. Star seemed as pleased to be around Anna as Anna was to be around her.

* * *

"She's doing beautifully," Dr. Twohy said a week later. "I wouldn't have expected her to improve so quickly."

Star had gained one whole pound and her coat was becoming sleek. Her eyes were clear, and her fleas were gone. She wasn't as docile at the vet's this time—she clearly wanted to be home—but she seemed calm as long as Anna touched her.

Dr. Twohy had asked for, and received, Star's records from her New York vet. She had the file open before her.

"There is no doubt," she said, "that this is the same cat. I'd like your permission to do some blood work and a few other tests. We saved the dead fleas from last week as well. We might be able to trace her path, using what she ate, what kind of fleas she had, and a few other measures."

"I don't want to make her uncomfortable," Anna said.

"All we have to do is take some blood," Dr. Twohy said. "It'll be the last time."

Anna nodded.

"I'd also like your permission to call the newspapers. This is such a wonderful story—"

"No," Anna said.

"But people love human interest, and it might bring in a few scholars—"

"No," Anna said. "A scientific paper, yes. But anything else, no. I don't want people to know what happened to me. They'll look at me differently. They'll know—"

"What? That you're a survivor? That you've gone on with your life after such a horrible thing?"

Anna shook her head. "I don't want Neil to see the article. And he will. It'll be online and in the New York papers. Please don't. I won't cooperate if you try."

The vet studied her for a moment. "Fair enough," she said. "You deserve your privacy like anyone else. But I will have to use your name and Star's in any medical paper."

"I know," Anna said. "You can do that, as long as you promise not to say where I live or answer any reporters questions should they come up."

"I promise," Dr. Twohy said. "In fact, you can look over the article before I send it off."

Anna smiled at her—her second real smile at another human being in less than a week. "I appreciate that."

She bundled Star into her new cat carrier. Star was happy to go inside.

"I am curious about one thing," Dr. Twohy said. "If you don't want press coverage, why are you willing to let me do the paper?"

"Because," Anna said after a moment's consideration, "you're my proof that what's been happening is real."

* * *

Pete was sitting on his porch when Anna got home. He waved. She nodded to him as she pulled Star's cat carrier out of the car.

She took Star into the house and let her out. Star immediately rubbed against her legs, happy to be home. Anna sat down and cradled her cat. Some things from the past weren't that bad. Some things were pretty darn wonderful.

She was so happy to have Star back. She couldn't believe how lucky she was.

There was a knock on her door. She set the cat down and stood. The knock hadn't surprised her—the first time since the murder attempt that she hadn't jumped at an unexpected noise. She went to the front door, and peeked through the curtain covering the small window.

Pete stood outside.

She opened the door. "Hi."

He smiled. "Hi."

"I'd've waved back, but I had Star."

"I saw that," he said. "I came by to see how you and Star were doing."

He seemed genuine. And nice. And he'd lived next door for a very long time, and never once got in trouble. He'd always had pets and had always been nice.

"Star's perfect," she said.

"What about you?" He asked that question hesitantly, as if he weren't sure whether he should broach the subject.

She smiled. It was getting easier. "I'm better."

And she was. She hadn't really realized it until now.

"Would you . . . like to come in?" A week ago, she never would have asked him. A week ago, she was terrified to have anyone in her space. "I could make some tea."

"I'd love some tea," he said.

She let him in. Star watched from the kitchen doorway, but didn't run from him like she had always done from Neil. She hadn't liked Neil from the beginning. She seemed willing to tolerate Pete.

That surprised Anna. Star hadn't tolerated any of her New York friends. Maybe Star had changed in some good ways.

Maybe Anna had, too.

She led Pete to the kitchen. Star stayed beside her, protective and welcoming at the same time.

Anna's therapist would be proud of her, taking small steps forward. Anna was proud of herself. But she couldn't take credit for the movement.

The changes had been inspired by Star. Star, who had taken a long and difficult journey to get where she wanted to be. Star, who knew what she wanted and who she wanted to be with.

Star, who had taught Anna the meaning of true love.

UNDER THE SIGN OF THE FISH

by Karen Haber

Karen Haber's short fiction appears in *Warriors of Blood and Dream, Animal Brigade 3000, Elf Fantastic,* and *Wheel of Fortune.* Her novels include the science fiction trilogy *Woman Without a Shadow, Sister Blood,* and *The War Minstrels.* She lives with her husband, author Robert Silverberg, in California.

TIMANDRA lived in the village of Zodz that was part of the Duke of Viridian's domain, in a small, slightly lopsided stone house that stood catercorner to the tall, narrow dwelling of Nestor, the village sorcerer.

She was an old woman, bleached and bent by time, slow of step and hard of hearing, but she was still capable of love. And love she did: her children and their children and even their children—although she sometimes forgot their names—and the first shy flowers that poked their purple heads through the damp earth at winter's end, and the brave green-breasted hummingbird that darted from petal to petal in search of his daily cup of nectar.

She loved her graystone house and her well-laid

hearth. She loved the soft cushions on her chairs and window seat. She even loved her tot of warm honey wine at day's end. But more than anything else she loved her black-and-white cat, Apollo, and her goldfish, Phineas. And they loved her.

She admired Apollo's noble head, his sleek black-and-white pelt, his large amber eyes, the black speckles along his long white whiskers. Truly, he was a prince among cats. And Phineas, with his elegant plumy tail, his orange-gold scales, his dark bulging eyes, well, he was a very special fish, there was no question of that.

The problem was, Apollo did not love Phineas.

Timandra was troubled by this, troubled that each time she passed the sparkling goldfish bowl she saw black-and-white Apollo, crouched nearby, tail swishing, watching Phineas. That wasn't love in his amber eyes. Timandra had lived a long time, and she knew too well the emotion she saw there.

Phineas, bless him, swam in meditative peace, unconcerned. But Timandra knew that danger was only a leap away.

Over her lifetime she had learned the ways of the world, of human beings, and nature. She had learned to be careful, to lock her doors and look over her shoulder. But one thing she had never learned was to lose hope. And she was hopeful now that Apollo could be made to love Phineas.

(I didn't say that Timandra wasn't foolish occasionally. But when she was foolish, it was often in the service of love, and what better reason is there for foolishness, after all?)

And so Timandra continued to hope that Apollo would love Phineas.

The days passed, and spring moved toward summer. Timandra especially liked to spend the twilight time sitting on the soft cushions by her window and watching the stars rise in the purple sky. Her favorite constellation, Pisces, the fish, was the last to climb above the horizon, and each night she waited eagerly for its blue-white stars to peep over the Earth's curve.

Apollo would always sit with her, studying the stars intently, purring all the while. Now and then he would lapse into solemn meditation.

Timandra imagined Apollo's mind leaping outward and upward, voyaging through the night sky. She was certain that Apollo possessed a special sort of cosmic consciousness. Often she had come upon him peering up at the stars, or lost in profound concentration. He was a philosopher, interested in the moon and the stars. His amber eyes contained mysterious depths and unfathomable wisdom. Surely he was a wizard among cats.

How disappointing, then, that this fabulous fur-covered sage also had a base craving: he desperately wanted to catch and eat Phineas.

As the sky darkened, Timandra shooed Apollo off her lap, stood, and prayed to the elder gods for wisdom. When she had finished praying, she turned and found Apollo dangling a paw in Phineas' bowl. His claw was extended like a fishhook. Phineas was examining the claw in a peaceful contemplative way.

Timandra clapped her hands hard. "Bad boy! Apollo, get away from there." Apollo looked up, pulled his paw from the bowl, shook it, and jumped to a stout beam near the rafters for a quick bath. She heard the low, sinister sound of his purr—the one that was the purr of anger, of cold catlike rage. Then he turned and cast his gaze out the window at the stars.

Mortified, Timandra moved Phineas' bowl into an alcove where it sat snugly and could not be tipped over. She put a smooth golden cutting board across the top of the bowl and weighted it with two flowerpots filled with purple-and-white pansies.

"There," said Timandra. "Let him try to get near you now."

Phineas floated in his bowl, unconcerned. Timandra felt better just looking at him. Dear Phineas. Such a sweet fish. So serene as he moved about his bowl, staring peacefully outward.

That night she locked Apollo in her bedroom and just before bedtime she gave him a lecture.

"You are a special cat, Apollo, I know that. And I understand that we are all just children of the elder gods. But you must leave Phineas alone. He doesn't threaten you, does he? No, he doesn't. And do you lack for food? No, you most certainly do not. We must all live together here in peace and harmony. Do you understand?"

Apollo purred loudly and gave her a deep, confiding look.

Timandra turned out the lamp and got into bed. Apollo snuggled next to her, his purr a sweet lullaby.

The next morning Timandra was especially busy. It was Fourthday and time for the market. She quickly fed Apollo and Phineas, swept the hearthstones, and bolted down her barley tea.

She put on her second best cloak, the green one with the deep pockets, picked up the lidded basket with the leather handle, and hurried out the door.

The market was choked with busy housewives buying up brown loaves of fresh bread, long ribbons of smoked fish, jars of fresh-churned butter and buckets of milk.

The smell of spice and honey, of blood and newly churned dirt filled the air. Chickens, their necks freshly wrung, hung like yellow pennants above Mr. Nielsen's stand.

Sacks of lentils and oats were fingered by sour-faced women determined not to be cheated. Fresh fruit was still rare this early in the season, but green jams and pink jellies added a welcome touch of color and sweetness to the spectacle. Every merchant sang out to the crowd to come and buy, come and buy.

"The best potatoes!"

"Sweet cheese, just try it!"

"Pepper and salt. Cloves and nutmeg. Come along, ladies. You can't cook without 'em."

"I've got sausages here, fresh sausages for sale!"

Timandra was a long time filling her basket. She chose carefully, two firm potatoes here, a yellow wedge of cheese, six fresh eggs, and four small sausages. Although the jellies were tempting, she decided against the indulgence. She could make her own come harvest time. Weighted down, she turned for home.

The sun warmed the air, flowers nodded their yellow heads, and the birds sang for joy. But try as she might to retain her good cheer, Timandra couldn't help but feel haunted by misgivings. What should she do about her pets? What should she do?

The Widow Pitke hove into view, a dominating vision in black-and-gray shawls. She was almost as wide as she was tall, and walked with a rocking gait. Many opinions were held by the Widow Pitke, and she shared them all freely, without waiting to be asked.

In a voice like grated iron she said, "There you are, Timandra. Have you seen Vronsky's apples yet? No? Then listen to me and save yourself the trouble. Such wrinkles I haven't seen since my mother-in-law was alive. He should be ashamed to sell last year's fruit." She sniffed and nodded, in full agreement with herself. "But his onions! As golden as the sun. And sweet? Look." She pulled a large yellow onion from her basket, bit into it, and offered it to Timandra.

"No, thank you, Violet dear." Timandra was not especially fond of raw onion although she liked onion well enough when fried in sweet butter with potatoes and eggs.

The Widow Pitke was only half blind, and with her good eye she saw more than you might imagine. What she saw now was her neighbor's unhappiness.

"But what's troubling you, Timandra? No, don't shake your head. You can't fool me. Out with it."

Overcoming her natural reticence—and her dislike of the scent of raw onion on the Widow Pitke's breath—Timandra blurted out her tale. "And all Apollo does is try to get at Phineas. I tell you, Violet, it breaks my heart."

Widow Pitke leaned upon her gnarled walking stick and nodded heavily. "You know what you should do? Go see the wizard. He'll fix you up. Remember when I had that problem with my Alfie boy? Always running after carts and getting under wheels, that dog. The wizard gave me a spell that settled him right down. You listen to me, Timandra, and go see our Nestor."

It was good advice; Timandra could see that. "Violet, when you're right, you're right. Thank you. I'll do just as you say, right now."

Timandra hurried home and put on her best

cloak—the pale one with the silken pink ribbons at the throat—and walked across the square to the narrow house of the village sorcerer.

The waiting room was crowded, but a gray-bearded gent in a ragged coat was courteous enough to give up his seat. Timandra thanked him and gratefully settled herself upon the hard wooden bench.

The consultation room was next door, the portal to it covered by arcane symbols graven into the wood, crossed lightning bolts set within a triple ring.

Nestor the sorcerer was known to be exceedingly impatient by nature. He was also a little deaf, and consequently he spoke loudly most of the time. Timandra could hear him now, talking—shouting, really—to a client: "No, I won't give you a spell to banish your bunions! Wear wider shoes and don't stay out dancing all night! I'm not some two-bit heal-all, you know!"

Nestor sounded even grumpier than usual. A young man whose cheeks were dotted by acne got to his feet and, his nerve failing him, dashed out the door, followed moments later by a frightened-looking woman in a blue shawl.

A hefty young woman with blonde hair in thick braids strode out of Nestor's room, halted to stare at her silent audience, blushed deep red, and hurried out into the street.

"Next!"

A small woman draped in widow's garb walked slowly into the wizard's room.

Timandra leaned back against the cold stone wall and closed her eyes. She could hear the woman's voice, but her words were indistinct murmurs.

"What do you think I am?" Nestor said. His voice had the quality of sandpaper against wood. "A miracle worker? Dead is dead, I told you that at the funeral! Stop blubbering. No, I'm not going to bring him back as a zombie. No! Now stop wasting my time. Nature is as ·.ature does."

Timandra felt her own courage evaporate. She had never heard Nestor in such a foul mood. Perhaps it was best if she came back another day. With an apologetic nod to red-haired Dora, the wizard's little apprentice, she slipped out the door.

When she got home, she found Apollo crouched low by Phineas' bowl, his ears straight back, his whole body tense.

He was watching the fish swimming back and forth, back and forth. His tail slithered back and forth, back and forth in matching rhythm, and his amber eyes were bright with wicked intent.

One of the flowerpots she had used to weight down the wooden cutting board had been knocked to the ground and broken, scattering dirt and pebbles—not to mention pansies—in a messy pile.

"Apollo! Get away from there."

The sharpness of her voice distracted the cat

long enough for her to grab him up and carry him across the room. Immediately Apollo began purring and preening against her shoulder. Timandra felt her annoyance melting away. What could she do?

She spent an uneasy night locked in her bedroom with the cat. Again and again the Widow Pitke's refrain came back to haunt her: "Go see the wizard. He'll fix you up."

Nestor. See Nestor.

She would go back tomorrow and be brave.

The next morning, just after her breakfast of grilled oatcakes and sweet barley tea, Timandra gathered her courage. She told herself that she had to see Nestor, regardless of how impatient he was. In her pale cloak with its pink ribbons she made her way back to the wizard's house.

The waiting room was empty.

Dora gave her a sweet smile and said, "You're in luck today. He's in a better mood." With an encouraging wave she sent Timandra through the symbol-laden door into Nestor's den.

The old wizard sat in a high-backed chair, reading from an enormous book. His booted feet rested upon a hot water bottle balanced on a three-legged stool. His hair was nearly gone, but his beard was white and long enough for a family of robins to nest in it. His thin lips and squinting left eye gave him a look of perpetual displeasure. Nestor looked up as Timandra entered and raised an eyebrow. "Well?"

"Good morning, Great Wizard." Her curtsy was made awkward by the ache in her knees. "Please, I want a spell to protect my beloved goldfish, Phineas, from my beloved cat, Apollo." In a breathless voice she described Apollo's daily efforts to catch Phineas and eat him. "If only Apollo could be kept from trying—"

Nestor's blue eyes flashed, and his mouth worked. For a moment he looked to be suspiciously on the verge of laughter. But his comment, when it came, was, as ever, dry and sardonic. "That is beyond the reach of magic, old woman."

"But —"

"Nature is as nature does."

Timandra stared at him in amazement. But Nestor was already waving a dismissal.

"Next!"

Sadly Timandra returned home and passed the day standing guard over Phineas. Apollo took up his position nearby, watching. Waiting.

It's not fair, she thought. *One's so big and one's so little. One's so strong and the other's so helpless. If only Apollo understood what it was like. . . .*

Sadly, she watched the sun move lower in the sky until the day had extinguished itself in a thin line of red along the edge of the land. The first stars of evening were peeping through the purple haze. Soon The Fish were shimmering over the horizon, blue-white Alresha the brightest knot in the Piscean string.

Timandra gazed at the springtime constellation. Pisces, the sign of the fish: it had to be an omen. Yes.

She sat up straighter than she had in a fortnight. A sign, yes, and one that she understood. She would gather her courage one more time, she would go back to the wizard, and she would ask him for a spell that would put Apollo under the sign of the fish.

The next morning Timandra presented herself yet again before the wizard Nestor. "Great Wizard," she said. "The stars have led me to your door once more."

"So I see." Nestor made an impatient gesture. "And?"

"Would it be possible for you to put a fish's soul in a cat's body and a cat's soul in a fish for perhaps half a day?"

"What would that achieve, pray tell?"

"The cat will experience the helplessness of the fish at first hand, and that will teach it pity for small defenseless creatures."

Nestor's eyes widened. "Interesting idea," he said. He gazed past her, musing. There was not a sound in the room besides the crackling of the logs burning in the stove. After a time the wizard stirred. "We could try it, I suppose." He picked up a white-plumed pen and began to write. In mid-scribble, he stopped, peered at her, and said, "Can you read, missus?"

"Yes. My children taught me."

"Hmm." His grunt was one of surprise. "Good." He handed her the finished incantation. "When you get home, read that once and then throw it into the fire. For twenty-four hours—and twenty-four hours only—the souls of your pets will be transferred into each other's body." He rang a tiny bell. "Dora! Next one!"

As she crossed the cobblestoned square, Timandra's spirit danced at the thought of having her problem solved. The sun was low on the horizon as she unlocked her front door.

Apollo had been sleeping in the front window. He yawned and jumped down to greet her. Phineas swam round and round in his sparkling bowl.

"Hello, my darlings!"

Timandra was so eager to invoke the wizard's spell that she didn't bother to cast off her cloak. And she ignored Apollo's urgent demands for lunch. She stirred up the fire until the flames danced merrily, took a step back, planted her feet firmly upon the hearthstones, and recited, "Caana. Feerum. Astorum."

Next she cast the scrap of vellum upon the fire and watched it burn until it had turned to a wisp of gray ash. She turned in happy anticipation.

Nothing had changed.

Apollo still sat and watched Phineas swimming in his bowl. Timandra felt deep disappointment seeping into the room with the evening shadows. Had Nestor made a mistake? Maybe he was getting old.

Then she looked more closely. Something was different. Yes. Very different.

Apollo sat on the floor, placidly watching the fish in the bowl. It was not so much his appearance as his aura that had changed. No longer did he seem to possess the mystic far-reaching perception that he normally had. In fact, he just sat there, dopily watching the fish without much interest. He did nothing. And why should he? He no longer possessed the soul of a special, mystical farseeing cat, but merely that of a fish.

Meanwhile, Phineas was swimming in tight panicky circles, eyes rolling back and forth, mouth working oddly. Timandra had never seen a more agitated fish.

All that afternoon, evening, and most of the next morning, the situation remained unchanged. The cat sat mildly, staring into space. The goldfish swam wildly, eyes rolling, tail flashing, nose butting from time to time against the wall of the bowl in what looked very much like desperation.

At the stroke of noon, Timandra put aside her knitting and watched eagerly.

Phineas ceased his frantic movements and once more swam placidly in his bowl.

Apollo shook his head, looked around the room in feline amazement, and licked his tail several times.

Then, without warning, he sprang at the fish-bowl, knocked it over. Water spilled everywhere.

"No!" Timandra cried. But before she could make a move, Apollo had seized Phineas and swallowed the fish, whole.

Weeping and angry, Timandra grabbed the empty bowl and hurried back to Nestor's house. Pushing her way through the crowd in the waiting room, she marched directly into his inner sanctum.

"Look," she cried. "Just look at what your spell has caused to happen!"

Nestor's expression was, for Nestor, mild. "Well," he asked. "what did you expect?"

Timandra was so angry that she stamped her foot. "Expect? You know what I expected!"

Nestor shrugged. "Very likely the cat didn't enjoy the experience. I suppose he meant to make certain that it would never happen to him again."

"But what about pity?" Timandra said. "You said the cat would learn pity by being a fish for a day."

"Oh, no, no, no." Nestor got to his feet. "Never would I say a thing like that." With each word he seemed to grow until he filled the room. "It was you who said that, old woman. Not me. You who wanted a foolish spell. How could you have lived so long and think that anyone could teach pity to a cat?" The wizard snorted with laughter. "It would be easier to teach a tree to dance! Go home, Timandra. Go home and sit with your cat. Play with it. Talk to it. But never, ever hope to teach it pity. That is beyond the scope of nature, magic, and even the stars."

Timandra's heart was sore in her breast as she trudged homeward. All day she ignored Apollo until, at sundown, she took her accustomed place upon the cushions by the window.

As blue-white Pisces rose in the night sky, Apollo leaped into her lap, purring, and curled into a cozy ball. He seemed to be watching the stars with fascination.

He was the same cat, thought Timandra. Just as lovable. Just as special and cosmically aware. But even philosopher cats have cat-souls. And cats know no pity. Apollo was what he was. She had no right to ask for anything else.

Nestor was right. She would never teach pity to a cat. Nature is as nature does.

She watched the changeless stars for a long time, until her eyelids grew heavy with the need for sleep.

The next morning she carefully washed out the fishbowl. She fed Apollo and swept the hearthstones. She put on her favorite shawl, the one with the pink ribbons. Apollo, she saw, was lost in his morning meditations, sitting in a puddle of sunlight by the window.

Nature is as nature does.

Timandra smiled at the truth of that thought. It was as true for humans as for animals. And it was simply her nature to love her pets, and to need them. Still smiling, Timandra went out into the fresh morning to buy a new goldfish—and a secure lid for its bowl.

EVERY LIFE SHOULD HAVE NINE CATS

by Mickey Zucker Reichert

Mickey Zucker Reichert is a pediatrician who has written numerous science fiction and fantasy novels, including two trilogies about the Renshai. Her latest novels are *Flightless Falcon* and *The Beasts of Barakhai*. Her short fiction has appeared in numerous anthologies, including *Battle Magic*, *Zodiac Fantastic*, and *Wizard Fantastic*. Her claims to fame: she has performed brain surgery, and her parents really are rocket scientists.

A WARM breeze heavy with damp wound through Wallinston's packed earth roadways, scant comfort from the heat. Qualin plucked at the strands of straw-colored hair that sweat had plastered to his temples and glanced at his companion. Heming marched steadily through the streets, head level, expression dispassionate, copper-and-white uniform crisply pressed and meticulous. Every hair lay in place, including his mustache, though gray mingled liberally with the black; his dark eyes revealed nothing. In comparison, Qualin felt like a bumbling fool. He cleared his throat. "So, why do we have to spend three days with this old lady?"

"M-check," Heming replied without looking at his partner. "Level 3."

"Level 3, huh," Qualin repeated. "M-check." He had no idea what any of those terms meant; and, so far, no one had given him any others. He glanced around at the awakening town. Women scurried to market or carried laden buckets, water sloshing as they moved. The distant mooing and bleating of animals carried on the wind, overladen by the thump of hammers on wood and the ringing clamor of the blacksmith's tools. Cottages stood in winding rows, blocks chinked with mud, wood roofs buried beneath tufts of insulating thatch. "Now, can you explain it in Wallinstonian?"

Heming drifted closer to Qualin, as if afraid of someone overhearing, though no one had given them more than a passing glance. "They think the 'old lady' might have magic."

Qualin nodded, waiting for the other shoe to fall.

Heming fell back into his rhythmical walk.

Suddenly left behind, Qualin jogged to his partner's side. "Just having magic? That's a crime now?"

Heming jerked to a sudden stop.

Now, Qualin found himself several paces ahead of his companion. He backstepped to meet beetled brows and a sour frown.

"Where have you been?"

Shocked by Heming's abrupt irritation, Qualin stammered. "Y-you stopped so suddenly. I-I couldn't—"

Heming laughed. "I mean, where have you been the last several months?"

"At Redsands. Training." The military had suffered heavy casualties during the recent war against a trio of powerful sorcerers. The town guard had stepped in to assist, and the cities had banded together to indoctrinate as many men as they could to take the places of those lost. Qualin had nearly completed his carpentry apprenticeship when he got called up and decided the guard force needed him more. "What did I miss?"

Heming continued their walk. "Did you miss Narvika, Haslawt, and Sharm slaughtering hundreds to gain control of the local government?"

Qualin resumed moving as well. "No, of course not."

"Did you miss the corpses, the injured soldiers, the towns in ruins?"

Qualin did not feel certain about how to answer that question. "I saw some. Heard of others." Inadequacy enveloped him, and he wondered if he had gone stupid. "I don't see the connection between three sorcerers gone mad and some quiet old lady."

"That's what we're going to determine."

"Oh." Qualin tossed his head, splattering sweat. "So . . . she knew them?" he tried. A sudden shiver wracked him. He remembered hearing stories of the Iberian market exploding into flames, wares thrown like droplets in a tempest, people charred like old match sticks. If this woman carried the powers they had, he did not wish to provoke her.

"Don't know." Heming stepped around a pile of horse manure left on the roadway. "But if she's got any kind of magic, we have to alert the M-squad."

M-check. M-squad. Qualin pinched his heart-shaped face between his callused, long-fingered hands. "The M is for magic?" he guessed.

Heming did not slow, but he glanced at his partner again. "Of course. You sure you're ready for this?"

"Yes," Qualin said from habit, though he doubted it. The idea of facing off with a sorcerer churned nausea through his gut. "I'm ready. Just—didn't know."

Heming adjusted his sword belt around his slender waist. "Not much to it really. Just observation." He headed down a side street away from the heart of the city.

A band of boys crouched in the road around a circle of irregular, unpolished marbles. They looked up, some waving, as the guards stepped around them and continued.

"What happens if we see anything magical?" Qualin asked as they reached the next crossroad.

"I told you. We report it."

Qualin made an impatient gesture. "Then what happens?"

"Execution."

Stunned by the revelation, Qualin stopped. "Really?"

Heming halted, then turned crisply. "Really."

For several moments, the two men stood, facing one another. "Why? She's just an old woman. She's not—"

Heming glanced past Qualin at the boys. Only the occasional excited shout wafted to them now. "She might."

"Might what?" Qualin held challenge from his tone with effort. Though shocked and bothered, he had no right to confront a senior partner. Heming placed a fatherly arm across Qualin's shoulders, steering him back down the path. "Narvika, Haslawt, and Sharm—not the first; but, by the grace of all the gods, the last."

The burden of the implications seemed too heavy to bear. "So we kill all users of magic because of three miscreants?"

"Magic is power, Qualin." Heming explained with a composure Qualin did not share. "Power so far beyond anything else in the world that it corrupts the wielder."

"Not always."

"Always," Heming said as the roadway grew stonier, weedy, and the cottages thinned. "It's just a matter of how they . . . express . . . that corruption."

At the end of the lane, a wooden fence surrounded a homey-looking cottage and garden.

"Always?" Qualin repeated, scarcely daring to believe it. He did not know anyone with magic personally, but it seemed impossible. "Always?"

Heming stopped walking, still several paces from the cottage. "Imagine yourself stronger than ten men and sword-proficient beyond logical possibility. Could you resist using your ability for your own wealth, glory, and might?"

"I . . ." Qualin did not know. "I would hope I could."

Heming patted Qualin's back, then removed his hand. "You're a good man." He frowned then. "But most aren't. With inhuman ability comes certain . . . burdens: loneliness, for example. And arrogance. Also, they're born with the same frailties we all have: desire, suspicion, greed." He sighed. "I said those three were not the first sorcerers gone power-mad."

"Yes."

"They were not the twentieth either."

That caught Qualin's attention. "More than twenty?"

"Just in my time as a guard."

Caught by surprise, Qualin swallowed hard. "I . . . didn't know."

"Most people don't. We like to keep it that way."

Qualin thought he understood. He would have found it hard to continue wrestling with the simple duties of his daily routine with the threat of some grisly death hanging over him. Farming might seem pointless, building a sham. "So," he finally managed. "What do we have to do?"

Heming led the way to the gate, tripping the well-oiled latch. "There're certain things we look for, beginning with animals."

"Animals?" It seemed odd to Qualin.

"All sorcerers have a pet, usually a cat."

"A cat?" Qualin said. A memory surfaced from childhood, himself begging his parents for a kitten and their gentle refusal. An animal meant one more mouth to feed. His suggestion that it could earn its keep catching mice and rats fell on deaf ears. Cats worked well for farms and granaries, but homes with no storage did not attract vermin. Realizing he sounded stupid just repeating the last word his companion spoke, he tried something more original. "But lots of people have pets. Not just sorcerers." It occurred to him that he had owned a cat many years ago, though the details of how he had got past his parents' objections remained sketchy for the moment.

Heming swung open the gate. "Of course. That's not the only criterion."

Qualin still hesitated to enter. "What else?"

"I've got a whole list." Heming gestured Qualin toward the garden path. "We can go over it tonight."

Qualin looked up. The cottage sat at the end of a short path lined with neatly tended flowers that waved in the breeze. Colors intermingled patternlessly, deep blues and startling pinks, brilliant yellows, oranges, and scarlets. The green stems added a dull contrast that made the petals seem all the more vivid. To the right, a vegetable garden formed a perfect rectangle, each food type in its individual plot. Vines snaked across, over, and through simple wooden trellises. Leafy tops stretched toward the sky in crooked rows, their bright emerald suggesting a healthy growth of root vegetables below.

"Nice," Qualin said, his tone revealing his respect for the woman's gardening skills.

Heming grunted. "A bit too nice if you ask me."

Qualin jerked his attention to his partner. "What do you mean by that?"

Heming did not answer, nor did he have to.

"You think . . . you think she might have used . . ." Qualin found himself whispering. ". . . magic?"

"I'm suspicious," Heming admitted.

Execution. Qualin swallowed. The idea of making a mistake pained. "Or she might have grown up on a farm. Or have gardened most of her life. Lots of natural talent or experience. Or—"

"Easy, boy," Heming interrupted. "I'm not going to make a judgment just based on one or two things. We've got three days to observe and as long as it takes to decide." He started up the pathway, lowering his voice. "I'm just saying that magic can take the place of talent and experience. Whether it's true in this case . . ." He shrugged. ". . . we'll see."

The responsibility seemed awesome. "So, by the end of our time here, we'll know for sure—"

"Impossible."

Another blow. Qualin clamped his hands and found them sweaty. He wiped them on his uniform breeks. "You mean we'll just have to . . ." He trailed off, allowing Heming to finish.

Dutifully, Heming did so. "Make a decision."

"And if we're wrong?"

"A sorceress goes free."

That mistake did not bother Qualin nearly as much as its opposite. "Or condemn an innocent old lady to death."

Heming sucked in a deep breath, then let it out slowly. "Qualin, we're guards. We make life-and-death decisions every day, and life doesn't hand us many certainties. I'm not going to declare someone guilty on a whim, all right?"

A friend of Qualin's father and a combat veteran, Heming had always shown common sense and good judgment. Qualin had been glad to draw the older man as a partner. "All right." He could not help adding, "But what if—"

Heming jumped in again, "—then 'if.' We do our best and live with the consequences, Qualin. It's part of the job." He stroked his mustache. "Wish we had it as easy as the *hivinators*."

The term meant nothing to Qualin. "The what?"

"The *hivinators*. The ones who check the newborns."

Qualin's heart skipped. For an instant, panic descended upon him, before it resumed its regular rhythm. "Are you saying they're sacrificing babies?"

Heming shrugged. "Only if they're magical." This time he grimaced, better revealing the feelings he had clearly tried to hide. "Better that than slaughter them as grown children or adults."

"I guess." Qualin shook his head. "But how do they know? That the babies are going to be sorcerers, I mean."

Heming shrugged again. "Not my area. Apparently, the newborns give off some sort of signal that certain people can detect. Once they get older, they suppress it."

"I can understand why."

"Yeah." Nearly at the front door, Heming paused. "But it sure makes our job harder. Puts innocents at risk. But eventually, with the *hivinators*, we won't have to do this at all."

Qualin understood. If they caught and exterminated the sorcerers at birth, they would no longer have to search and judge adults.

As the two men reached the lintel, the door whisked open to emit the crisp, enticing odor of baking bread accompanied by cloves and tubers. A plump, grizzled woman in an apron beamed at them from the doorway. "Welcome, welcome, good sirs. You look hungry."

Heming paused, his expression startled.

Qualin smiled and answered for both of them. "Thank you, good woman. Smells delicious." He took guilty satisfaction from his partner's shock. Heming bested him in weapons practice every time; for once, Heming had been disarmed instead of him.

Heming recovered quickly, trailing his partner into the cottage while the woman closed the door. The entrance opened into two rooms. To the left, a sturdy frame held a pallet neatly covered with blankets. A strongbox with polished copper bands and hinges lay at the foot of the bed. A chest of drawers took up most of one wall beneath a window that admitted tepid air and a bright beam of sunlight. A chamber pot sat in one corner, and a table and chair took up most of the center portion of the room, covered with cloth dyed a cheery lilac, matching thread, and three needles stabbed into the wood.

In the room to his right, Qualin saw another table, this one surrounded by stools. Clay plates and bowls sat at three places. A wrapped loaf steamed in the center, a jug beside it, and a basket held cold spiced tubers. Storage barrels lined the wall nearest a remarkably clean hearth. A full ash bucket sat nearby, a soot-blackened broom leaning against it. Smaller cooking utensils peeked over the edge of an enormous black kettle in the unlit hearth.

The woman gestured toward the table. "I'm Sarrie. Please sit. Help yourselves."

Though the manners his mother had taught suggested he do as his hostess bade, Qualin took his cue from Heming, who bowed politely to acknowledge the invitation, but did not move.

"Ma'am, you do understand why we're here?"

"No," Sarrie admitted, her expression still bright. Heming opened his mouth, but she continued over him. "I mean, I know the reason; but I don't understand why you've chosen me."

Qualin watched the exchange curiously. It seemed only fair to warn the subject of their observation, though he thought it counterproductive. Only a foolish sorcerer would reveal himself while he knew those with the power to execute him watched.

"It can only be because someone has raised suspicions about you," Heming proclaimed, still watching her.

"Ah," she said.

The smell of the fresh bread brought saliva to Qualin's mouth, and his stomach gurgled.

Though surely equally enticed, Heming maintained his stiff formality. "Ma'am, you have every right to withdraw your offer of hospitality."

Sarrie reeled as if struck, her face a pinched mask of affront. "Certainly not, sir. Even had I anything to fear from the loyal and honest guardsmen of Wallinston, good manners would not allow it." She gave the senior guardsman a piercing stare. "Surely you have enough years behind you to understand that."

Heming smiled stiffly, then waved toward the food. "I'm not sure I like being called 'old,' but I thank you for your unexpected hospitality."

Feeling it necessary both to dispel the awkwardness as well as defend the manners of the youth of Wallinston, Qualin added, "I prefer to accept the compliment she gave all of us. Loyal and honest." It was not exactly true. Although Qualin believed he and Heming embodied those words, not every one of Wallinston's guardsmen did so. Guards had all the shortcomings that came with being human—some cruel, some foolish, some grasping or inconsiderate. Qualin presumed the governor took pains to select men of character, but the recent crisis had to make him less meticulous. Sometimes, too, combat or speaking skill accounted for more.

Oblivious to Qualin's train of thought, Heming responded only to his words. "You can afford to take it as a compliment. She didn't call *you* old."

Sarrie patted her white hair into place. "You get used to it." She inclined her head toward the prepared table. "Now, sit. Sit, please. Help yourselves."

This time, Heming headed for the table, Qualin and Sarrie just behind him. They all chose places and sat. Sarrie unwrapped the bread, releasing a cloud of savory-scented steam, and raised a knife tucked into the basket beside it. She sliced off several thick pieces, then passed the basket around. Each man placed a hunk of bread onto his plate, waiting until Sarrie bit into her portion before trying their own. The caution made sense in this situation; the old woman had every reason to attempt to poison them.

Crunchy crust gave way to a soft center that seemed to fall apart in Qualin's mouth. When she added the sweetly spiced tubers and grape juice, it made a meal the like of which Qualin had not tasted since he left his mother's home. *If I could only find a woman my age who cooks like this, I'd marry her in a moment.* He suppressed a smile at the thought. A common saying suggested that men preferred regular good food to beauty, youth, even sex. For the first time, he felt he understood the saying.

With an apology for the accommodations, Sarrie placed the men in her drawing room for the night. Beside the kitchen/pantry and catercorner from Sarrie's sleeping quarters, it seemed the ideal place for the two to talk without worrying whether the woman could overhear them. Heavy coverings separated them from the eating area and the smaller room that held washbasins, chamber pots, and tubs. The center of their room contained two fresh piles of straw covered by finely woven woolen blankets washed to supple softness. Each had an intricately embroidered cat in its center, one an orange tabby, the other white. Two tables had been pushed against the hearth wall, chairs shoved beneath them holding pallets, dyes, and paints. Parchment and canvases covered their surfaces, deeply stacked. The walls supported nine pictures, every one of a lifelike cat. In one, a slender calico pounced on a mouse wide-eyed with terror. Another depicted a black-and-white queen attending a litter of five. A black kitten nursed while another batted at her tail. A calico snuggled between her paws. Two gray tabbies suckled beside their darker sibling. Heming hefted canvases partway from the table, glancing at the pictures.

"I like her," Qualin said softly.

Heming continued sifting through the stack. "I like her, too." A frown deeply scored his features. "But you know we're not here to determine if we like her."

Qualin sighed. "So tell me what we're looking for. And what you think so far."

Heming laid down all the canvases and sat on the blanket with the embroidered white tabby. "Every picture's of a cat."

"Yes?" Qualin took a seat beside Heming, who had not answered his question.

"Magic and cats go together."

Qualin studied his companion. In the moonlight seeping through the only window, he looked older, burdened. "These aren't real cats," he reminded.

"No."

Silence fell. Qualin glanced around the hanging pictures again. One caught his eye, a thick-faced ginger tom sitting with a look of catty smugness. Once it caught his attention, it would not let go.

Qualin knew that cat.

Heming addressed the query at last, his voice jarring. "I'm not used to . . . kindness . . . from these people." He hurried on, "Not that I blame any of them. If they're innocent, they have a right to resent the intrusion. If guilty, they have everything to hide. This . . . this hospitality. I'm not sure how to read it."

Qualin grunted. He wanted to say more, but the picture held him spellbound. Long-suppressed memories from his childhood flooded back with such vivid clarity he wondered how he could have forgotten them. His parents had not allowed him to keep a cat, but a cat had kept him. It had come to him at twilight, through the window of his room, and lain with him through the night. Its satiny fur had yielded so smoothly to his touch. Its purr had become the ultimate lullaby. Every night it had come, and every morning it left. With the creativity of a young child, he had given it the name Oxcart, another fascination. He could spend hours studying the great ox-drawn vehicles of the Iberian merchants, their massive axles, their sturdy wheels, their travel-stained chassis.

With age had come a realization that his parents had explained for years. Oxcart was not a real cat, just a figment of his imagination. And, as he grew to adulthood, reality overcame fantasy. The need for a cat disappeared and, with it, the solidity of his whimsy. In the ensuing years, he had pushed the fantasy-cat to cobwebbed depths of memory. And now, this picture brought the animal home.

Finally, Heming's voice broke through Qualin's reverie. "You know, if you're not even going to listen, I'm going to save my breath."

Qualin shook his head, forcing his attention back to his companion. "I'm sorry. I'm just . . . tired . . . I guess." He caught his gaze drifting toward the cat again and jerked it back.

Heming yawned. "Me, too. Probably best we get some sleep. We've got two more days to finish the assessment and as long as it takes to talk out our decision."

Qualin shifted to the other pallet, taking closer notice of the embroidered tabby. Though also a ginger, it did not draw him into remembrance as the picture had done. He lay down and rolled to his side, his back to Heming, comparing the two pictures. He had never before considered the differences between cats, other than the obvious coloring. The cat on the blanket had a narrower face, a tighter pattern of stripes. Though just as realistic, it was not Oxcart. He looked at the picture again, no less fascinated than the previous time. He could not quite define the differences in the shape of the face, the eyes, the set of the nose, yet it definitely defined his imaginary pet. He realized he could not have described the differences between the faces of his sisters either, yet he would never confuse one for another.

The problem bothered Qualin long into the night. Heming's gentle snores rose above the creaking of crickets, the deep whirring of foxes, the higher-pitched warble of owls. He redirected his thoughts, at first gently, then with irritation; but, always, they returned to the cat he thought he had permanently forgotten. Rolling from side to side brought him no nearer to sleep and also broke the pattern of Heming's breathing. Seeing no reason why neither of them should sleep, Qualin rose, traipsed through the hanging, and used a rough-hewn clay chamber pot. Then, worrying their hostess would find it first and feel obligated to empty it before he could, he carried the pot out the back door.

The sounds of the night intensified. The moon carved a gentle crescent through the black velvet of the sky, and stars sprinkled the heavens in the clear patterns he had learned in childhood: the Ocean Waves in the eastern sky, the Bear in the northwest, pointing the way to the North Star, the paired Oxen to the south. The wind bowed flowers around a bench carved from stone, loosing sweet-smelling pollen. Surreptitiously pouring out the contents of the chamber pot, he sat on the bench and placed it beside him. Not yet ready to return, he alternately watched chips of quartz glimmering in his seat, the yawing flowers, and the great expanse of the heavens above him.

"Beautiful, isn't it?"

The gravelly female voice caught Qualin utterly by surprise. He lurched and spun clumsily, sweeping the chamber pot forward. It slammed against an edge of the bench, shattering, and fragments of clay tumbled to the ground.

Sarrie carried a blanket over her nightdress, and a kerchief covered her hair. "I'm sorry," she said, catching his elbow. "Did I frighten you?"

"How could you tell?" Qualin sheepishly studied the hunks of clay littering the walkway. "Caught off guard. Some guardsman, huh?"

"Actually, I find you more pleasant than most."

Qualin blinked. It seemed to contradict her previous compliment of the entire force. "Honest and loyal?"

"I hope so." Sarrie moved gracefully to the bench and sat. From the back she looked like a much younger woman, her spine straight, head high, her figure voluptuous and full.

Horrified, Qualin forced the thought from his head. *I am tired to be looking at an elderly woman that way.* Hurriedly, he gathered hunks and chips of clay, piling them on one end of the bench.

Sarrie took no notice. "You never answered my question."

Qualin tried to remember it.

Sarrie assisted. "Beautiful, isn't it?" She made a broad, arcing gesture. "I mean the sky, not my garden."

"Your garden is beautiful, too."

"I'll assume that's a yes." Sarrie studied the heavens, and Qualin found himself doing the same. Though he was twenty-five years old, it seemed like a century since the lazy nights of his childhood when he had puzzled the pattern of the stars from his window, Oxcart in his lap.

Qualin blurted, "Are you a sorcerer?" He had not meant to ask the question, but now that it had fallen from his mouth, he looked to Sarrie for an answer he did not expect.

To his surprise, she smiled. "No more than you are, Qualin."

The odd response caught Qualin nearly as unprepared as her arrival.

Before he could comment on it, Sarrie pointed. "What do you see there?"

Qualin set the last chunk of pot on the bench, then followed Sarrie's gesture to the constellation. "You mean the Bear?"

Sarrie's grin persisted. "Yes, the . . . Bear." She emphasized the last word as though to make a issue of it, though she did not continue in that vein. "Qualin, you're obviously reluctant. Why do you do this?"

"This?" he pressed.

"Evaluate possible sorcerers."

Qualin gave the only answer he could. "It's my job."

"And if it were your job to execute those people, would you?"

Qualin refused to lie. He had never killed anyone, yet he had already contemplated the possibility that he might during the course of his duty. "Yes."

"What if you knew, for a fact, that they were innocent. Would you still execute them."

This time, Qualin considered. "No."

Sarrie finally faced him directly, the moonlight kind to the wrinkles on her cheeks. "What would you do?"

It seemed obvious. "I would talk to my superiors, get them to free the innocents."

"And if they wouldn't listen. Would you do as your duty required?"

Qualin shook fatigue from his thoughts, seeking a clear answer. He yawned. "You mean kill them?"

"Yes."

"No. And I'd try to see to it no one else did either."

Sarrie's grin broadened. "Loyal and honest."

Qualin was not certain whether Sarrie meant he would be violating his loyalty to Wallinston or upholding it to the innocent. He merely shrugged. "I could never slaughter those I knew to be innocents, no matter my duty."

Sarrie jabbed a finger toward the constellation again. "What do you see?"

Qualin looked up. "Do you still mean the Bear?"

"The Bear, yes." Sarrie continued to point. "But tell me, Qualin. Have you ever seen a bear with a tail?"

"No," Qualin admitted. "But the legends say they used to have one. Back when the patterns of stars first formed and—"

Sarrie caught Qualin's arm. "Look harder."

Qualin did so, staring at the Bear until its form blurred and the stars that defined it became indistinct. A shadow superimposed itself into the outline, dim, orange, and indeterminate. He blinked, vision clearing to an unmistakable image. Where once had appeared the familiar pattern of stars someone long ago had named a bear, he now saw a ginger tomcat. *Oxcart*. The more he stared, the more he tried to clarify his vision, the more definitive the image became. "Lady Night," he breathed, startled to his feet. "Lady Night, it's . . . it's—" Suspicion thundered down on him, and he whirled on Sarrie. "What have you done to me?"

Sarrie looked at Qualin, smile wilting to bewilderment. "I've done nothing but asked you to open your eyes. You did so with no help from me."

Qualin swallowed and glanced back into the heavens. Now that he had seen it once, the Cat would remain there forever. "You bewitched me," he accused.

Sarrie's hands flew to her hips. "I did nothing of the kind. And you know it."

Strangely, Qualin did know it. No sorcerer he had heard of could influence a person's memories, and Oxcart remained *there* as well. "You *are* a sorcerer."

Sarrie said nothing as the rest sifted into focus.

"And so . . . so am . . . I?"

Sarrie neither confirmed nor denied either accusation.

Qualin's heart quickened at the dilemma. Duty bound him to report Sarrie and himself as well. He slammed his fist against the bench, pain hammering through his knuckles. "Why did you tell me? Why did you have to tell me?" He whirled, caught in a tidal wave of frustration, terror, and rage. "Do you want to die?"

"Did you think a hundred-and-seventy-year-old woman would fear death?"

Qualin froze. "A hundred and seventy?"

"Approximately. I might have missed a birthday or two." She shrugged. "Why do you think they suspected me of sorcery when I have performed not so much as a healing spell in all my time?"

"Why not?"

"Healing is not my talent. I'm a keeper. The Keeper, in fact."

The term meant nothing to Qualin. Lightheaded, he dropped back to the bench, deliberately slowing his breathing. "The Keeper?"

"Cats are magical animals. It's my job to hold them safe, link them with those who cannot link themselves."

"Like . . . me?"

"Like you."

"Oxcart?"

"Look for yourself."

Qualin did not have to. He knew the animal still beamed down upon him from the sky and understood, without knowing how, that he could conjure the living ginger tom to him with nothing more than a thought. "I'm a sorcerer." He looked at Sarrie, hoping for direction. "Do I have a talent?"

"Yes." Sarrie placed a motherly arm across his shoulders. "You read what's in people's hearts."

Qualin considered that. He had always had a knack for selecting good friends, honest merchants, loyal companions. He looked at Sarrie and knew she told the truth, that she was right. He had liked her for a reason; she had a good heart, one that deserved to continue beating.

"I am a sorcerer," Sarrie finally admitted directly. "For more than a century and a half. Yet, there is nothing I can do about this situation. Good people will die. Honest people will lose their lives. All for the ambitions of a few." She tightened her grip. "I've placed my life into your hands, Qualin. And yours, too. That's obvious. But what's less obvious are the lives of so many unborn." She caught and held his gaze, her eyes lacking the watery thickness of age. "And it's not as simple as the governor believes."

Qualin nodded to indicate he still listened.

"The *hivinators*, they're magical. Once they die out, no one can replace them . . ."

". . . because the babies . . ." Qualin inserted slowly.

"When that happens, no one can determine whether a child will have the talent. Things will return to the way they were, except for one great detail."

Qualin figured it out. "Bitterness. Prejudice." The possibilities boggled his mind. "Future sorcerers more likely to try to seize power, to make up for the crimes of the past."

"I'm helpless to do anything about it. But you, Qualin, you're a guard. You have a platform. Some small power." No hint of the smile remained on Sarrie's face. "And, with your friend in the stars, the ability to make the just decisions."

Imbued with new hope, Qualin looked to a future that did not exist a moment before, speaking his plan aloud. "The *hivinators* can find the babies destined for magic. As to those discovered grown up, I can search their motives on a regular basis, help find those consumed by selfishness and greed, and . . ." . . . *and what?* The answer did not immediately follow. Though clearly more fair to execute only those with cruel hearts and magic than just anyone with magic, it would still result in destroying people who had not yet, and might not ever, do anything wrong. Qualin looked at Sarrie, who wore a hopeful expression. ". . . then I tell you. If you don't supply them a cat . . . ?" he wondered aloud.

This time, Sarrie finished for him. ". . . they never recognize their powers."

It seemed the perfect solution. "Now, all I have to do is to get the governor to listen to a fill-in guard want-to-be." Qualin shook his head, hopeless.

"What's in his heart?" the sorceress whispered.

His heart. Qualin looked at the sky. Oxcart beamed back at him. "His heart is good." Something soft touched Qualin's leg and purring filled his ears.

Oxcart was back.

ONCE, WE WERE WORSHIPED

by Diane A. S. Stuckart

Diane A. S. Stuckart has been caretaker to numerous felines over the years. Her current cat companion is Moonpie, a plump orange tabby whose favorite pastime is lying in areas of high foot-traffic and tripping the unwary. She—Diane, not Moonpie—is the author of five critically acclaimed historical romances written as Alexa Smart and Anna Gerard, as well as other short fantasy and romantic suspense pieces penned under her own name. When Diane is not busy catering to Moonpie's demands, she is working on another writing project or else practicing martial arts in an attempt to cultivate feline grace. She and Moonpie share their Dallas area home with Diane's husband, Gerry, and various dogs, birds, and fish.

New England
Summer, 1912

STARLIGHT pierced the shadowed canopy of ancient oaks and splashed like silver raindrops across the darkened courtyard. The resulting glow did little to illuminate the mossy expanse of faded brick that paved the tiny square. Still, it was more than sufficient light for Thomas Moonraker to make out the mummified corpse that lay there like a discarded haunch.

He studied the grisly object from his concealed perch high atop the courtyard's surrounding wall of stone. Until tonight, the body had reposed in the same spot where it had lain for the last dozen years, stacked with numerous other forgotten antiquities upon a shelf in Professor Winthrop's musty storage room. Thomas, himself, had been enlisted to drag the long-dead creature from its academic lair. Now, it lay exposed to the night, its carved wooden mask tossed aside, and its pitch-soaked linen wrappings shredded to reveal the withered body within.

A gust of wind caught at the fragile remains, so that they skittered a bit along the uneven brick. *Almost as if the thing were alive.* Thomas swiftly disguised his reflexive shiver with a careless stretch of his long, gray-striped torso. He wasn't superstitious . . . well, no more so than the average feline. True, he always left behind either a foot or a tail—never both—of any prey he consumed. And, certainly, he always made sure to lick a paw before running in or out of a doorway. Still, these rituals were more feline tradition than any precaution against bad luck. He'd never given credence to the old cats' tales of witches' familiars, nor had he ever met the black cat that could bestow bad luck. And, until last night, he had never believed that the dead could return to life.

But if Selena's claim proved true—that she, like

numerous of her feline ancestors, could summon the magical powers of the stars—he soon might witness that very corpse wandering about the courtyard, alive again, and after so many centuries.

To prove to himself that he wasn't unnerved by the entire situation, he eased through the overhanging branches and made the leap down into the courtyard. Then, as he padded his way toward the body, he reluctantly recalled what had led him to this pass.

Of course, the entire thing had been Selena Quicksilver's idea. Thomas gave a soft purr of appreciation as he pictured her . . . sleek black, tipped with a white chin and feet, and with eyes more golden than any he'd ever seen on a feline. They'd known each other since they were kittens, wrestling together in the garden. And, from the first, he had admired her.

Indeed, she was the cleverest of cats. She could do everything from snatching a tidbit from the butcher's window while evading that man's foul-tempered wife, to tipping a milk bottle so that the cream splashed out but the glass container never shattered. When *he* attempted the same feats, he always earned a swat from the butcher's wife's broom, or sent the milk bottle rolling off the stoop and into the street. And while he was reconciled to the fact that they would never be mates—Selena was far too self-centered ever to be any cat's per-

manent companion—he never lost hope that she
might one day consider him a good friend.

Lately, however, it seemed that she thought of
Thomas as little more than a nuisance. She had
been in this unsettled mood ever since spring, hissing and growling at the slightest provocation. True,
she had always been difficult. Professor Winthrop
was her third human caretaker . . . Selena having
summarily abandoned her first two families after
short tenures with each. Each time, she had huffed
that, if they expected drooling submission, the humans should find themselves a dog, instead. And
Thomas knew that she refused, on general princi-
ple, ever to purr when a human petted her.

But now, her arrogance had reached the point
that it even had begun to prickle whiskers in the
local cat community. Only Thomas, of all the neighborhood felines, would have anything to do with
her any longer. Still, it had been only the night before, as they'd sat beneath the stars in this same
courtyard, that he had screwed up his courage
enough to ask her what was wrong.

"Wrong?" she'd caterwauled in a tone that immediately made him regret the question. "Is it not
obvious what is wrong? The world has turned upside down. Once, we were worshiped by humans.
Now, we are their chattels, expected to sit in their
laps, rid their houses of rodents, and come when
they call our names."

At that inopportune moment, a scratchy human

voice had emanated from the ramshackle cottage at the courtyard's other end. "Mittens," Professor Winthrop called, sticking his bearded face out a half-open window. "I have a nice saucer of milk for you. Come inside, Mittens."

Mittens. Thomas saw Selena cringe, as always, at sound of her mundane name . . . the informal appellation given any cat by his or her human caretaker. Her white-tipped paws, which flashed in the dark whenever she padded her swift way across that starlit terrace, were the reason for the second portion of her nom du cat, Quicksilver. Unfortunately, the professor had been able to equate her precise coloring with nothing more interesting than a human item of clothing.

"Really," she'd huffed, slanting an evil golden eye in the direction of the house, "one would think that a human so well versed in the history of the Great Ones would have the courtesy to address their descendants with a bit more respect."

Thomas, while not exactly sure what she'd meant by that last, still had hidden a commiserating grin behind one fluffy gray paw. His human family had no clue as to his own nom du cat. By the greatest coincidence, however, they had dubbed him "Tom Kitty," to which name he answered as happily as his own. Most cats of his acquaintance did as he did and responded to their mundane names . . . particularly when cream or a nice bit of fish was at stake.

Selena, however, had ignored the professor, deliberately flopping onto the cool bricks to bask in a ray of starlight. Thomas did not immediately join her. Instead, absently rubbing an ear with one paw, he began, "You said that once we were worshiped. Do you mean that they once admired us in the same way that dogs admire their caretakers?"

"Dogs admire anyone or anything that will spare them the time of day," she had spat in a scornful tone. "If a bit of bone bounced off the garbage wagon and landed at a canine's paws, the silly beast would admire the garbage wagon. No, I'm speaking of worship. Do you know that once, we were the humans' caretakers . . . that we ruled and they obeyed?"

"Really?"

Thomas' wide green eyes had grown wider. His knowledge of feline history was limited to what had been passed down to him by his mother. In addition to teaching such practical skills as how to choose the sunniest spot for napping, she'd related tales of their ancestors . . . brave cats who had sailed the seas on foreign ships before settling in America generations earlier. As a kit, he'd found the stories quite thrilling though, as he grew older, he came to suspect many of those ancestral exploits. But even the wildest of those anecdotes could not compare to the tales with which Selena had begun to regale him.

He had listened in rapt amazement for much of

the night as she dreamily spoke of a magical cat kingdom she called E-Gyp. It was a land of mice and cream, a heaven on earth for a long-ago feline generation . . . the Great Ones, as she called them. There in E-Gyp, clouds never shrouded the night sky, so that a cat could dance beneath the starlight until dawn. There, too, a cat was never roused from a peaceful nap by a human intent on reclaiming a favored chair.

"The humans did as we cats bade them," she had pronounced in satisfaction. "They brought us offerings, built marvelous temples and tombs in our honor, and they mourned us most wonderfully when we died."

As if her stories had not been enough to confound him, she'd waited until Professor Winthrop had retired for the night. Then, she had motioned Thomas over to the same half-opened window from which the old man earlier had called.

"Come inside," she'd hissed, "and I'll show you how I learned of this."

Thomas had followed her lead. He'd found himself inside a musty room, the walls of which were lined, floor to ceiling, with all manner of books. Deftly, Selena wove her way through the equally numerous volumes stacked along the threadbare rug. She leaped gracefully onto the broad wooden desk, and Thomas had leaped after her . . . though he'd had to shuffle a bit as he landed to keep from sliding off the other side. Selena, for once, did not remark on his clumsiness, busy as she was pawing through a volume that lay open before her.

The starlight that shone through the window was bright as sunshine to Thomas' feline eyes, so that he had no trouble making out what was on the pages. Each was filled with lines and lines of what he knew humans called writing. That writing was interspersed with pictures of oddly dressed humans and even stranger looking cats. Some of the latter were adorned with jewelry; others were wrapped in some sort of cocoon, like a butterfly, and wore painted masks; still others seemed to be part human and part feline!

"These books all belong to Professor Winthrop," she had explained while Thomas stared at the pictures in amazement. "He used to be what the humans call an archaeologist . . . someone who digs up old things."

"Like a dog digs up a bone?"

"That is the general idea," Selena impatiently replied, "though humans finds objects far more interesting than just bones. But the point I am trying make is that he used to study this place called E-Gyp . . . and that is how I learned about it, too, from reading his books."

"You can read?"

Thomas' amazement had broadened into wonder. For his own part, he often had examined the funny markings on the pages of the occasional book left open on his caretaker's table, but he had never been able to decipher their meaning. To him, books were primarily an excellent source of claw-sharpening material when no handy tree or table leg was at hand.

Selena, meanwhile, had given a dismissive flick of her tail.

"Of course I can read. Do you think I sat curled on the professor's lap all those hours because I enjoyed his company? Certainly not. You see, the silly old man often whispers the words as he reads, so I simply followed along as he moved his finger down the page and learned that way. I am quite literate now in English, have a passable knowledge of French and Latin, and can even decipher almost a hundred E-Gyp signs," she finished proudly.

Thomas' wonder had transformed into outright awe. Never had he known another cat so accomplished. Indeed, he could barely believe that Selena would deign to talk to him, gifted as she was. Quite humbly, he ventured, "Your stories of E-Gyp and being worshiped are interesting, but those times are past, are they not?"

"Past to some," she had hissed, "but not to me."

She fixed Thomas with a sharp golden gaze. "Surely you must agree that it is time for us cats to resume our rightful place in the scheme of things. That is why I want to learn how we came to rule over the humans . . . and learn, too, what caused us to lose that power. Certainly, the best way to find out is to go straight to the source. And that means—" she paused for dramatic effect, "—I shall raise an E-Gyp cat from the dead and learn its secrets."

"R–raise it from the d–dead?"

Thomas had stared at her in consternation. He'd witnessed the passing of enough felines in his time to be certain dead was, well, dead. "But how can that be possible?"

"Really, Thomas, you didn't think that the saying about us having nine lives was just an old cat's tale, did you?" she asked and flicked a sleek black ear, indicating disbelief.

When he gave a sheepish nod, she amended, "Well, perhaps we don't have quite as many as nine lives, but those cats who are clever enough to know how it is done certainly have more than one. My mother had at least two lives, and *her* mother lived four. *I* intend to have as many as possible. And for those cats who cannot manage it on their own, there are those of us felines who know how to nudge them into another lifetime. All it takes is a starry night and the right incantations. And that is what I am proposing to do with one of the E-Gyp cats."

She pointed to a picture of the cocooned creatures that earlier had held Thomas' attention. "These cats are what archaeologists call Mum-Mees. When an E-Gyp cat died, the humans wrapped him in cloth and poured perfume all over him, so that—"

"—so that he wouldn't stink like a dead mouse?" Thomas interjected helpfully.

"—so that everyone would know how important the cat was," Selena finished with quelling glare. "And I happen to know that Professor Winthrop is the caretaker of several Mum-Mee cats. I've seen them on a shelf in his basement."

She had gone on to explain the rest of her plan. They—or, rather, Thomas—would remove one of the Mum-Mee cats from its resting place and bring it out into the courtyard the next night. Selena would wait until the stars were right, and then recite the incantation that would bring the long-dead E-Gyp cat back to life. And afterward . . .

"And afterward," she had finished in triumph, "I shall learn from the E-Gyp cat what I need do to gain domination over the humans once more."

Thomas, while impressed by her ideas, still had expressed doubts as to the wisdom of this scheme. Supposing that her spell *did* work . . . what if the Mum-Mee cat was not pleased to have been roused from its centuries-long nap just so that Selena could question it? He knew that he, himself, did not appreciate being prodded awake in the midst of a pleasant sleep. Why, it might bite and scratch and, generally, act unpleasant.

And even if Selena did learn its secrets, what then? He had no wish to rule over humans, he'd told her. He was quite content lying about his caretaker's house, catching the occasional mouse, and accepting the daily saucer of cream. Why, changing the way things were might mean that *he* had to provide cream to the humans . . . an unsettling possibility.

Selena had offered reassurances on his first question. The spell she had found was deliberately designed so that the one who cast it would hold sway over the cat that had been revived. In answer to his second, however, she had given a disdainful sniff. Like it or not, she told him, she intended to restore the feline species to its proper place. He could either join her, or be left behind with the dogs of the world.

Thomas sighed now at the memory. Unfortunately, he could never say "no" to Selena, not even when it was in his best interest to refuse her. And that was why he was standing beneath the midnight stars in Professor Winthrop's courtyard, with only a Mum-Mee cat for company.

A hiss of sound no louder than a falling leaf made him start. He glanced around and saw Selena padding silently toward him, white paws flashing in the starlight. Thomas' furry gray jaw dropped as he took in the exotic change to her appearance. Tiny gold rings dangled from each sleek black ear while, around her neck, a broad collar of gold mesh gleamed against her black chest. Indeed, adorned as she was in jewelry, she looked remarkably like pictures of the E-Gyp cats that she'd shown him the day before.

She paused before him, head tilted at a regal angle. "I thought it best, since I will be raising an E-Gyp cat, that I use an E-Gyp spell I found in one of the professor's books." She touched a white paw to the necklace she wore. "Luckily, the professor had a bit of E-Gyp jewelry in his basement that I could wear."

"Y–You look very nice," Thomas managed, hoping she would not notice the blush that made his ears turn red . . . and feeling quite glad, all of a sudden, that he had agreed to help her. Indeed, if Selena wanted to resurrect a dozen Mum-Mees, then Thomas was her cat!

She waved away his awkward compliment with a flick of her tail. "We'd best hurry," she proclaimed. "The stars should be in the right position now. You wait over there," she pointed toward the wall, "and don't make any noise until I tell you so."

Only slightly deflated by her dismissal, Thomas trotted back to the wall and settled on his haunches in a bright patch of starlight to wait for whatever might happen next. He still was not convinced that her plan would work . . . but just in case, he would keep both green eyes peeled.

A soft caterwaul abruptly wafted through the courtyard. Selena stood wrapped in the shadows, chanting in a tongue he did not understand. Then, still cloaked in darkness, she began circling the E-Gyp cat. Every so often, she rose on her hind legs and batted at the stars with her silvery paws; then she would drop back to all fours and continue to pace about the still figure. Thomas watched it all with great interest. He would be ready, he assured himself, should the Mum-Mee cat leap to its feet and join Selena in her starlight dance.

But two circles later, she was still dancing by herself. Thomas stifled a yawn and settled into a more comfortable position, belly to the ground and paws tucked neatly against his chest. This business of reviving a cat into its next life seemed a tedious task; that, or else it was an impossibility. Perhaps Selena had deluded herself into believing she could accomplish something that was, in reality, beyond the abilities of mere mortal cat.

He brightened a bit at the thought. Once she conceded defeat, surely she would need a bit of friendly comforting to soothe her feelings over her failure. And since Thomas was her only friend, anymore, that meant he would be the one to—

A ragged yowl tore through the night, abruptly banishing Thomas' pleasant fantasy. He leaped to all fours, neck and tail bristling as he swung about, searching for the source of that sound. The howl hadn't been Selena's—she was still chanting and circling—but it seemed to have originated from somewhere nearby. Ears flattening, he moved a few steps closer. If he hadn't cried out, and neither had she, then that could only mean the sound had come from—

"The Mum-Mee cat," Selena abruptly hissed,

halting in her steps and sitting. "Look, I think the spell is working!"

And, indeed, a change *had* come over the shriveled remains. The body rippled like a saucer of milk that had been patted by a careless paw, and then began to broaden, lengthen. An unsettling moment later, it had split free of the remaining linen wraps. Thomas could see that dark fur was spreading swiftly as spilled ink across its torso and limbs. Then, slowly, it gathered itself onto its haunches.

Thomas swallowed back a panicked *me-reoow*, fur fluffed to full alert. He should run, he frantically thought as he stared at the horrible shadow parody of a cat . . . but how could he leave Selena behind? Not that she was frightened, he realized as he glanced her way. Her golden eyes were not wide with dread, as surely his were, but instead gleamed with triumphant satisfaction.

He returned his attention to the Mum-Mee cat in time to see that an odd, silvery mist had enveloped it. He gave a hopeful little purr, not bothering to wonder at the cloud's source. Now was the time to run, he told himself . . . now, while the creature, presumably, could not see them any better than they could see it. If only he could convince Selena to make a dash for it, perhaps they could—

Another yowl split the night, and the silver mist abruptly parted. Thomas stumbled back onto his haunches, his green eyes blinking in disbelief. The horrid Mum-Mee cat was gone, replaced by a long, sleek brown feline, the likes of which he'd never seen before. It yawned and gave a luxurious stretch, its cinnamon-colored fur shimmering beneath the starlight. Then, moving forward on delicate paws, it surveyed Thomas and Selena through a pair of narrow amber eyes.

"Ah, yes, my loyal slaves," it—or rather, she—spoke in oddly accented tones that made Thomas' fur bristle again. She halted and sat, long tail wrapped neatly about her and head tilted at a regal angle. "I am glad to see that, lowly as you are, you still were able to follow me to the afterworld. But now, I am hungry. Bring me a portion of fish and a vessel of milk."

"S–slaves? B–bring you . . . fish . . . milk?" Selena sputtered. She rose and stalked toward the E-Gyp cat, white paws flashing against shadowed brick. "You don't understand, Mum-Mee. I am the one who brought you back to life. If anyone is the slave, it is you!"

"Impudence!" the other feline yowled. "Do you not know that it is Hasheptiri, Feline Queen of the Lower and Upper Deltas, to whom you speak? Guard your words, or I shall have you put to the canines!"

"Really?" Selena spat by way of reply. By now, she and Hasheptiri were nose-to-nose, and Selena had raised a white paw in a threatening manner. "If anyone deserves to be thrown to the dogs, it is—"

She broke off with a hiss of pain and skittered

back several steps, gold mesh necklace jangling and ears flicking in anger. Thomas promptly forgot his fear and bounded to her side, his wide green gaze swinging from Selena to the E-Gyp cat and then back again. "What's wrong?"

"Sh–she did something to me," Selena sputtered in tone of mingled anger and puzzlement. "I started to bat at her and, suddenly, it was as if a wasp had stung me on the paw. I know that she didn't bite or claw me . . . but she did something."

Thomas stared at Hasheptiri, who sat as still as if she'd never been unwrapped from her linens. Indeed, he was certain that she had not moved a single cinnamon-colored hair from the moment that Selena had approached her. So what had just happened?

"Very good, slave," the E-Gyp cat spoke again, her tone regal as she stared down her long muzzle at them. "I see that you are learning some manners. Perhaps it is just as well that I did not use my full powers upon you. Now, bring me my milk and fish, and be swift about it."

Thomas gave Selena a doubtful look. "Maybe we'd better get her some milk and fish, like she wants," he suggested in a meek undertone.

Selena spat wordlessly in the E-Gyp cat's direction and then fixed Thomas with an angry yellow gaze. "You go get food, if you like. I intend to figure out what went wrong with the spell, and then take care of this Mum-Mee, once and for all."

But when Thomas returned a few minutes later with a choice fish head that he'd saved from his supper, the situation had not improved. Indeed, he found Selena crouched against the stone wall in apparent retreat, ears flat against her sleek black head, and her golden eyes blazing with resentment. As for the gold necklace and earrings she'd been wearing, that jewelry now adorned Hasheptiri, who sat in the center of the courtyard, her manner one of regal aplomb.

He approached the E-Gyp cat on cautious paws, then carefully set the fish head before her. "And there's a saucer of milk by the door," he nervously added with a nod to the spot where Professor Winthrop always left Selena a generous bowlful.

Hasheptiri made no reply but pounced upon the fish with rather less dignity than he would have expected of a queen . . . but then, she hadn't eaten in a few hundred years, he reminded himself. She finished the bowl of milk with equal speed, and then began to groom herself with a long pink tongue.

"You are dismissed, slave," she told him between swipes with a damp paw at one chocolate-colored ear. "When I am finished bathing, I shall take a nap . . . but I expect you and the other one to be ready to attend me when I awaken again." Not waiting for his reply, she gave the fur on her chest a final lick, then curled up upon the brick and promptly fell asleep.

Thomas waited until he heard a royal snore, and

then tiptoed back to where Selena still crouched against the wall. "I think this Hashep-whatever-her-name-is is not an ordinary cat," he whispered. "I think she has some sort of magical powers."

"How very astute of you, Thomas," Selena spat, her outraged yellow gaze directed at him as much as at the E-Gyp cat. She rose, white paws flashing as she stalked in tight figure eights about him. "Tell me, what gave you that idea? Was it the way she stopped me from swiping at her with nothing more than a glance, or was it the way she levitated the jewelry right off me without lifting a paw?"

"Er, I missed the jewelry part," he replied in some disappointment, certain that the sight of a flying necklace would have been most interesting. "But surely you can send her back from where she came from . . . can't you?"

"I don't know. I'd have to find another spell. Come on, let's take another look at the professor's library while she is sleeping."

But, to both Thomas and Selena's dismay, none of the books explained how to return a previously mummified cat to that state. "Something *must* have gone wrong," Selena muttered, flipping page after page. "That spell was meant to give me control over her, not vice versa. I must have translated a word or two incorrectly and reversed that power."

"Maybe her powers are just temporary," Thomas suggested in a hopeful tone as they pawed shut the last volume. "Maybe when she wakes up, she'll be an ordinary cat again."

"Maybe," Selena muttered in a tone full of doubt.

Unfortunately, she was proved right. If anything, Hasheptiri's abilities seemed to have strengthened as she slept. Indeed, by the next morning, the E-Gyp cat had expanded her powers beyond Professor Winthrop's courtyard, beginning to form what Thomas could only call an army of cat slaves.

The first recruits had been a pair of orange tabby toms . . . strays that Thomas had encountered on the streets a time or two before. At first light, they leaped atop the courtyard wall to sit like stone sentinels, not even acknowledging Thomas' greeting. More felines joined their ranks throughout the day. Come nightfall, he had counted perhaps twenty cats perched there, silently waiting on what he could only assume were orders from Hasheptiri. Another score joined them over the next two days, and the next. Soon, perhaps a hundred felines were under her control. They noiselessly gathered at the courtyard each evening and then dispersed come dawn, only to return again the following night.

"So, what do you think Hasheptiri plans to do now?" Thomas whispered to Selena late one afternoon when almost a week had past since the E-Gyp cat's resurrection.

As on previous evenings, the cat army was silently assembling atop the wall beneath the surrounding canopy of branches. Thomas had slipped into the courtyard earlier while the E-Gyp cat slept, flanked by the original orange toms that he privately referred to as her sergeants-at-arms. Oddly enough, he, of all the felines in the township, seemed immune to Hasheptiri's powers. He had puzzled over that fact, but had yet to discover the reason for this invulnerability. Even knowing that he was safe from enslavement, he would have preferred not to set paw in that courtyard at all. The only reason he daily did so was for Selena's sake.

Selena, however, proved less grateful for this covert visit than he might have hoped.

"I know what she plans to do . . . she plans to make my life miserable," she spat in reply to his question. She flopped onto the mossy bricks, shutting her golden eyes. "Do you know, I've had only sixteen or seventeen hours of sleep each day ever since that evil beast came into my life? All I hear from her is, *Bring me another bowl of cream, Selena* . . . or else, *The bricks are too damp, Selena, spread some dry leaves about for me.*" She paused, opened one eye, and added in an outraged tone, "Why, she even had me chase a mouse about the courtyard yesterday."

"That's awful," Thomas commiserated, frowning as he studied his friend.

Indeed, she did look rather the worse for wear. Her usually sleek black fur stuck out in tufts behind her ears, and a cobweb clung to one dark whisker ... deficiencies in grooming that Selena normally would never have allowed herself!

"And that is not all," she went on with a sigh. "I found out from her that cats never did rule over humans, not even in E-Gyp. Oh, yes, we were worshiped ... but so were birds and dogs and crocodiles and almost every other animal that you could think of. The only ones that cats ruled over were other cats—and dogs, of course—and Hasheptiri was that ruler. But the humans were masters over everyone, just like they are now."

"So there aren't any secrets to learn from her, after all," Thomas replied. "And in the meantime, she's made you and half the cats in this township her slaves."

"Not for long. I'll find a way to get rid of her, or my name isn't Selena Quicksilver!"

On that note, Thomas left her napping in a rapidly fading patch of sunlight. Instead of slipping back over the wall as fast as he could, however, he paused. He was certain that Hasheptiri soon would not be content with simply gathering her slaves. How she might extend her powers, he could not guess, but her continued presence surely did not bode well for anyone in the township ... feline, canine, or human. And as Selena seemed unconcerned with anyone's fate beside her own, that meant it was up to him to put a stop to Hasheptiri's reign.

But how?

He rubbed his chin with one furry gray paw and glanced at the library window. Selena had yet to discover why her spell had gone awry and, caught as she was under Hasheptiri's iron paw, it seemed unlikely that she ever would. But surely it couldn't hurt if he pawed through the professor's books, himself. True, he could not read . . . but he *could* look at pictures. With a bit of luck, he might even stumble across something within those pages that Selena had missed.

The stars had risen by the time Thomas had perused the last of the archaeological volumes still stacked atop the desk. He yawned and stretched; then, with a single powerful leap, he landed back on the windowsill. After making certain that Hasheptiri was not in sight—doubtless, the E-Gyp cat was making yet another nighttime foray in search of new slaves—he settled onto the narrow perch of worn wood and reluctantly conceded defeat.

How could he ever have hoped to find a solution to this dilemma when Selena, who was far cleverer than he, could not do so? He sighed and looked up at the stars, which seemed to twinkle back at him with mocking glee. Had E-Gyp slave cats once gazed up at that same night sky, dreaming of the day they might be free to sleep and hunt as they wished?

That same night sky.

Thomas' green eyes widened. Abruptly, he

turned tail and bounded back onto the professor's desk, scattering papers everywhere. Paying no heed to the disarray, he swiftly pawed open the last book on the stack and began searching for one particular illustration. Perhaps he might have stumbled onto the reason for Hasheptiri's great powers, after all. And if he were right, maybe there *was* a way to reverse Selena's botched spell . . . or, at least, to counteract it.

A moment later, he had found the page he sought. He studied the picture for a long while, and then gave a soft *mrmph* of satisfaction. He had been right. Now, all that remained was explaining his discovery to Selena, so that they could concoct a plan of action.

"The stars were wrong?" Selena's golden gaze narrowed as she paced the professor's desk. "That can't be. I checked before I began the spell, and they were in the right location."

"The right location for our time," Thomas agreed, "but not for the time of the E-Gyp cat. I saw a star diagram in one of the professor's books. Their moon and constellations were in a different place in the sky than ours."

He pointed at the topmost book, which was opened to a crudely rendered illustration of the Egyptian night. With an eager paw, he pointed out several constellations familiar to even the youngest of kittens . . . the Running Mouse, Dog with a Bone,

Cat Balancing a Ball. "See, in this picture, they're not quite where they should be at this season. It's as if the sky shifted . . ."

". . . or as if the calendar changed," Selena finished his thought for him as she began flipping through the book again. "Unlike the feline calendar, which has remained constant over time, the human accounting of days has changed quite often throughout their history."

She paused at one page and began to read, nodding to herself a time or two as Thomas fidgeted from paw to paw. Finally, she raised her golden gaze from that volume and gave him an admiring look.

"Why, Thomas, I do believe you are correct. It says right here that there were two calendars followed by the humans of ancient E-Gyp, and they differed by about five days. That must be why things went wrong. Our stars were in the wrong place that night for an E-Gyp spell," she paused to count on one paw, then nodded, "but now they are in the right spot."

"And, speaking of spots," Thomas eagerly added, "remember that I was sitting in a patch of starlight the entire time you were saying the spell. Maybe that's the reason that I'm the only one not affected by Hasheptiri's powers."

"Maybe." Selena gave him a speculative glance. "But whatever the reason, you will be the one to say the spell when we try our magic again tonight."

"Are you certain that this is a good idea?" Thomas fretfully whispered from their shadowed hiding place in a corner of the courtyard. "I–I've never done magic before. What if something goes wrong?"

"Things can't go any more wrong than they have," Selena snapped and gave him a none-too-gentle nudge forward. "All you have to do is repeat the words I taught you, and walk in a circle around her. Every third time you say the words, you must stand and reach for the stars. It's simple enough that even a dog could do it. Now, hurry . . . it's almost midnight."

Too bad there wasn't a dog foolish enough to volunteer for the task, Thomas told himself. If the plan went wrong, and he couldn't reverse Selena's original spell, then things might go badly for both him and Selena this night. Gathering his courage, he padded on nervous paws toward the center of the courtyard, where Hasheptiri was busy organizing her latest recruits.

As always, she was flanked by the same two orange-striped toms who had joined her that first night. The pair abruptly swung about to face him, twin growls rumbling in their throats as he approached. Hasheptiri turned as well, her gold jewelry flashing in the starlight.

"Ah, yes, I remember this slave," she announced, her harshly accented tones sending their usual, unpleasant shiver all the way down his back. Her amber eyes narrowed as she looked down her long muzzle at him. "Why aren't you lined up with the others? Go now, and swiftly, before I grow angry."

Reminding himself that Selena and every other cat in the township was depending on him, Thomas opened his mouth and let out a yowl that made even him jump. Then, the words spilling out as fast as he could summon them, he began the chant that Selena had taught him.

He'd circled halfway around Hasheptiri before the toms recovered from their initial surprise. Steeling himself for their attack, Thomas yowled the words a third time and rose on his hind legs to bat at the stars, just as the pair pounced. But rather than tumbling him to the ground, both felines landed in a heap on either side of him, neither having laid a paw upon him.

"What are you doing?" Hasheptiri rose to her full height, fangs bared and tail slashing. "I command you to cease now!"

"Keep on chanting, Thomas . . . don't stop!" Selena cried from the shadows.

And, indeed, he had no intention of stopping, not when he could feel an odd sort of vibration that seemed to radiate from his nose to the tip of his tail. Something was happening, and the E-Gyp cat obviously did not like it. He yowled the words three more times and rose again, stretching even higher this time to reach the stars.

From the corner of one eye, he saw the orange-striped toms scramble to their feet and scurry away, heedless of Hasheptiri's furious demand that they attack him once more. He dropped back to all fours and continued circling and chanting, aware now of a faint chorus of hisses from the dozens of cats gathered atop the wall. The E-Gyp cat heard the sound, too, and gave an angry cater-waul.

"All of you are mine to command! Destroy this slave, before I destroy all of you!"

The hissing intensified, but not a cat twitched a paw to obey. Hasheptiri yowled again, but this time Thomas could hear a note of fear in her voice. "Cease!" she cried again, but in a weaker tone now. "I am Hasheptiri, Feline Queen of the Lower and Upper Deltas. You must obey me. You must."

It was as he reached for the stars a third time that he glimpsed it . . . the same odd, silvery mist that had risen while Selena was casting her original spell. Now, it again spun its tendrils about Hasheptiri, who hissed and caterwauled but could not shake herself from its filmy grasp.

"I am Hasheptiri!" she frantically mewed as the mist reached her chin and continued to rise. "You must obey me. You must . . ."

Thomas halted in his tracks as the cloud enveloped her from tail to ear tips. Then, just as abruptly, the silver mist split. For the space of a heartbeat, a motionless Hasheptiri stood silhouetted against it. Then the cloud dissolved, and with it went the E-Gyp cat, her elegant form collapsing into a pile of fine sand upon the courtyard's faded brick. A few seconds later, a breeze scattered those remains to the night, leaving behind only the golden necklace and earrings. The jewelry glinted a moment longer beneath the starlight before it, too, crumbled into dust and was carried away by another gust.

"You did it, Thomas," Selena cried as she bounded toward him, pausing to give him a quick lick on the jaw. "And look, her spell over the slave cats is broken, as well."

Too surprised by her unexpected show of affection to say anything, Thomas could only follow her gaze to the wall, where the cats gathered there had fallen silent. Now, they gave a collective yawn, flicking their ears and rubbing their eyes with their paws as if they'd just awakened from a nap. Then, one by one, they slipped back down the wall, until only the overhanging canopy of tree branches ringed the courtyard.

"It did work," Thomas finally managed with a sigh of relief. "But from now on, I'm leaving the magic up to you."

"And just as well," Selena answered, sounding more like her old self again. "Magic can be a dangerous thing in the wrong paws, even when the stars are right."

"Mittens, where are you?" a scratchy human

voice interrupted before Thomas could reply. The door to the courtyard opened, and a nightcapped Professor Winthrop hurried to where Thomas and Selena sat. "Ah, there you are, Kitty. Are you all right?"

Before Selena could protest, the old man had scooped her up in his arms and was cradling her, a smile on his bearded face. "So, it's only you and your handsome gray friend," he said with a nod toward Thomas. "With all that caterwauling I heard, I thought an army of cats was prowling about. Now, since we're all awake, why don't both of you come into the kitchen and have a saucer of milk?"

As he spoke, the old man scratched Selena beneath her white chin, only to pause as a rusty rumbling abruptly echoed through the courtyard. His bushy eyebrows rose in astonishment, and then his smile broadened. "Why, Mittens, you're purring. I don't think I've ever heard you do that before."

And, to Thomas' great surprise, the sound did appear to be coming from none other than Selena. She peered at him from over the crook of the professor's elbow, her golden gaze narrow.

"I'm only purring to be polite," she declared in a peevish tone. "And if you want that bowl of cream, you'd better promise never to mention this incident again."

"I won't, I promise," Thomas replied, smothering a grin behind a fluffy gray paw. Of the quite magical incidents that had occurred over the past week, the sight of Selena purring had to be the most amazing one of all. With a final glance up at the stars, he rose and trotted after her toward the brightly lit doorway and his waiting bowl of cream.

PRAXIS

by Janet Pack

Originally a native of Independence, Missouri, Janet Pack now resides in the village of Williams Bay, Wisconsin, in a slightly haunted farmhouse with cats Tabirika Onyx, Syrannis Moonstone, and Baron Figaro di Shannivere. Her extensive rock collection adorns her living room. Janet's two dozen plus short stories, interviews, and nonfiction articles have been published by DAW, Ace, HarperCollins, Thorndike Press, FASA, Xerox Corp., *At the Lake* Magazine, and TSR/Wizards of the Coast. Her musical compositions can be found in Weis and Hickman's *The Death Gate Cycle* and in *Dragonlance R* sourcebooks from TSR/WotC. Janet works as the manager's assistant at Shadowlawn Stoneware Pottery in Delavan, Wisconsin, and when needed at the University of Chicago's Yerkes Observatory in Williams Bay. During free moments she sings, reads, embroiders, walks, cooks, watches good movies, plays with her companions, and does as little housework as possible.

FEELING like a rodent under the hungry eyes of a hovering hawk, Lucien Tirysthenes slunk down the sunlit street until he reached the back door of his friend Dracus Manorum's small house on the outskirts of Athens. As he moved, his bright-eyed cat Praxis peeked from beneath his clothing. He wasn't supposed to be in the city—all mathematicii had been banished last year after the city-state had branded astrology as "foreign drivel," and ostracized those who practiced it. But Lucien couldn't stay away from the verve and energy of Athens, just as he couldn't stop watching the stars and trying to determine what those glimmering silent bodies in the night sky were trying to tell him. Lucien was sure that their movements held important messages, messages he could decipher if only he tried hard enough.

Melothesia, the universal sympathy linking the microcosm of man with the macrocosm of nature, had to be influenced by the movements of the stars. Lucien believed that every limb, organ, and human body function was subject to the pull of the planets and signs of the zodiac. All he needed was peace to watch the heavens, the patience to note his observations consistently, and the time to apply the necessary mathematics—then the information they held would be his.

But the Greek government had disallowed him that peace. Afraid the new practice imported from Egypt would unduly influence the populace, Athens and many other city-states had banned astrology. The city's soldiers had been instructed to gather up all practitioners of the Egyptian art and banish them. Thirteen months ago, with only scant moments to gather together what he could carry

from his belongings and to grab his beloved cat,
Praxis, Lucien had been snatched from his dwelling
in the city and then marched to the border under
guard with six others, all of whom shared his fascination with the stars. He'd been told in forceful
words never to show his face again near Athens,
and informed of the terrible price he'd pay if he
did. So he'd made the best of it. Lucien had begun
traveling the world, accompanied as always by his
furry friend Praxis. But his feet kept returning him
to Athens. At great personal risk, his friend Dracus
had saved Lucien's library of precious scrolls and
secreted them in his house. Given the current polit-
ical climate all over Greece, the astrologer couldn't
afford to take them with him. Possession of those
scrolls could be a death sentence. But Lucien
couldn't live without them either.

His copious notes on Egyptian decans had cost
him many years of hard travel and study when he
was younger. The documents were the envy of all
the mathematicii of his acquaintance. When other
astrologers encountered difficulty in their equa-
tions, they sought out Lucien. His carefully detailed work often provided the answers they
needed, and his kindly guidance redirected those
who floundered along the way.

And Praxis helped. The cat, one of the tawny
tick-coated Egyptian Mau breed used as temple
guardians in that distant land, had been born in the
home of a renowned astrologer, and had a peculiar

affinity for the art of calculating the movements of the stars. Odd as it seemed, she had a knack for finding the occasional mistakes that crept into his calculations despite his best efforts to avoid them, and she would attract Lucien's attention to them by batting the offending line with an insistent paw. She would dance in tight circles on star charts, and when he examined those charts, his studies would always lead him toward a path he hadn't previously considered. And the cat's quickly vibrating tail frequently pointed out important information the mathematici had either overlooked or discarded as irrelevant. Sensitive as he was to cosmic influence, he knew his cat could access higher powers he could only guess at. And he couldn't deny that his cat had often been his savior in his studies. He valued his companion's odd behavior, and over time had learned to recognize and understand her silent signals. Her uncompromising attitude toward mistakes was a mirror of Lucien's own constant search for perfection.

The astrologer hugged his pet close to his body as he entered the cool interior of the house through the back door on the alley. Once again, he'd negotiated the perilous journey safely. Instead of praising the Greek gods, he muttered thanks to the stars that the pair had encountered no challenges during their trek through Athens' outskirts. Finishing his prayer, Lucien set the cat on the tile floor.

"This is home for a time, Praxis. We need to be invisible here. Do not stray."

His friend gazed at him with wide gold eyes as if she completely understood his words, then miaowed and wove her way fondly around his ankles, her tail brushing softly against the folds of his clothing. She followed Lucien as he made his way into the study, hopping into a cushioned chair for a nap while he searched for his scrolls. Dracus frequently moved them about, all too aware of the consequences he'd face if they were found.

Lucien finally located them in a wooden box nearly hidden beneath a small table on one side of the room. Reverently he took one out, unrolled it, and read the first few lines of his crowded script. Carefully replacing it, he took out another. This time he took it to the mosaic-surfaced reading table that dominated the center of the study, and became so engrossed in the information in it that he had no sense of the passage of time until darkness finally made it impossible to see.

"Anyone here?" The soft voice startled them both, coming from the back where they'd entered. "Hello?" Lucien glanced at Praxis. She didn't seem disturbed, only alert—perhaps she knew that if the invader had been a soldier, he'd have barged in the front and made no effort to keep quiet. The cat had more sense than most of his acquaintances. If it had been a soldier, she'd have disappeared without a sound until the danger was past.

Lucien grabbed a lamp from the table and ignited the wick. With it in hand, he left the study to see who was calling on them.

The visitor stood near the storage room where wine and olive oil were kept. The man had politely remained in the back of the house until he found out if someone was there and received permission to come farther into it.

"Mathematici Tirysthenes?" The sudden light from Lucien's lamp made the visitor squint, casting deep shadows into his dark eyes. "You *are* here. I heard a rumor you had returned to Athens. I have been seeking you for some time. I would like a chart from the best of astrologers. I can pay." The man opened his hand and revealed two large coins. Silver glimmered in the lamp's glow. This was a princely fee for the casting of a single chart.

How had this man found him? He'd been so careful. Lucien's initial reaction was to deny his own identity and refuse the man's request. If a whisper of his return made it through the streets of Athens, soldiers would not be far behind this visitor and Lucien's death was assured. Then he noticed the harsh lines mapping his visitor's face. The man was clearly at his wit's end, exhausted with worry and care. How could he refuse to help a man so burdened with pain?

"Why do you seek this chart? Business or personal reasons?" the astrologer asked.

"Both."

Lucien's caring nature had almost convinced him to help when he felt the cat at his ankles. Perhaps it was time for a second opinion. Setting his lamp down in a convenient niche, he picked up his pet.

"What do you think, Praxis?"

The feline squirmed beyond his reach, jumping to the floor. She marched up to the visitor, her attitude brimming with typical cat curiosity, but showing no signs of nervousness. The intruder offered his fingertips for her inspection. Praxis sniffed, considered, and scratched her chin against them, signaling acceptance.

"We will do your chart," answered Lucien.

"We?" The dark-haired man looked up, startled.

"Praxis is my partner," Lucien smiled, indicating the long-limbed cat with a nod of his blond head. "She knows astrology almost as well as I do." He picked up the lamp, and sought another in the storage area. "Come into the study and we'll get started."

The astrologer lit the second lamp's wick from the burning one in his hand and gave it to his visitor to carry. He led the way back to the quiet sanctuary at the heart of his friend's house. Praxis leaped onto the reading table as the visitor seated himself at the long side of the table nearest the door where he'd entered. Rummaging in a box, Lucien found a quill pen, a cake of ink, and several parchment sheets on which to take notes. He sharpened the pen with a small knife, spat on the cake of ink to moisten it, and set his mind toward the familiar discipline of getting the information he required to construct the chart.

His questions to the visitor were pointed. He needed the man's birth date, and how far the day had advanced when the visitor had been delivered into the world, if the visitor knew that. He needed to know what this visitor sought to discover in the chart, the specific questions he wanted answered about his life, his family, his business, his relationships. Was there anything else the seeker might like to know that the stars could reveal? Ferreting out all the necessary information from his visitor took a bit of time. At first the man was reticent to the point of silence. He never did reveal his name. But by halfway through the session, Lucien and Praxis had put him at ease. From then on the man offered more details than were strictly necessary. The information the visitor gave reassured Lucien. It was clear that this man's life was indeed precarious, and often endangered. Perhaps the chart would offer the man the help he needed to change his lot.

Lucien finally sat back, satisfied that he'd learned everything he needed to plot the chart. "I hope that the stars will be auspicious. Return at midday tomorrow," he told his visitor. "I should have your chart finished by then."

"So soon?" The visitor looked surprised. "It will be detailed?"

"Very detailed."

The man rose with obvious relief, as if a weight had dropped from his shoulders just from knowing that the information he needed would soon be forthcoming. "Thank you. Thank you very much. I shall see you tomorrow, then." He placed one of the pair of silver coins on the table, saying, "For your efforts on my behalf. I shall give you the rest when you've finished your work." Then he picked up the second lamp and exited the study. Lucien listened to the slap of the man's sandals against the stone floor as he left the house.

"Well, Praxis. It seems we have a task at hand." The cat's purr filled the room as Lucien searched his box for the copies he'd made of Hipparchus' preliminary findings on star movements and precession of the equinoxes. Laying them across the mosaic table, he began searching for the information his client needed.

Time became meaningless to him. He carefully noted details on his scraps of parchment as the stars whirled in their patterns above the roof and the night passed on toward dawn. Between naps, Praxis watched him through slitted eyes until, deep in the chill of early morning, Lucien fell asleep between the precious scrolls of Hipparchus and the complicated new chart.

Rising and stretching, Praxis leaped down and patrolled the edges of the house. Satisfied nothing was wrong beyond a mouse in the storage area, she returned to the study and jumped onto the table. She padded to the new chart and looked at it. Not much wrong there either. With that smile of satisfaction only a cat can give, she lay down with her paws on the parchment, sighed, and allowed sleep to overtake her also.

The visitor from last night called at the back door around noon, just as he'd promised. Lucien greeted him and escorted him to the study. Carefully the mathematici explained all he'd learned, and interpreted the information on the parchment. That took some time. Judging by the visitor's reaction, and the number of times the man nodded and said, "That's right," or, "Of course," Lucien's words were useful and accurate in the context of the man's life. Lucien could only hope his client found what he sought. Excited and ebullient, the dark-haired stranger thanked Tirysthenes profusely, paid him the remaining coin, exited the house, and disappeared into the narrow streets of the district.

"Dracus Manorum, or whoever is within, come out in the name of the city of Athens!"

The strident, commanding voice from the avenue in front of the house made both Lucien and Praxis start. The human headed for a shuttered window where he could peek out without being seen. Ever practical, the cat bounded for the study.

"Soldiers," groaned the astrologer, wheeling to run in the same direction as his pet. Grabbing Hip-

parchus' scrolls, he stuffed them into their box, and
shoved that into the shadows beneath the small
table. "They've found us. What led them to us
now?"

Clinking drew his attention. Praxis had a paw on
the silver coins the dark-haired man had left as
payment.

"You think we were betrayed." Lucien sighed as
the cat jumped to the floor. He was suddenly weary
beyond words, and so frightened his voice shook.
That a client should ask for an astrological chart for
fallacious purposes was a sad commentary on how
far humanity had to go to achieve enlightenment.
"You're probably right. I suppose doing his chart
was a stupid idea, but I couldn't help myself. It was
as if it was meant to be. As if my fate was in the
stars to do it." Praxis turned in a nervous circle on
the floor, tail twitching.

"You, within the house! Come out now, by order
of the government of Athens, or we shall come in
after you!"

Lucien trembled at the imperative voice. "Stay
with Dracus and save yourself, Praxis, my faithful
companion. This is a journey I must make alone.
I'm going out the back. They've undoubtedly got
someone posted to prevent just such an event. I'll
probably not escape." He traded a long look with
the feline. It seemed almost as if there were words
written in her steady gold stare, words he could

read with a bit more understanding, a little more effort . . .

Lucien wrenched his eyes away from the cat's gaze as heavier pounding sounded against the door. "Stay," he urged her. "Stay!"

But Praxis leaped through a partly shuttered side window as her partner headed for the rear of the house. The astrologer stopped, listening. It was quiet, other than the constant noises of the city. The hammering at the front door had stopped. He slipped quickly through the doorway and out into the back alleyway. Not a soul was in sight. Perhaps this was his lucky day. He'd done some of his best work in forming that stranger's star chart last night, and now he might even elude the soldiers sent to arrest him. Full of optimism, Lucien turned right and began walking down the alley between houses.

"Where you goin'?" A hard hand crashed down on Tirysthenes' shoulder. *By the stars! Is this what the touch of death feels like?* Fear ran through Lucien, as cold as the snow on Mt. Olympus' peak. "Din't ya hear, th' Prelate wants ta talk ta you." The soldier raised his voice and called to the others. "Got 'im here!"

"Good work, Minomides." The apparent leader of the group called from the entry to the alleyway. "Form up, men." A small band of soldiers appeared behind him.

Lucien was marched through the streets of

Athens with a wall of soldiers surrounding him, like a man accused of a capital crime. People gathered to watch the tiny procession, whispering and pointing. The astrologer wanted to shout at them, to tell the onlookers that he wasn't a bad man—his only crimes were loving astrology and wanting to help others with the knowledge he obtained through his star observations. But Tirysthenes' heart was full of shame at being suborned and caught so easily; he walked through the streets with his head bowed and his throat tight, overcome by his grief.

Lucien didn't notice until they were halfway along its length that they were passing the market. His brow furrowed, and he raised his head. If the Athenian leaders planned to kill him now, his escort was going in the wrong direction. Confused as well as worried, the astronomer paid more attention to his surroundings.

They were definitely going the wrong way. They passed fine houses now, though not the grand ones of the wealthy traders, but the substantially smaller ones of teachers and sages. His escort halted before one. The leader knocked deferentially on the door and called out, "He whom you sought is here."

The portal opened. Lucien stepped through, backed by two of the soldiers. The astrologer looked through the foyer to an atrium larger than his friend Manorum's house. Sunlight spilled in, warming, comforting. Perhaps he wasn't about to die today. This certainly wasn't the right kind of place for a state-sponsored killing.

"Come in, and welcome." The voice belonged to an elderly man with short graying hair and sparkling brown eyes. Despite his age, life vibrated throughout his body. His countenance and tone seemed friendly, but Lucien didn't dare relax yet. He had too many questions that needed answering, and too much at stake to let down his guard. "This way. Please."

Lucien was escorted to a chair in the atrium. His host sat opposite him behind a small marble table. A pitcher and two low cups made of beautifully glazed pottery awaited them. The elderly man poured, a slight smile on his lips that reminded the astrologer of Praxis. A pang of loss stabbed him as he thought of his cat. He hoped she would find a good new life somewhere in Athens, that she wouldn't be killed or crippled out in the bustle of the busy city streets.

"Wine?" Tirysthenes' gentle captor handed him a cup and sat back in his chair. Suddenly realizing he was both hungry and thirsty, Lucien drank. It was good wine, only slightly watered. Its strength meant his captor must have guessed what his mental state would be. He swallowed more.

"I owe you an explanation. Several, actually." The gray-haired man sipped from his own cup. "Let me begin with an introduction. I'm Phillides

Mellitus, poet, playwright, and orator. Also, for a time, the leader of the Athenian government."

Lucien's eyes widened. He couldn't help it.

"Yes, I see my reputation precedes me. And I have a favor to ask you, but that will come later. First, let me apologize for any trouble or anguish my actions have caused you. My little ruse with the chart seemed the best way to tell if you were the correct astrologer for my needs." He reached behind his chair and brought out the chart Lucien had made last night. "From what the agent who visited you last night tells me, you seem to be both competent and knowledgeable in your field, as well as being willing to help someone in need despite considerable risk to your own life. That takes courage and a good heart. And you're the only one he found with these. I commend you on the scope of your collection."

Lucien sucked in his breath as Mellitus set his precious box of scrolls on the marble between them.

"I'm going to ask you to do a chart for me, and also one for my daughter. She's rather taken by the idea of your art, and can't be persuaded to see a sibyl or priest of any god for a vision of the future instead. So I will try things her way. Advice from the stars. Interesting."

"But—but I'm made criminal here just for practicing."

"Yes, the law against astrology." The poet-orator

waved a deprecating hand. "It will be rescinded. The populace has changed its mind on the matter; it is therefore time for the law to reflect that change. One of the joys of democracy is its lack of consistency."

"I'm free to work?" Lucien felt shaky.

"You can even have your Athenian citizenship restored should you wish it." Mellitus' glance was shrewd, assessing. "Shall I call my daughter?"

"Yes!"

"This will please her greatly." The poet-orator rose. "And in doing so, it will please me also. This way."

Lucien grabbed the box of scrolls and followed as his host led the way to his study, a spacious room filled with racks of orderly scrolls, lying just off the atrium. Pens, ink, and parchment sat ready for his notes on a beautiful wooden table. The astrologer organized them to his taste while Mellitus fetched the girl.

Saffron-haired and beautiful, she bounced into the study with energy equal to her father's, but unconstrained by the wisdom of age. "My daughter, Callista," the Athenian leader announced.

Lucien questioned the girl with great care, then her father. These would be the most detailed and careful charts he'd ever rendered. When they left him alone in the room after he'd finished his inquiries, he set to work with a will. Determined to do an exceptional job for these people who offered him the hope of his life returned to normal and the

chance to do the work he loved, he didn't realize at
first that there was something missing. The fact hit
him with crushing force when he began his mathe-
matical calculations. His hand halted on the parchment.

"Praxis!" Tirysthenes groaned, dropping his
head in his hands. Ink smeared his cheek. He didn't
care.

"Is something wrong?" Mellitus' voice sounded
concerned. The poet-orator stood in the doorway, a
tray of fruit and wine in his hands. "I thought you
might need refreshment, so I brought this, but from
the sound of it, you may need more help than I
have in hand."

"My partner . . . my cat Praxis," the astrologer
forced out. "An Egyptian Mau, a temple guard cat.
She's always with me when I do charts. I told her to
stay when the soldiers came for me, but she leaped
out the window, terrified." His voice took on a
bleak edge. "She's probably lost by now. I didn't realize I depended on her so much."

"Can I help? I could send people to look for her.
Did you see her run away? What direction did she
go?"

"I don't know." Lucien shook his head. "I don't
know. The shutters were half closed, and it's been
so long she could be anywhere by now."

"Perhaps the cat has returned to your friend's
house. Callista might accompany a soldier to in-

quire. She's good with animals—she'll be able to entice your cat to come with her if Praxis is there."

"That could work," the astrologer said slowly. "If I sent something of mine with your daughter that Praxis would recognize, a bit of clothing perhaps— Or could I go? The cat would come if I called . . ."

An irregular series of noises including a bellow of human rage sounded near the front door of the poet-orator's house. Mellitus reacted first, moving very fast for a man of his age. The orator ran from the study across the atrium, with Lucien only three steps behind him.

A soldier Lucien recognized from the escort party stood in the foyer, blood running down his leg from multiple lacerations. His sword was in his hand. Before him snarled one immensely irritated Egyptian Mau cat, every whisker and hair on her body extended to its maximum length, making the normally slick and slender feline look three times her actual size. The cat had one paw with blooded claws raised to strike again.

"Praxis!" Lucien sagged to his knees, arms out.

The soldier didn't hear him. The man's sword sliced through the air on a downstroke aimed at the feline's raised back when Mellitus snapped out "Halt!" The soldier's hand opened and the weapon hit the floor with a clatter. The cat sprang for her owner and was cradled, still snarling, in Lucien's arms.

"So," Mellitus gasped, clearly amused and trying not to laugh. "What happened here? What mortal enemy has bloodied my army?"

"It's this cat, sir," replied one of the soldiers standing by the doorway. "It walked in like it owned the place. When Anaxeris barred its way, the cat attacked him."

"Of course she did," smiled the older man. "She has come on a mission, you see. She has work to do here."

"Work, sir?" the wounded warrior asked. "What work?"

"She is an associate of the astrologer, who is my guest. He finds her essential to complete his task at hand. Get those scratches attended to, soldier." He turned and faced the others. "Do we pay you men to stand around my house, or to guard my door?"

Grudgingly the soldiers returned to their posts, exiting into the sunshine. Mellitus turned to Lucien.

"Is your cat well?"

"She seems to be. Thank you, sir."

"What did I do? Nothing. Except watch a fine animal with an appropriate name hold her own against a foe many times her size. Praxis, meaning action." Mellitus reached out a hand to gently ruffle the feline's soft fur. "That was a great scene for a comedy. I believe I shall use it in one of my poems. But now, let's return to those charts." He smiled at the astrologer. "Do your work well, and

I'll be sure to commend your skills to my friends. It will be the making of your fortune, I prophesy. I have a great many friends who'll be interested in their own charts if mine and my daughter's ring true." The poet-orator let a few heartbeats pass. "If you can handle that much work, of course."

"It will be a privilege. And there's no time better to start than now," Lucian said, looking down at the cat, who was rubbing the top of her head against his chin. Her purring warmed his heart. "No time better."

DEATH SONG

by Bill McCay

Bill McCay shared an apartment with a cat for almost a year and a half without realizing he was seriously allergic—he just thought he had a lot of colds in that period. In spite (or maybe because) of such obliviousness, Bill went into publishing, achieving the dubious distinction of becoming the only freelance editor-in-chief he's ever heard of. Bill has authored more than sixty books, mainly for juveniles, under a multiplicity of pseudonyms. As himself, he has written a number of science fiction novels, including five books carrying on the action of the movie "Stargate." His *Star Trek* novel *Chains of Command,* co-authored with Eloise Flood, enjoyed several weeks on *The New York Times* bestseller list.

THAT *damned* cat!" Glenn Warriner leaped up from his seat as a gray-furred figure flashed along the back of the couch.

"Tom does seem a little antsy tonight," Karen Warriner admitted, leaning forward as she tried to catch the cat's eye. "Hey, Tom. What's the matter?"

The old tomcat paid no attention, dropping soundlessly to the plush carpet. He continued his restless circuit around the living room.

"The way he's going, I'm surprised the old fur-ball hasn't worn a track in the rug." Reassured now that the cat was in view, Glenn sat back.

He glanced sidewise at Karen. "You know what the trouble is. Tom was used to a house in the country, lots of room to roam around. The new apartment is getting on his nerves." He left unspoken the thought, *The furball is getting on* my *nerves*, but both of them knew it was there.

"We knew it would take a little acclimation time," Karen said in placating tones.

"Acclimation?" Glenn echoed. "Look at him! Tom moves around this place as if he's a caged prisoner. He's shredded the side of the new couch. I stepped in a pool of puke this morning on the way to the bathroom. About the only thing he hasn't done is pee in my shoes." Glenn cast a suspicious look over the cat. "At least that I know of."

"Tom's old," Karen tried to defend her pet.

"And it looks like you can't teach an old cat new tricks," Glenn said. He watched as Tom completed the circuit. This time, the furball didn't take the route along the back of the couch.

"I meant it's a little late in his life to try to have him declawed." Karen looked at her husband. "Putting him under—" she shuddered. "He might not make it."

"Karen," Glenn hesitated, then went on, "maybe that would be for the best. Tom was what—twenty-something on his last birthday? He's had a long life for a cat. If he's not happy . . ."

Karen looked from her husband to her cat. She'd barely been five when Tom had adopted her out at her grandfather's farm. She remembered him as the half-grown kitten spotlit in a beam of sunlight on the barn floor, dancing on his hind legs as he batted at breeze-borne bits of chaff.

Tom had always been an adventurer, carving out his own territory among the hills and valleys around Karen's childhood home. He was always getting into trouble. Karen had cried the first time he'd come back wounded from some epic fight. But then there'd been the night she'd taken out the dinner debris and inadvertently trapped a raccoon between the trash cans and the wall of the house. To her nine-year-old self, the cornered coon had seemed enormous as it came at her. Tom had appeared as if from nowhere, emitting a strident war cry.

At the cost of a severe clawing, he'd kept the raccoon at bay, letting Karen get away. She could still find the scar from that escapade snaking through his belly fur, a souvenir of Doc Sohlsen's patch job. After that, it had seemed a small enough repayment to clean up the messy wounds he'd received over the years from encounters with snakes, woodchucks, and rival felines. Weekends had been spent home from college so she could be with Tom—and see what escapades he'd gotten up to during her absence.

Karen remembered those country days fondly. This wasn't the way things were supposed to go when Glenn got his shiny new job in the big city.

"And what do we tell Katie if we do that?" she asked quietly.

For their two-year-old, Tom was a best friend and playmate. Just today, Karen had laughed at the sight of the toddler single-mindedly pursuing Tom, wobbling on her chubby legs.

"Tom! Tom!" Katie had run as fast as she could, trying to catch Tom's tail as he stalked away from the ruins of the block "house" she'd tried to build around him. Astonishingly, Tom put up with Katie's assaults on his dignity with a certain amount of good-humored acceptance. Not many cats, especially older ones, would do that.

Glenn didn't meet his wife's eyes. Instead he looked at Tom, who'd assumed one of his favorite perches, on the living-room windowsill. The cat stared out impassively at the view of the upper West Side of Manhattan, as seen from the thirty-first floor.

"Don't you ever worry about what might happen to Katie if Tom—well . . . snapped?" Glenn asked uneasily.

Karen didn't reply. She merely watched the grizzled fur of Tom's tail tip as it twitched back and forth, back and forth, like a nervy, sinuous pendulum.

Tom paid no attention to the humans on the couch, although even from this distance he could taste their soured emotions. Not surprising, that. What leaked through the portal opening in this room could poison the sweetest nature—even the temperament of his beloved Karen.

Still worse was the danger to the little one, Katie.

Tom stared up into the night sky, not that he could see anything. The lights of the building blotted out all but the brightest stars from his view. But he sensed the steady progress of the red wandering star up in the heavens—the planet Mars was in retrograde, and proceeding through the constellation of Scorpio. The sign of strife . . . the time when the Greater Banes could reach into this world.

As a kit, he'd been amazed by the two-legs' blindness to the workings of the Banes and the Benigns, and so many other phenomena that were clear to him, yet obviously invisible to human eyes. His mother had taught him this wasn't always so. According to the motherwisdom of her lineage, their ancestors had once served as eyes into what the humans called the Unseen World. Familiars, those long-ago kindred had been named.

But it had been long and long since any of the two-legs had enjoyed even a halting insight into the Unseen. Ten hundred and more of mothers had passed along the old stories to their kits, keeping the knowledge alive.

Tom's tattered right ear twitched as a Bane passed behind him—a lesser one, which he could easily have dispersed. They grew bolder as their stronger brother came near. Fewer and fewer Benigns had attempted to penetrate the slow, poisonous leakage of shadow into this home.

Tom perceived Benigns as glowing presences that lightened the world and the spirit. They could only affect the physical world in the most tenuous ways, barely able to move motes of dust. In his younger days, Tom had played with them, leaping after bits of fluff spiraling under Benign guidance.

Banes were just as tenuous, deeper blacknesses hiding in the shadows. It wasn't the darkness of spirit they engendered that set Tom and his kindred against them. It was the sick hunger that radiated from them. Banes craved form, solidity . . . sensation. Sometimes they succeeded in possessing creatures that lived in the dark—the six-legged scuttlers, the red-eyed tribes, mice and rats.

These vermin smelled bad enough normally. But the presence of a Bane inside created a special psychic rankness. Chasing off disembodied Banes was a duty. Killing the possessed was a kindness.

Then there were the Greater Banes, who sought larger prey. These were powerful enough to ensnare humans, especially children. The motherwisdom told of some of these—the dreadful emperor of the French so long ago, and more recently the German monster who'd nearly destroyed the world.

The saving grace of human existence was that the Greater Banes lived at a farther remove from this world. Their contacts with the two-legs were limited in time and space. During the last period of contact, humans had been more aware of the spirit world. Then, humans and their feline familiars had charted the portals, and they had gathered during certain stellar conjunctions, denying access to these creatures of darkness.

Today, the cat-kindreds carried on alone, even braving two-leg disapproval to keep the invisible predators at bay. Many times Tom had joined with his brothers and sisters, psychically resisting an incursion while suffering curses, missiles, and even gunfire from oblivious humans.

He studied the picture in the sky. Yes, tonight would be the conjunction. The portal would open . . . and only Tom would be there to contest the Greater Bane's passage. Tonight, Tom would die.

He didn't fear the coming battle, even though the outcome was foreordained. His only hope was to extend the fight long enough for the conjunction to pass—or to leave his opponent too depleted to reach out to Katie.

Mostly, Tom felt anger at himself for not realizing the danger until it was too late. This was a portal that none could have known of or charted in those olden days. High, high in the sky—how frustrating it must have been for the Bane, to have a vantage over so much prey, and yet be unable to touch it and consume it. To watch the little people on the little island carry on their existences obliviously, just beyond the reach of the creature's power, must have been maddening for the creatures of evil. The only possible hosts they could subsume from this place had been birds or bats.

But then the humans—the blind, heedless humans—had built themselves into range of the portal.

Even now, after months of occupation, the raw newness of this place his people had occupied jarred Tom's perceptions. That was why he hadn't noticed the wrongness in the living room. That, and age.

Tom knew the moving star was red, but he couldn't see it, even though the planet Mars was one of the few celestial objects bright enough to glow in the Manhattan night sky. His sight was fading, like so many of his abilities. He hadn't noticed the wrongness, hadn't realized its gathering strength until it was too late. Now the shadow of the Bane blanketed the apartment, smothering any hope for psychic communication with the cat-kindred out in the city.

And even if he could have called for help, how

could they gather in this place, sealed off and perched so absurdly high in the sky?

No, Tom would face the Bane alone, and he lacked the power to defeat it.

Old . . . useless . . . deserve to die.

Did that come from the Bane? Or was it merely his own inner conviction of his imminent death? Tom tried to push the negative emotion away.

Noises from the sofa made him turn his attention to his people. Karen and her mate turned on the box of pictures, the television, and sat watching things-that-were-not-there.

Tom climbed onto the couch and arranged himself in Karen's lap, butting his head against her hand. He knew he could hope for no help there, but he wanted to enjoy a little comfort before the impending battle.

Karen absently stroked his fur, and Tom tried to relax under her touch.

Then came a spasm of nausea. Tom leaped from the couch, managing to reach the tile floor of the kitchen before his stomach vented its contents. He lay on the floor, panting for breath after having his guts wrenched, as Karen came in. Beyond, he was barely aware of the surly tones of her mate. Karen answered softly, cleaned up the mess, and cradled Tom in her arms. She didn't bring him back to the couch, though. Instead, she left him in his bed.

Tom closed his eyes, trying to regain some portion of strength. In the weeks before the portal manifested, minor Banes had constantly turned up, many of them in six-legged hosts. Tom had killed the vermin, but the Banes had evidently been serving their larger brother. The possessed hosts had dined liberally on insecticide. In killing them, Tom had slowly been poisoning himself.

He hadn't been able to keep food down for the last two days, although he'd hidden that fact from Karen.

It seeks every advantage. The thought was as bitter as the taste in Tom's mouth. He longed to lose himself in pacing, in movement, but he forced himself to remain still, conserving his energy.

At last, Karen and her mate rose from the couch and turned off the lights. Tom reentered the darkened area, leaping to the back of the couch, and then to the shelves of the wall unit, seeking the highest point in the room.

Below him, the darkness seemed to coalesce, to coil together in a pulsing mass—

—And then it burst like an abscessed wound, spewing the stink of Bane.

Tom hurtled down to face it, longing to respond with a battle cry. But the last thing he needed was to draw Karen into this. He raised a paw in a clawing gesture—purely symbolic, he knew—as he lashed out psychically at the entity beyond the portal.

The Greater Banes were powerful. It took many cat-kindred to drive them back. Fighting alone,

Tom had only one advantage. He'd taken part in many of these battles. This would be his enemy's first fight.

Blackness recoiled before him, and Tom lanced it with another psychic thrust. His whiskers caught the barest trace of movement, another smell—

The dark shape leaped on him from beneath the couch, tearing at his flank with sharp teeth before darting away. Tom caught the stink of rat as he turned to face this new foe. It was a monster of its kind, easily half Tom's size. It was young, and strong—and Tom caught the psychic whiff of Bane inhabiting it.

The newcomer hadn't just reached out to the least of its brethren. It had found a powerful physical ally. Tom wondered what the lesser Bane expected to gain from its service. Then there was no time for thought. The rat was darting forward again.

Tom sprang, aiming to bring the vermin down between his paws. But he landed on nothing. The rat skittered to the side, leaving a gash on Tom's shoulder. Tom tried again and again, each time pouncing where his enemy had been an instant before.

Old . . . too old! Five years ago . . . even two . . .

Still worse, Tom knew that every moment wasted on this physical foe allowed the Greater Bane to consolidate its foothold in this reality, to reach out—

For Tom, the very air seemed gummy with the stench of Bane. *It extends its power,* he thought as shadow seemed to press on his very brain. *Karen . . . her mate . . . Katie. They wouldn't even hear if I cried aloud.*

And then he did cry out, as the rat went for the ankle of his right forepaw, trying to rip the sinews and hamstring him.

With a desperate jerk, Tom managed to shake the rodent off. He leaped, not so much trying to pounce as to trap his opponent under his body.

Darkness seemed to congeal around him, slowing him. Tom landed badly, his wounded foreleg almost collapsing. The rat managed to squirm free, setting its teeth in the ankle joint. A yowl escaped Tom's lips at the searing hurt.

Twisting onto his back, he kicked out with his rear feet. One caught the rat, sending it flying—but at a cost. The flesh of his foreleg tore. Tom smelled blood in the air—his blood—as his world was lost in a glare of agony.

Have to move while the damned beast is stunned, Tom thought. But his attempted attack failed ignominiously before it was even launched. He fell on his side, his forefoot flopping, useless.

Tom barely managed a three-footed stance before his adversary was back at him, darting in and out with slashing attacks. *Trying to strike the vermin with only one paw is even more useless than what I was doing before*, Tom realized hopelessly. He tried to roll, bringing his rear legs into the fight.

The rat dodged, feinted, and came in again, boldly climbing Tom's body to go for his face. Tom's attempt to bat the vermin away failed. Only a desperate twist of his head saved his left eye.

But his attacker's teeth dug into the flesh of Tom's cheek. The sensitive nerves connected to his whiskers blasted his brain with an onslaught of pain. He writhed, blood and mucus smearing across his muzzle as the rat hung on. Again, he'd have to pay in anguish to get free of his attacker.

Tom stumbled against a table leg, ramming the rat against the obstruction more by accident than design. The agonizing grip on his cheek let go, and Tom almost toppled at the sudden release of weight.

His adversary skittered back, its red eyes full of mocking, rattish laughter.

The world shrank to those two little red beacons in the darkness—right, left, forward, back—feinting, but inevitably piercing his defenses to draw a little more blood and strength from the cat.

Tom's nostrils clogged. He panted for air through his mouth. Should he try for the advantage of height, jumping to the top of the table? Not with a virtually dead foreleg. If he fell, the damned rat would be all over him.

The barest sound of a footfall sent his eyes twitching to the entrance. Katie!

Her body moved stiffly, with a sleepwalker's gait. Katie wasn't asleep, though. Her face was blank, but her eyes were aware—and shining with terror. The thing was drawing her to itself!

Tom turned to the portal, to find that the Bane's formless blackness was now extruded in a tangle of waving tendrils. They surged at Katie like a thousand misshapen tongues, eager for the first taste of flesh.

The little one took another slow, stiff-legged step toward them as the rat moved in for the coup de grâce.

Tom had a bare instant to interpose his shoulder where the soft flesh of his throat had been.

The impact knocked the weakened cat over. Tom scrambled to his feet at the cost of yet another wound. Katie took another step. The wormlike mass of blackness squirmed closer.

Tom tried to shamble over to protect the two-leg kit, only to be blocked and driven back by the rat.

The cat's fur was becoming clotted with blood. His breath wheezed, and he tottered as he tried to move. Finally, Tom overbalanced, falling on his bad leg. The rat moved in for the kill.

And as it moved, Tom thrust himself up again, then fell on his adversary. His feigned collapse had been all too real. After going down, Tom hadn't been sure he'd be able to get up again.

His rear legs scrabbling for purchase, Tom pushed himself and the trapped rat toward the portal . . . and the Bane. Beneath him, he could feel small, sharp teeth savagely ripping into his vitals.

The tendrils of almost-palpable blackness turned toward Tom as he came nearer.

Tom pushed himself up, freeing the rat. With his good forepaw, he batted it directly into the squirming darkness. The tendrils struck instantly. Yes. The Bane couldn't help its own hunger. It drove out the lesser possessor.

And in the instant that the rat's body froze, as its possessor dealt with a flood of physical sensation, Tom struck. A moment before, the Bane had been discorporate, untouchable.

Now it possessed a body—with all the vulnerabilities inherent in flesh.

The rat gave vent to one horrified shriek as Tom's teeth penetrated its neck. The vermin died, and in the shock of death, the Bane recoiled back through the portal.

Tom, his psychic teeth still set in his prey, was pulled along.

The other side of the portal was a tiny pocket of existence, a darkness so intense that its shades seemed like layers of phosphorescence, reacting to the comparative brilliance of earthly night.

Tom could understand why the Bane was eager to escape such a prison to an earthly body. He suddenly realized that he, too, was bodiless. Yet somehow he maintained a fierce hold upon the Bane. Greater or not, the malign creature seemed much smaller on this side of the portal. Or was it that Tom had somehow become bigger since leaving the corporeal world behind?

Perhaps the shock of undergoing a physical death had disassociated the being he fought with. Despite being on its home ground, the Bane couldn't seem to get free. Its struggles were spasmodic, each attempt to escape weaker than the one before. Suspicious of a ruse, Tom persisted with his psychic death grip as the Bane diminished, and diminished, until . . . it was gone.

Tom raised his head in the victory cry of his people—a cry that made no sound in this little pocket universe.

Tom broke off in mid-yowl. Victory cry . . . or death song? He had no body, although it seemed he could survive here. Tom turned—or, rather, directed his disembodied attention to the portal. He could "see" the connection to his world shrinking—the conjunction must be passing.

What to do? Return to a decrepit, mortally wounded body, or survive—at the cost of staying in this dark existence?

Never to see Karen—Katie—unless the stars line up correctly in their lifetimes, Tom thought. *Never to have a body . . . is this the birth of a Bane?*

He needed no more consideration. The same mental impulses he would use for a leap sent Tom's bodiless consciousness back through the portal. Back to his world . . . back to death.

*   *   *

Karen watched her daughter laughing and dancing in the frame of sunlight from the living room window. Katie reached up, trying to catch the motes of dust swirling on the random air currents. Her childish laughter soothed Karen's worry over the awful events of the other night.

Katie's frantic cries had roused Karen and Glenn. The two-year-old was incoherent about what had happened, but it was obvious that old Tom had made the ultimate sacrifice, protecting the baby from that enormous rat.

Glenn was already pursuing the co-op board with a major lawsuit. He and Karen were debating whether to find another place to live. That was for the future, however. Karen's present concern was all for Katie. How would her daughter cope with the traumatic experience she'd undergone?

Karen had feared nightmares and grief over the death of Tom. Instead, the two-year-old had displayed a—well, "sunny disposition" was the best description Karen could come up with.

She watched as Katie left off her dust-pursuit. The toddler headed away from the window toward the far corner of the room. There the sunlight was cut off by the bulk of the wall unit.

Katie stepped into the shadow, stamping hard in the middle of the relative gloom. "Bad Bean!" she announced—a new word she'd been using lately.

Then Katie turned and smiled up at the golden vortex rising in the sunlight. "Right, Tom?"

AFTERWORD

This confection of cats and bogles was sold on a simple premise. "The little Banes possess vermin. The big ones create Hitlers." Then I started doing some research and found a list of historical figures with a strong cat aversion: Napoleon, Mussolini—and, yes, old Adolph. Convenient? Yes. But also, perhaps, just a little bit disturbing. . . .

A LIGHT IN THE DARKNESS

by Pamela Luzier

Growing up, Pamela Luzier read everything she could get her hands on, sampling every genre. But, finding she preferred stories that ended with an optimistic outlook, she narrowed her reading down to fantasy, science fiction, and romance stories, especially those that include a touch of humor. Now an engineer turned writer, she enjoys writing stories that contain as many of these elements as possible. She's published seven romance novels and a novella under the name Pam McCutcheon, and writes her fantasy stories under the name Pamela Luzier. Her work has previously appeared in the DAW fantasy anthology *Creature Fantastic*. The cat in this story is heavily modeled on the one that currently rules her house.

GAIL Atherton pulled off into a cul-de-sac, cursing. It was almost midnight and she felt frustrated, angry, and totally lost.

No wonder. Up here in the mountain subdivisions west of Colorado Springs, the roads were still unpaved and streetlights were nonexistent. Towering pine trees and ghostly white aspens shielded the houses from view on acre-plus lots, with only a few pools of light here and there to show anyone was at home. How the heck was she supposed to read the road signs, not to mention the house numbers?

Despite the full moon, finding the streets she needed had proved difficult on these tortuous winding roads. And naturally, she couldn't read the map since the dome light had burned out two hours ago. But Gail needed to take another look at that map if she was going to find her louse of a husband tonight.

She pulled over in front of a house with lights in its windows and left the car running as she got out and stretched. The gentle soughing of the wind through the trees silently implored her to enjoy the peace and silence of the woodland setting, but she fought it, not willing to give up her righteous indignation just yet. She would need all she could muster when she finally found Richard.

She squatted in front of the headlights to peer at the hand-drawn map, wishing she had questioned Liz more about it. But Gail had been so angry, she'd just grabbed it and headed off.

She squinted at her friend's scribbling. Was that word Valley or Galley? Hell, it didn't matter. Gail hadn't seen either street in her wanderings. Glancing up at the brilliant starlit sky, she made a silent plea for help.

A sudden movement nearby made her jump, but she relaxed when she realized it was only a cat—a beautiful white, long-haired cat with a delicate triangular face. It looked incongruous out here, as if it should be a pampered pet instead of a carefree roamer of the back woods.

The cat stopped about two feet away, just within the light, its green eyes assessing her gravely. Now that she could see it better, Gail realized it wasn't completely white—its ears and tail were gray, and it had one large gray splotch on one side. But it wore no collar or anything else to suggest ownership.

"Hi, kitty," Gail murmured, holding her hand out for it to sniff. "Isn't it a little dangerous for you to be out all by yourself?" Foxes and other predators roamed these woods, only too willing to make this pretty kitty into dinner.

The cat rubbed its head against her hand and Gail scratched its ears. "Well, I'd love to stay and chat, but I have to find my husband and daughter."

Gail started to straighten, but before she could do so, the cat nipped the map out of her hand and took off with it.

"Hey, come back here," she shouted. "I need that."

The cat paid no heed, but bounded off through the underbrush up to the house beyond and disappeared through an open window.

"Damn," Gail muttered. *Didn't it figure?*

But at least the lighted house appeared inhabited. Sighing, she turned off the car, grabbed her purse, and walked up to knock on the door. It opened immediately, though the man who stood inside surprised her.

Somehow, she had expected jeans, a flannel shirt, and sturdy hiking boots. Instead, he wore some kind of short silk robe in an ornate black and gold design over a pair of loose black silk drawstring pants and bare feet. The robe was unbelted and where it gaped open, his skin was a light creamy brown. His chest was smooth and hairless, and so was his head—he had shaved it. How exotic. And even more weird, he looked vaguely familiar.

Her stupefaction must have shown on her face for he smiled at her, kindness flooding his features so he no longer appeared so strange. "May I help you?"

"Uh, y–yes," she stuttered. "A cat stole a map out of my hand and jumped in through your window."

His smile widened. "Did she now?"

She relaxed. If he knew this cat, it must be his. "Yes, and I really need that map. Could you get it for me, please?"

"Of course," he murmured. "But it might take a little time to find out which one of her hiding places she's used this time. Why don't you come inside while I search?"

She hesitated, then remembered where she had seen him before—with Liz. "Haven't we met before?"

He blinked, then smiled. "Yes, of course—at Liz

Summers' picnic. Well, then, you are doubly welcome. Please, come in."

Gail relaxed. If he was a friend of Liz's, he should be a good guy . . . and she needed that map. As he headed off into another room, she entered tentatively and received another surprise. A sense of peace and remarkable well-being washed over her. She frowned, not sure she was ready to let go of her anger just yet, but the ambiance drew her in, cradling her in its welcome warmth.

Where was the feeling coming from? The decor didn't seem to generate that kind of response. Rather than the rustic cabin she'd expected, this modern home held sleek furniture with a decidedly Egyptian feel, done primarily in black and gold with touches of bright jewel tones. Subtle hieroglyphics showed in the fabrics and furnishings, but instead of the expected Nefertiti or Tutankhamen busts, there were a number of cat statues scattered about, as well as some with the body of a woman and the head of a cat.

It all seems benign, but if a mummy shows up, I'm outta here.

Her host arrived then from the other room, shaking his head.

"Did you find it?" she asked eagerly.

"I'm sorry, not yet. Pasch must have a new hiding place."

"Pasch?"

He smiled and gestured down at the thieving cat

who now stropped herself on his legs. "I'm sorry, Pasch is the one who took your map. I'm Jonathon. And I've forgotten your name . . . ?"

"Gail Atherton. Look, I really need that map. Isn't there something you can do?"

"There might be." He gestured her to a seat on the couch while he took a chair. The cat sat between them, staring at her unblinkingly. "What are you looking for?"

Oddly enough, Gail didn't feel in any danger. The guy practically radiated goodwill and kindness despite his strange appearance. "I'm looking for a cabin."

"Do you know the address?"

"No, I don't remember. It was on the map."

"And why do you wish to reach this cabin?"

She thought it was a weird question to ask but shrugged it off. "My daughter's there," she said shortly. Richard had taken Angela and his girlfriend and had run off for the weekend to a cabin somewhere in these benighted woods.

"I begin to see why you were brought here."

"I wasn't brought here," Gail insisted. "I was trying to find the cabin and got lost. Then when I stopped to read the map, your cat stole it out of my hands." She glared at Pasch, but the cat seemed totally unconcerned as she groomed her dainty white paws.

"There are no accidents," he chided gently. "You were brought to my door on this night because I can help you achieve your heart's desire . . . if you are willing."

What was this New Age mumbo jumbo? "Look, all I need is the map, then I'll go away and leave you alone." She stared pointedly at the cat, hoping she would take the hint, but Pasch just yawned, revealing a small pink tongue and sharp white teeth.

"If that is all you wish, I can probably accommodate you, but I sense there is more to it than just a desire to reach a specific destination. If you tell me what you really want, I can help you find it."

"How?" Gail asked jokingly. "With magic?" That was the only thing that would help her now. That, or the map.

He smiled serenely. "As a matter of fact, yes, I'm speaking of magick."

"Huh?"

He rose. "Magick with a 'k,' to distinguish it from the illusory magic of stage magicians. Come," he said, beckoning. "Let me show you."

He led her into another room that was even odder than the first. At one end of the room stood what could only be an altar, covered with a starry black cloth and set with a goblet, a couple of candles, another statue of a cat, a few other objects she couldn't immediately identify, and a cat-handled knife.

"What is this?" she asked suspiciously. "Are you some kind of voodoo priest or something?"

He cocked an eyebrow at her. "Not voodoo. I practice Wicca."

Until Gail relaxed, she hadn't even realized she'd been tense. Liz dabbled in Wicca, and though Gail didn't know much about it, she did know that there was nothing to fear in the witches' practices. That meant the knife must be an athame. At least, that's what Liz had called hers.

"So, I guess that makes you a warlock," she said in relief.

He frowned. "A male witch is still a witch. Warlock means oath breaker—we never use that term."

"I'm sorry, I didn't realize."

He waved away her apology. "I showed you this to explain that I was just getting ready to perform a ritual when you arrived."

"By yourself?" Didn't witches come in covens?

"Yes, I prefer solitary practice, partly because I work with an uncommon deity."

"Let me guess," Gail said. "A cat god."

"Yes, the Egyptian goddess, Bast. She appears as half woman, half cat, or in fully feline form, and is the goddess of animals, children, the home, and bountiful positive energy."

It was Gail's turn to raise her eyebrows. "Children and the home?"

"Yes, and it is on just such an errand you have come tonight, isn't it?"

"Yes," Gail breathed. Could it be wholly coincidence that had led her to this house and this man?

Could he help her regain custody of Angela? Why not? She'd tried everything else, and Gail prided herself on being open-minded. It wouldn't hurt to try a bit of magick. And it might even help.

Especially since Pasch was doing her inscrutable cat thing and acting like she'd never even heard of a map. "Do you really think you can help me?"

"Perhaps," he said. "It depends on exactly what you're looking for. Come, let us sit comfortably in the living room and talk."

Pasch led the way for both of them, her gray plume of a tail waving gently as she preceded them into the living room. Then with one of those swift, lithe movements only a cat could make, she twisted upside down and lay on her back, front legs outstretched to leave her underside exposed.

Jonathon obeyed her silent command and knelt to rub her furry exposed tummy. Then when she had had enough, Pasch turned on her side and regarded Gail as if to say, "You see who's in charge here, don't you?"

Gail suppressed a grin. Yes, it was quite obvious the cat ran this household.

To her surprise, Jonathon shared her amusement. "She has me well trained," he murmured.

Gail laughed. "That's the nature of cats, I understand."

"Especially Pasch." He settled back in his chair and said, "Now, I may be able to help you find your heart's desire, but only if I know what you seek."

"What I seek?"

"Yes, what is it you want? Why are you looking for this cabin?"

Gail grimaced. "To expose my lying husband for the cheat he is." Her answer emerged with far less heat than she'd expected—this place must be exerting some kind of calming influence on her.

"That I cannot help you with," he said flatly.

Surprised, Gail asked, "Why not?"

"Our creed is to harm none, and the threefold law says that whatever is sent out in the way of good or evil will come back on the perpetrator threefold." He and Pasch regarded her gravely. "So, you see, I cannot wish harm to your husband."

"Then how am I to get my daughter back?"

He raised an encouraging eyebrow. "Perhaps you should tell me the whole story."

Gail shrugged. "There isn't much to it. My husband and I separated several months ago when I found out he'd been seeing someone in his office on the sly. We plan to get a divorce, but Richard is fighting me for custody of Angela." Though Richard's betrayal upset her, the thought of losing her little girl was far more painful.

"Is it likely he'll succeed?"

"Maybe. I've been a stay-at-home mother since we married, and I just reentered the workforce, so he thinks he can give her a lot more than I can. Me, her own mother!"

Both Jonathon and Pasch looked appropriately

sympathetic, so Gail continued. "Then when I learned he had borrowed a key to Liz's cabin from her husband and took Angela there for the weekend, I knew he was bringing his girlfriend as well. Since we haven't filed for divorce yet, I figured if I caught him in the act, so to speak, I could prove he was an unfit father and I could get custody."

"I see," Jonathon said impassively. "So your true goal isn't to expose your husband's indiscretion, but to . . . ?"

"Gain custody of my daughter."

He frowned, giving Gail the distinct impression that she had just given the wrong answer.

"What's wrong with that?" she demanded. "I just want what's best for Angela."

He brightened. "Ah, better. And if it would be best for her to be in her father's custody?"

"It's not," she said indignantly. "She should be with me."

Jonathon made a negating movement. "Set aside your own feelings and prejudices for a moment and think of Angela. If it really were best for her to be with her father, wouldn't you want that for your child?"

"In whose opinion? The male-dominated courts?"

"No, I speak of an objective personage—someone who would truly have the child's best interests at heart. An all-knowing deity. Would you trust a goddess to make that decision?"

A goddess? Was he kidding?

No, the earnest expression on his face showed he was absolutely serious. Even Pasch seemed to be on the edge of her seat, waiting for Gail's answer. "Well, as a purely hypothetical question, yes, I would trust a goddess to make the right decision. What's this all about?"

"And would you abide by that decision, no matter what it is?"

"I guess so." If she truly thought Angela would be better off with Richard, Gail wouldn't fight giving him custody. But not to worry. No goddess in her right mind would give Angela to a cheating louse like Richard.

He nodded. "Then let us ask Bast for help to do what is best for Angela."

That's right—he had said Bast was the goddess of children. "Do you think She can really help?" Gail was too polite to say it, but what she really meant was, *Do you honestly believe this?*

Oddly, he answered her unspoken question. "Think of it as another form of prayer. Together, we will pray to Bast to do what is best for your daughter."

Gail thought about it for a moment. Prayer could do some miraculous things . . . and Liz had told her of some amazing results that had come from Wiccan rituals. Maybe this guy really could help.

And it sure couldn't hurt. Until she found that

map, she couldn't find Richard anyway. "Okay, why not? What do I need to do?"

He beamed at her and even Pasch seemed pleased with her answer. Somehow, that made it feel like the right thing to do.

Jeez, what's wrong with me? Now I'm worried about the approval of a cat?

"We can proceed right away if you wish, but the ritual will be more powerful if you have a sacrifice to offer."

Gail stared down at the beautiful Pasch in horror. "You don't mean . . . ?"

He grimaced. "No, of course not. I'm speaking of a personal sacrifice—something you are willing to give up in order to gain your desire."

She relaxed, glad that he didn't expect her to harm any small creatures . . . or large ones, for that matter. "I'm not sure what you mean."

"For example, if a friend in the hospital asked you to help her heal quickly, your sacrifice might take the form of a donation to a medical research foundation, volunteering a few hours a month at the hospital, or merely visiting your friend during her illness. Your freely given sacrifice of time, money, or anything else that belongs to you shows you care enough to make some effort yourself . . . and that makes your ritual, or prayer, that much stronger."

"Ah, I see." It even made sense. Gail thought for a minute, wondering what sacrifice would be appropriate to obtain Angela's happiness. Heck, it wasn't difficult to figure out. Ever since the separation, Gail had been so worried about a job, money, and the prospect of losing Angela that she hadn't had much time to spare for the child herself.

Feeling guilty, Gail realized the best thing she could do was spend more quality time with her daughter. "I've been too busy to play with her much. Maybe if I set aside at least an hour each day just for her—to make it our special time together?"

"Perfect," Jonathon said.

Gail relaxed. That wasn't so hard . . . and it was something she should do anyway. Even if Richard gained custody, the court would surely allow her visitation rights, and she could make sure Angela knew her mommy loved her. "Okay," she said, feeling better already, "what do we do now?"

"Just follow my lead—I'll do most of the work." He led the way to what she thought of as the Wicca Room and glanced back with a smile. "We're in luck. There is a full moon tonight, and the sun—Ra, Bast's father—is in Leo, Bast's special sign. It should make the ritual even more powerful."

He went to a drawer and pulled out blue-and-pink candles, scratched hieroglyphics into the wax, and rubbed some oil on them as he murmured something.

"What are those for?" Gail asked when he was done.

"These are to set your intention, to let Bast know what you're asking for."

"I see," Gail said, though she wasn't at all sure she did.

"Do you have a photo of your daughter with you? it will help us concentrate the energies."

"Yes, of course." She pulled out one of the several she kept in her wallet and he placed it on the altar.

He smiled at her, then held out his hand. "Are you ready?"

Ready as she'd ever be. "I guess so."

He helped her learn how to ground and center first, then when he was satisfied, Pasch claimed a vacant spot on the altar and Jonathon declared them ready to begin.

With a look of utmost concentration and solemnity, he drew the athame from the altar and extended it out and up, chanting in a language that sounded vaguely Egyptian as he used it to slowly draw an imaginary circle around them. When he reached the point at which he had begun, Gail heard the circle close with an almost audible snap, as if he had just created an impenetrable force field around them.

Awed, Gail froze, wondering what would happen next. Jonathon didn't keep her in suspense long. Raising his arms, to the heavens, he began a chant that started out low and gained more force as he sang. As the volume rose, so did the crackling feel of energy in the air, not to mention on the small hairs on Gail's arms and nape.

She stood stark still, amazed. This must be the magick he spoke of. Even Pasch seemed to feel it, as she sat upon the altar with her eyes closed and her face raised in an expression of bliss, for all the world as if she were basking in the flow of power.

Suddenly, when the sparkling energy seemed to be at its peak, he broke off and switched to English. "Oh, mighty protectress, we have come this night to honor thy presence and to bring peace and happiness to Angela Atherton. Let your wisdom and benevolence guide the decisions of her parents and help them do what is right for their daughter."

He then turned to Gail and handed her a lighter, saying, "As you light the candles, state your intention and sacrifice."

She expected to stumble through this part, but something in the power of the circle gave her the ability to state her hopes clearly. "I ask for an end to the custody fight in whatever manner would best help Angela, and promise to devote at least an hour each day we are together to being with her and making her feel loved and cherished."

Jonathon nodded approvingly and Gail even heard a rumbling purr from Pasch.

"Repeat after me," Jonathon said. "As I will, so mote it be."

Obediently, Gail did as he said, and felt the energy suddenly decrease, as if part of it had zoomed off to take care of her wish. Gail shook her head, amused at her whimsy.

After they shared cake and wine, he rose to his full height once again and declaimed, "Bast, we thank you for presiding over this ritual and participating in our rites tonight. As we open the circle and go about our daily lives, remain in our hearts, watch over us, and guide our feet along the paths that are best for us. Blessed be."

"Blessed be," Gail murmured in response, feeling as if it were the right thing to do.

Jonathon drew his athame from the altar once again and traced the circle in reverse order. "The circle is now open," he said with a smile. "Once the candles you lit have burned down, your wish will be answered."

The energy ebbed, leaving Gail feeling strangely drained, as if she had just put her whole substance into the ritual.

Seeming to sense her problem, Jonathon guided her to a couch in the living room where she sank into the soft pillows. "I'll make you some tea," he murmured.

She nodded and closed her eyes to rest for a moment. The next thing she knew, a soft touch on her face woke her from a sound sleep. She opened her eyes to find daylight streaming in through the windows, illuminating Pasch, who sat watching her curiously, patting Gail's face with light feather touches.

"Hi, Pasch," Gail said softly, stroking the cat's soft, long fur. So the events of the night before weren't a dream. How odd. She lay still for a moment to assess her feelings. Now, in the bright light of day, those experiences seemed surreal. But, if nothing else, the ritual had helped eliminate her bitterness and made her feel good about her relationship with Angela once more. And since it was morning, the candles must have burned down by now. Did that mean her wish was granted?

As if in answer, Pasch dropped a piece of paper in front of Gail's nose, and Gail blinked at it. The map . . . But it was unreadable now with tooth marks, cat saliva, and dirt smeared all over it. Oh, well, it was too late to find Angela anyway.

She rose to use the bathroom she had seen earlier and splashed some water on her face, exiting to find Jonathon, looking more normal in jeans, a T-shirt, and tennis shoes.

"I'm sorry," she said, embarrassed. "I fell asleep."

"It's all right." And once again he gave her one of those supremely serene smiles. "Would you like some breakfast?"

"No," she said, mortified. "I'd better get going— I've imposed on you enough." Grabbing her purse, she blurted, "Thanks for everything."

"You're welcome." He escorted her to the door, watching with Pasch while Gail made her way up the walk to her car.

There was another cabin nestled in the sheltering trees across the cul-de-sac, and as she glanced at it, she saw a young girl with short dark curls skip up the driveway. Could it be . . . ? "Angela!" Gail cried.

Angela stopped and stared, then ran to her, yelling, "Mommy, Mommy!"

Gail scooped her up and hugged her tightly. How strange—Angela and Richard had been across the road the entire time. Richard emerged from the cabin now, looking warily toward Gail. He had cause, she supposed. She had been a bit of a shrew lately. But he didn't matter any more—Angela was the only important thing.

"What do you want?" Richard asked.

"I just wanted to see my daughter," Gail said calmly. No need to go into the events of the night before.

Pasch ambled up the walk and Angela squirmed when she saw the kitty. Gail put her down, so she could speak privately to Richard without worrying about what Angela would hear.

He looked perplexed at her mild reply. "It's just as well. There's something I want to talk to you about."

"What's that?" Despite her newfound peace, Gail felt herself tensing, wondering what demand he would have now.

"I want to file divorce papers right away."

"Fine." What they had together was dead now and there was no sense dragging out the funeral.

Seeming relieved at her ready acquiescence, Richard added, "And, uh, Cynthia and I want to get married."

"So?" What did he want, her approval? No matter how good she felt, Gail couldn't bring herself to wish her husband happy with the woman who'd stolen him from her.

He shifted uneasily, and glanced back at the cabin where Gail could see a shadowy figure in the doorway. "So, uh, Cynthia and Angela don't get along very well. Since you've been wanting full custody, I think it would be better for everyone concerned if I let you have her."

Elation filled Gail. "You mean it? I can have custody of Angela?"

"Yes," Richard said, and glanced at his daughter with some pain in his expression. "But I want visitation rights—she's still my little girl and I love her."

"Of course," Gail exclaimed. "I wouldn't deprive Angela of her father."

"Good," Richard said, looking relieved. Apparently, he'd been fearing a much more contentious discussion. "Then why don't you take her now, and I'll bring her things home later. Cynthia and I have things to discuss."

"Sure," Gail said, not believing it had been so easy.

While Angela kissed her daddy good-bye and Richard turned toward the cabin and his girlfriend, Gail could do nothing but stand there, stunned. She'd gone from anger and despair to joy in a few short hours. How had it happened?

Jonathon, that's how.

She turned back toward his house and saw him approaching. "Did you hear?" Gail asked joyously. "Richard has agreed to give me custody of Angela!"

"That's wonderful."

"And it's all due to you and your ritual. How can I thank you?"

"Your joy, and Angela's happiness, are thanks enough. But it wasn't due to me."

"What do you mean?"

"Your pledged sacrifice had something to do with it, but most of it was Bastet's doing. She brought you here."

"Bastet?"

"When Bast is in fully feline form, she uses the name Bastet . . . and sometimes Pasch."

Incredulously, Gail stared down at the cat who was bearing up very well under the not so gentle ministrations of a three year old. Naw, it couldn't be . . . could it?

In answer, Pasch tilted her head with an amused expression, looked directly at Gail . . . and winked.

MU MAO AND THE COURT ORACLE

by Elizabeth Ann Scarborough

Elizabeth Ann Scarborough is the Nebula Award-winning author of *The Healer's War,* as well as twenty-two other novels and numerous short stories, including several novels coauthored with Anne Mc-Caffrey. Her most recent books are *The Godmother's Web* and *Lady in the Loch,* as well as an anthology she edited, *Warrior Princesses.* She lives in a cabin on the Washington coast with four lovely cats who find her useful for the inferior human DNA that granted her opposable thumbs for opening tuna cans. When she is not writing, she beads fanatically, and is also the author/designer/publisher of a bead book of fairy-tale designs called *Beadtime Stories.*

MU Mao became Aware as he was reborn yet again. That is to say, once more he became embodied, for his rebirth occurred not at the body's physical emergence from the mother's womb, but from the time Mu Mao realized, *Here I am again. Here I go again. What now?* The current body gained Awareness as it was dumped unceremoniously into a cage with three siblings, all as hungry as Mu Mao, reincarnate, suddenly was.

Just once it would be nice if rebirth took place in a lovely home, somewhere warm, with soft blankets laid down for the arrival of the sweet little much adored and wanted kittens. Instead, Mu Mao the Magnificent found himself in an animal shelter, among many other cats and kittens.

He knew it at once by the smell—it was clean, which was a blessing. And at least there would be some food. Often he was born into the wild, or into some great colony of feral cats. Being a Bodhisattva and helping others work out their destiny and achieve Enlightenment was no easy task when one had to skitter up trees to avoid being eaten by larger predators. Worse by far was having to avoid being eaten by other larger and more aggressive cats. Mu Mao was now born into perhaps his thousandth lifetime, the first several hundred of which had been devoted to evolving into the wise person, shaman, healer, priest, lama, hermit, monk, and counselor he had ultimately become, the latter thirty devoted to his reward—being born into the highest possible life-form, that of a cat. He found it particularly upsetting when others of his exalted species aimed their teeth at his own helpless little kitten tail. True, even some cats had to evolve, but he found their process unnerving.

Did *no one* in charge of fate think it necessary for Mu Mao to help his fellow life-forms from the standpoint of being a companion animal to some doting two-legged being with opposable thumbs?

When he had slaked his hunger and thirst, he researched his current situation by closely examining the papers covering the floor of his home. They looked fresh and current and he could still smell the ink, so he knew they must be no more than a day old at the most. It was the year of the Cat, according to Asian astrologers, and from the date, within the sign called Leo in Western astrology. The sign of the cat. Very catty. Reeking with cattiness. Very clearly, Mu Mao's current mission would be concerned with events unfolding in the realm of his fellow felines.

"Ahem," his Mother of the Moment said. "What do you think you are doing? Tear up that paper at once! Cats can't read!"

"I beg your pardon, gentle mother," he said politely, "But I can. In several languages actually. Which I also speak, though only after judicious consideration for the sensibilities and circumstances surrounding me. However, other than the information I have already gleaned, the reading matter lining our cage tells me nothing of value concerning our current situation. Perhaps you can enlighten me. Is there some great event in the making within the realm of cat-kind?"

His mother, a calico of undistinguished markings, reached out a hard paw and swatted him across the cage. "Don't get saucy with me, young kit! While you drink my milk, you go by my rules. Cats don't read, and cats of our clan don't meddle in the affairs of the realm. What business have we with royalty? Did royalty step in and prevent my farmer's land from being sold, keep the barn that has been the personal domain of generations of my ancestors from being torn down to make a parking lot for a shopping mall? Did it keep my elders from being put down and you and your brothers and sisters and me from being put in here where no doubt we'll be gassed as soon as the kits take the kennel cough? Don't speak to me of matters of the realm!"

"I beg your pardon," he said with what sounded like a small pitiful mew as he washed his face very quickly to try to wash away the pain of the blow. It didn't take much to hurt you when you were five and a half inches long from nose to tail tip.

However, a small thing like personal discomfort could not obstruct his duty, and so he sought other sources of information. The cage beside theirs was filled with what looked like a vast black-and-gray-striped fur pillow. Mu Mao reached out a paw and touched the pillow. "I beg your pardon, sir or madame, as the case may be," he said to the pillow. There was no reply. It might have actually been a pillow—it might have been dead, except that there was some warmth emanating from beneath the fur and the coat twitched ever so slightly as Mu Mao touched it.

"Hey, little fella, don't bother the poor old guy," a man said. Mu Mao turned. The man was looking sadly toward the cage containing the inert animal.

Mu Mao, sensing that there was something for him here, rubbed himself against the front bars of the cage and gave a small, cute mew. Manipulative and disgusting perhaps, but effective.

The man undid the latch of Mu Mao's new home and lifted him out, holding him in one hand and stroking his head with a finger. It felt very good. Most nice things that happened to Mu Mao felt very good. Feeling very good when at all possible seemed to be one of the benefits of possessing the qualities of Catness.

"Would that older cat have hurt that little baby kitten?" a woman's voice cooed from somewhere to the left and slightly behind the man.

"I doubt it. But the poor old guy has enough problems without being harassed by a little punk like this guy," the man told her. He wore a name tag. It said "Andy."

"Oh?" the woman asked without much interest, and sneaked a finger around Andy so that she could tickle Mu Mao's chin.

"Yeah, poor old cat is a sad case. He's lived with the same guy for almost twenty years and now his master is dying. The guy thought maybe if the cat came here, he'd have time to find a new home before his master died. But the old cat ain't havin' any. He sits like that with his face to the back of the cage."

"Maybe he needs more attention," the woman said. Her voice carried no reproach that Mu Mao could hear, but Andy reopened Mu Mao's cage and returned him to his siblings, then opened the adjoining cage and extracted the other cat.

The other cat lay like a lump in Andy's arms, unresisting, but also indifferent and stiff, a deeply resentful look in his narrowed eyes.

He did not respond to Andy's voice or touch or to the woman's. He just sat there and glowered, and pretty soon Andy put him back into his cage.

Mu Mao's heart went out to him, but when he tried to speak to the old cat again, his siblings pounced on him and rolled him around the cage and his mother began to wash him with more energy than was strictly required.

After that, he needed a nap. When he woke up, the people had gone home. The first time he lived in a shelter, he thought that when the people went home, all of the animals would go to sleep. He was wrong. This was when the cats gossiped through the bars and wires of their cages.

"Did you hear?" asked a bobtailed black tom two levels down. "The King of the Cats is dead and nobody knows who the new king is or where he might be."

"That's silly," said a fluffy neutered calico spinster. "How can anyone mislay a king?"

The tom tried to lash his bobbed tail and thumped it against the bars. "It's more a case of the king mislaying his mistresses—and potential heirs.

Tom Gamble was a very busy cat. The ladies always liked him and he hated to disappoint them."

"Perish the thought," Mu Mao's mother said, yawning and settling her chin on her paws. "The world never has seen such a lot of scruffy long-haired tawny-striped kits as His Majesty sired. And which of them is the crown prince, well, that's anyone's guess."

"His Majesty wasn't much to worry about details," sniffed a gray tabby. "He never did appoint a court oracle."

"You don't *appoint* one of those," a white almost-a-Persian said loftily. "They are born, not made. Not even by kings."

"Well, whoever was made didn't get recognized anyway. So now here we've got Bast-knows-how-many potential heirs and nobody to sort them out. There'll be fur flying for sure, bloody civil war because of it, I tell you." The black bobtail was warming to his subject.

Mu Mao peered carefully down through the screen of his cage. He wondered if black bobtail tom had any idea what a real war was like. By now, many generations of cats had come and gone since the end of the World. The warlords had made way for governments which were, if no less rapacious than they were, at least more peaceable about it. These governments were extremely polite to each other. For now. A cat civil war wouldn't involve nuclear devices, probably, but it could still be an ugly and horrible thing. As the many times great grand-sire of almost all of the cats in existence today, Mu Mao mourned any carnage among them.

A frightening thought occurred to him then, and he checked his own body. Whew! He had a little sooty black tail and a white chest and paws, black back with a white spot, white belly with a black spot. His face would either be black or have a mask, he supposed. It didn't matter. He was not a ginger cat as Tom Gamble and his likely heir were. So the heir was not him. Nor did he feel especially oracular. Therefore, he was free to pursue whatever business seemed to call for him to put a paw in.

As soon as the others settled down for the night, he began.

The first thing to do was get from his cage into the adjoining one, to confront the terribly depressed cat.

This presented only a small difficulty for Mu Mao, who as the most esteemed of lamas had excelled in the Tibetan psychic sports, which naturally included breath, and even molecular, control. He simply exhaled all of the air in his body. His mother was not watching. Perhaps if she had been, she would have been alarmed, for when he exhaled, he exhaled the air between his very atoms, becoming so small as to be virtually invisible. Thus he could easily slip through to the next cage, after which he inhaled mightily and regained his former kitten size, perhaps even adding an additional inch or two of air. Then he padded forward to confront the bitter old cat.

The old one was not sleeping, but brooding with both green eyes slitted resentfully.

"My dear sir, you simply cannot continue like this," Mu Mao told him. "Your unfriendly demeanor frightens away those who would save you. I have it on good authority that it is nearly impossible for an adult cat to find a home from one of these places as it is."

Mu Mao thought for a moment the old cat would swat him, but the poor fellow seemed to lack the energy, and instead sighed, letting much of the air out of himself, though not to the degree that Mu Mao had done.

"Don't speak to me of homes. A home is nothing but an illusion based on the whim of a fickle and callous race. I should know. From the time I was smaller than you, all through kittenhood, I was with him, his true companion, loving him when others rejected him, bringing him mice and birds when he was hungry, licking his wounds. I even submitted to the veterinarian's knife so that my natural urges to mate and sire children would not interfere with my closeness to him. And now, after all these years, he has betrayed me. Dumped me like so much feline garbage, given me into the hands of these people who cage me here, without my pillow or dish, without my weekly treats or my toy, without the drug that gave me the feeling of being wild and free—and without that cruel un-worthy man I have loved for so long. He doesn't want me anymore. I don't care. I hate him now. I hate all humans, and I don't want to live with them. If I must live with another one in order to live, then I prefer to die."

"Oh, you will die if you keep this up," Mu Mao said. "But then you will be with your friend if you do, I suppose."

"What do you mean?"

"You heard Andy. Your friend is dying. That is why he had you sent here to find another home."

"You understand what they say? It means some-thing?"

"You mean you don't? You lived all those years with one man and didn't understand what he said?"

"Well, no. Not really. It didn't matter. I didn't ac-tually need to. He would say things in a kind voice and I knew I could do as I wished, and if he sounded stern and pointed at something I knew I shouldn't go back to it until his back was turned. Otherwise, he fed and petted me and babbled to his heart's content, and I sat on his lap and purred for him and meowed when I wished him to do some-thing in particular. I must say, he spoke better cat than I did human. But then he stopped speaking to me, would not lift his hand to pet me, and finally turned away from me and allowed others to take me from our bed and put me into a vile case and bring me to this place where you see me now. Perhaps he was bored with me, do you think? I have heard others here speak of how their people became bored with them when they no longer performed kittenish antics such as someone like yourself might do. When that happens, I understand it is not uncommon for the people to simply dispose of one, as has happened to me, and get a newer edition."

"No," Mu Mao said firmly. "That is not what happened at all. Andy explained it to the woman. Your friend was dying. He wanted to see you in a good home before he had to leave, to make sure you would be cared for. Even as he dies, he cares for you and worries for your welfare."

The old cat stared at Mu Mao, and a large tear ran down the short fur along the side of his nose. Mu Mao noticed that he had black circular stripes that joined on the bridge of his nose, like spectacles. "He will be all alone and he sent me away to spare me. But I don't want to be spared. I want to be with him. I want to go to him. If I die, too, I don't mind. But I can't bear to be locked up in here when he needs me." The old cat stretched briefly, then rose to his feet and began pacing in a manner that was extremely tiger-like. "Tomorrow I will raise such a ruckus that the man—Andy—would unlock my cage to see what was wrong and then I would give him a great scratch and make him release me and I will run out the door very fast and home again."

"Oh, good! You can find it again?" Mu Mao asked hopefully, for he was sure now he knew what his first mission in this young life must be.

"Well, it must be around here somewhere!" the old one snapped. "I know I will find it only—only, now that you tell me what is happening, I suddenly have a feeling."

"A feeling?"

"Yes, I think—I feel Fred is still here but I don't feel he will be here tomorrow. He needs me *now*. Of course, it is all his own doing that I am here, but you and I both know this isn't working. I need *out*." The "now" and the "out" were drawn out and agonized, and meant the same thing in cat as they did in English.

"Calm yourself," Mu Mao said. "I am here to help you. First, we must release you from your cage."

"Yes, but how?"

"Patience," Mu Mao said. He thought about it. He could make himself small again and slip through the front of the cage, but that would not release the old cat. If he were full grown, and the cage on the lowest level, he could easily undo the latch with his teeth and paws and the cunning of thirty remembered feline lifetimes and prior lives as a holy man. But this was not the case. "Hmmm," he said to himself and then, "Hm?" That was it. A simple mantra, a chant—a purr, done with great concentration and deep vibration.

He leaned against the lock and purred with all his might and all his energy and all of the depth of his tiny being. The lock never stood a chance. It shuddered open within moments, and Mu Mao and the old cat leaped to the floor.

Instantly, all of the other cats were awake and scratching at their cages. Mu Mao's new mother was particularly vociferous. "Ungrateful spawn of a lecherous tomcat, why are you liberating that washed-up old alley cat and not your own family?"

"Mother—friends, at least here you will have a warm place to sleep and food. Outside you will have nothing."

"Except our freedom," said the bobtail black. "And a certainty that nobody will pluck us helpless from our cages to take us to a gas chamber. I've heard about what they do in these places. I like it out here. Where do you think I was before I came here if not out there?"

The old cat was pawing and mewing at the door and Mu Mao turned from him to the others and back again while the old fellow went frantic trying to escape.

"Very well. There's no time to argue." He went to the door and jumped up on the handle and said to all of the other cats. "Repeat after me:" and began the purring Mantra of Liberation once more.

Moments later two dozen cats and kittens were straggling at various speeds behind the tail of Mu Mao, who was struggling to keep up with the old cat, his nose never catching up with the butterfly spirals of black stripes on the old cat's gray sides.

Mu Mao's mother continually lost ground as she shifted kittens and at last Mu Mao in his tiny voice told three of the other adult cats that if they wished to go in the same direction he was, they should help carry the young. Much to his surprise, they agreed. But even more surprising, the old cat turned for the only time since their escape, and scooped up Mu Mao by the nape of the neck. After that, their caravan progressed much more quickly.

The old cat was not lost, nor was he confused. He unerringly homed in on his former home. A strong chill wind blew them along, but it was not yet raining or snowing and the night was clear, with many stars Mu Mao could not properly appreciate from his berth under the chin of the old cat.

The cortege of cats passed over and under a series of back fences, alleys, and yards until they came to a small house with high grass. A light shone through a back window. The old cat dropped Mu Mao, hopped up to the sill and scratched, mewing.

Mu Mao jumped up beside him. The others started to do the same, but the old cat hissed warningly at them and then modulated his tone to another plaintive meow.

Inside the room was a bed full of tumbled covers and a small, frail person. The person turned toward the window, as Mu Mao looked on. The man seemed to have no attendant or helper however, and had barely the strength to raise his hand. Someone had brought him water and tidied the place recently, from the look of it however. Perhaps he had help come in during the day, or perhaps they slept elsewhere in the house, though it scarcely looked large enough for two people.

"Let me in, Fred! Let me in!" the old cat cried over and over and Fred seemed aware of him but unable to move. Finally the old fellow jumped down, narrowly missing Mu Mao's mother and two of his brothers.

"If he won't open the window, then I will take a run and break through it," the old cat declared.

"Oh, that will be a grand surprise for your friend. A concussed, unconscious, perhaps even dead cat lying cut to ribbons and bleeding all over his floor. I believe there is a better way," Mu Mao said. "A moment please." He began his chant of levitation, aiming at the window. It was a tricky business. Once he himself rose into the air and he had to start all over again. Another time he saw something move from the corner of his eye and looked around to see all of the other cats lifting from the ground. Once more he started over. Fred lifted once, briefly, too, but then Mu Mao at last chanted with the correct intonation and the window creaked, jerked, and flew open. The old cat flew through it as if he had wings, landing on the bed beside his friend and purring madly, rubbing himself so hard against the fragile body in the bed he threatened to crush it.

"Gently, old one," Mu Mao cautioned. "His fires burn low. You wouldn't want to extinguish them entirely before you had a proper reunion."

Just then, however, Mu Mao heard paws on the sill and turned back to the other cats. "It's a private moment," he told them. The bobtail black tom sauntered saucily forward, and had to bounce unceremoniously back to the ground to avoid losing his nose as the window flew shut again.

Mu Mao saw with surprise that the communication between Fred and his feline friend did indeed consist only of cat noises on the one side and human murmurings on the other. It seemed to suit them fine, however, and he decided not to offer his services as a translator.

Fred was immediately enlivened by the presence of his feline friend, and gave the cat weak strokes and spoke to him while the cat purred and rubbed. Mu Mao found such extravagant affection almost distasteful, as he himself had learned to practice detachment in all things. However, in his heart he knew that love was not merely a great catalyst to many important changes and events, but the only catalyst if such things were to have Merit.

Slightly bored, nonetheless, Mu Mao looked about him while man and cat reunited. He noticed many framed photographs on the dresser. They were all of Fred and the old cat, who in some of them was a young cat, and Fred a younger man. In one of them the old fellow were respectively a mere fluffball of a kitten and Fred himself barely dry behind the ears. Most of the photos said, "Me and Delf" although one, a portrait of Delf as a kitten, said "Delfy, seventh son of Alison Gray." Delfy himself was very gray in that picture. The dark stripes would have come in later life.

Photographs also covered the walls, but they were too high for someone of Mu Mao's diminutive stature to see. Photograph albums were piled on the table beside the bed, as if Fred had been looking at them before his caretaker tidied up. Mu Mao jumped up on the table to see if any of them were open, but none was and they were too heavy for a small kitten to manipulate. He didn't want to knock one off the table and disturb the reunion.

However, from his fresh vantage point, he saw a computer sitting on a table in one corner of the room. This was something even a kit with the right know-how could use. After all, it involved only the pushing of a few buttons and something called a mouse.

It was a small computer, and its power button responded readily to the touch of a tiny paw. Fred was not a secretive man. No password was required to see what concerns he filed on his machine. One choice said "Delfy" and Mu Mao pounced on the mouse. A number of things happened inside the computer with the result that soon there was a chronicle of Delfy's life from the time he was born until Fred became too ill to be Delfy's biographer any longer.

Man and cat had been intertwined throughout their lives to the extent that it was amazing to Mu Mao that Delfy had never learned more of Fred's language or had mistaken Fred's intention when the man sent his cat companion to find a new home. Actually, according to the sad note in Delfy's chronicle, Fred had given Delfy to a friend who promised to find him a home. Apparently the friend had simply dumped the cat at the shelter.

But from the time Delfy was born, a Gemini in the year of the Dragon, when Fred had helped Alison Gray deliver her kittens and had wiped the caul from little Delfy's face, they had been together. There were snapshots of the house Fred and Delfy lived in before and after the earthquake. Fred wrote that before the earthquake, Delfy had leaped from his arms and flown back and forth to the frame of the door, hooking his claws into Fred's pants and insisting that Fred follow him. Fred credited Delfy's instinct for survival with saving his life. There were the women friends that Delfy didn't like who eventually broke Fred's heart and the man friend that Delfy hated, who turned out to be a crook. Fred even spoke sadly of when he first began to feel ill and Delfy began shredding a magazine that had an article about bladder cancer in it. Had he paid attention at the time Delfy did this, Fred believed the doctors could have treated it.

A Gemini in the Year of the Dragon. Well. Yes. Auspicious? Certainly.

Mu Mao gave the mouse a final, rather unenlightened bat, and jumped down from the table.

Fred's initial joyous greetings had dwindled to incomprehensible murmurings. His pets grew feebler as the joy that had flooded him with adrenaline could not sustain his strength, and his hand faltered, and lay still.

Delfy stopped in mid-purr and looked into Fred's face. His eyes, so fond and full of happy memories before, were now glazed and empty, though his lips still curled in a slight smile.

Delfy gave a mew that was half a whine and nosed at Fred's limp hand.

Mu Mao jumped up on the bed and with his tiny tongue began grooming the old cat's head. "We were just in time," the kitten with the old soul said. "And you did a good thing for Fred. He was very glad to see you and had missed you very much, as you saw for yourself. I have read his words concerning you, and it is true that he only sent you away to save you. But you didn't want to be saved, so now what?"

"You who can open doors with your purrs, make yourself invisible, and levitate windows ask me what's next?" Delfy asked in a dispirited voice.

"I do," Mu Mao said. "We are all wild again. The

others seem to wish to stay together for the time being. How about you?"

The old cat sank his chin into his paws. He remained snuggled next to Fred's body. Mu Mao licked and licked, projecting calming and healing thoughts as he did so. "I don't care."

"You cannot stay here, friend. I know the ways of people. Soon they will come and take Fred away and someone new will live here. Probably you will not be welcome and will find yourself back in the place where we were. I think you and I both know you have a life with and a duty to your own kind now."

Delfy turned away to lick Fred's ear, and tried to groom his hair.

A horrible wild yowl sounded from without and Mu Mao jumped upon the windowsill in time to watch a gang of strange cats descend upon the refugees from the shelter, tearing into them with ferocity meant to kill. The fur flew, screams and spits, hisses and the sound of ripping flesh met him. For just a moment, the small feline he was in this life thought it best to stay put, but he saw a grizzled calico with one ear leap upon his mother and try to get at one of his littermates. He levitated the window with such force that the pane rattled in its frame.

The bobtail black tom flew into the grizzled calico and tore her from Mu Mao's mother's back. Mu Mao was levitating his small siblings to the relative safety of the windowsill when Delfy sprang up beside him.

The striped cat's fur bristled until he was enormous, ten times the size of Mu Mao and his brothers and sisters. With a roar like a lion's, a roar so unlike his mewlings and purrings to his former companion that Mu Mao could hardly believe this was the same cat (the dual nature of a true Gemini, he reflected with satisfaction), he stilled the furor of battle. "HEAR ME AND BE WARNED!" he snarled. His eyes were rolled back in his face, and the black spectacles around them became a spiraling infinity knot that hypnotized the cats below and quite surprised and pleased Mu Mao with the definitiveness of its declaration of Delfy's unique status.

"The King is Dead. You anarchists who would rend the kingdom apart for lack of leadership, beware. The new king is among us now. Long live Bobtail Black Tom, the only legitimate and non-neutered heir to His Former Majesty, Tom Gamble!"

The strange cats slunk away from those they were mauling, just far enough to roll onto their backs, as did the other refugee cats one by one, while Bobtail Black Tom strolled among them licking their faces or giving their bellies a warning tap with his paw. Mu Mao's mother, having made her obeisance, brought her youngsters from the sill one by one, the last being Mu Mao, who jumped down unaided.

Beside him, Delfy landed but neither of them showed their bellies to the bobtailed black king. Nonetheless, the king graciously sauntered forward, quite full of himself now, Mu Mao noticed, though he doubted the black cat had had any idea of his own royalty prior to Delfy's announcement. With great ceremony he licked Mu Mao's forehead and then lowered his own head for Delfy to lick his ears, which Delfy did in the feline equivalent of a coronation.

"Great Oracle," the king asked when this was done, "You took your own sweet time about announcing yourself. What kept you?"

Just then Fred's caretaker, who apparently had been asleep in another room in the house and been aroused by the racket, came to the window. "I never saw so many damned cats in my life. Shut up, you lot! There's been a death in this house and—why, Delfy! You came back. Come on back inside, kitty, and we'll find you a good home. Fred wouldn't want you to be a stray."

But Delfy, a true Gemini now joined with his second path, turned his tail to her and nosed the king, who led his court back into the dark backyards and over the back fences and across the shadowed alleys that were his new realm. Mu Mao, his small body weary from his exertions, begged his mother for a ride.

STAR SONG

by Nina Kiriki Hoffman

Nina Kiriki Hoffman has been writing for almost twenty years and has sold almost two hundred stories, two short story collections, novels (*The Thread That Binds the Bones* and *The Silent Strength of Stones, A Red Heart of Memories,* and her most recent novel, *Past the Size of Dreaming*), a young adult novel with Tad Williams (*Child of an Ancient City*) a *Star Trek* novel with Kristine Kathryn Rusch and Dean Wesley Smith (*Star Trek Voyager 15: Echoes*), three R. L. Stine's *Ghosts of Fear Street* books, and one *Sweet Valley Junior High* book. She has cats.

"**I** HATE it here," said July's thirteen-year-old daughter, Claire. She lay sprawled on the sofa, feet up against the back, head hanging back over the edge, streaky blonde hair brushing the floor, and glared at her new world upside down.

Open white Chinese food cartons sat here and there around the living room. Chopsticks stuck out of the tops. The air smelled like stir-fried vegetables and disturbed dust. Outside, the winter sun had dropped into the southern California ocean, and night gathered beyond the windows.

July studied the armful of books she had just

pulled out of one of the boxes stacked around the room. She had had a dream that she would actually organize her books now that she was moving them, but . . .

Here was *The Magical Household*—she put it on top of the bookshelf; she'd need to do some basic clearing and wards around the house right away. Here was *Herbs for Use and for Delight*. Here was a photo album from last year, up on the mountain, with all the family in the pictures, including Martin, her soon-to-be-ex-husband, and Tim, her older son. Here was *Comparative Cultural Analysis*. Here was a very battered copy of *The I Hate to Cook Book*. She set that aside to take to the kitchen. Here were four novels she had bought over the past three years and hadn't found time to read.

Wait, one of them was somebody else's book. She'd have to take it back to the commune. She set it aside, too, and put other books on the shelf. Maybe once they'd unpacked everything else she could come back and organize the books.

Yeah, right.

"Did you hear me, Mom? I hate, hate, hate this house!" Claire pulled gum out of her mouth in a long string that led back between her lips. She stretched the gum until it drooped dangerously near the floor. "I hate, hate, hate this yard. I hate this neighborhood!"

"I heard you." July grabbed another armful of books. She didn't say what she really wanted to say.

Wasn't Claire the one who always wanted to go downtown while they lived at the commune? Now they *lived* downtown, within walking distance of movie theaters, the library, the school, and the new downtown mall! Even more important, there was a music school just two blocks away where Claire might find a voice teacher. Claire's wish had come true.

But July couldn't say that. Given any opening at all, Claire would explode.

"Hey, Mom!" Ten-year-old Orion raced into the room, brushing past stacks of boxes. A top box teetered and thumped to the hardwood floor. July hoped it contained books and not china. "Now that we have our own house, can we get a dog? Can we? Huh?"

"We'll get an animal if we're lucky," July said.

"We will?" Orion jumped up and down with joy. The floor shook. Then he stopped, a frown on his face. "I don't want an animal you cast a spell for, like ugly old Frizzis!" he said. Frizzis was the family familiar, a mean, ancient, skeletal cat who snarled at everybody but Martin and Tim. Maybe because Frizzis knew that Martin and Tim were the only members in the Rhodes family who treated the craft seriously. Frizzis had stayed with Tim and Martin. "I want a regular animal. I want a dog that loves me and can learn tricks."

"We'll see," said July.

Claire stuffed the gum back in her mouth. "I want to go home."

"Well, you can't. You have to stay with me. Your father and I flipped a coin for you, and I lost."

Claire rolled over, tumbled to the floor, stood up, and screamed. She had a powerful and piercing scream, and really good lungs; she sustained an ear-torturing pitch and volume for what seemed like ten minutes before she ran out of the room.

Out the back window, a faint yowl echoed Claire's scream.

Orion stared at July, his big brown eyes tear-bright. "Did you flip a coin for me, too?" he whispered.

July put down the books she had just taken out of the box and hugged him. "No, no, my bonny boy. Your dad and I fought over you, and I won."

"What about Tim?"

July sighed and released her son. "You know Tim's studying craft with Uncle Lucas," she said. "He didn't want to leave. Your dad and I talked it over with him."

"Tim got to choose?"

Oh, Goddess. She and Martin had agreed they wouldn't tell the other kids that Tim had made his own choice. Each decision had been so painful and difficult. They had done their best. "When you're fourteen, you can choose, too, sweetie."

Orion glanced at the door Claire had disappeared through. "Does that mean that next year she—?"

"We'll see." A fib. July cringed inside. She hated fibbing to the kids. The truth was, like it or not, Claire was stuck in town with July.

Martin didn't want Claire around. He had no parenting skills with teenagers or girls. He wouldn't have to do much for Tim; Lucas had accepted Tim as a son of the craft, and would treat him as a son of the body.

July wasn't sure she had girl-and-teenager parenting skills either. At this point, she wasn't sure she had any parenting skills. At the commune, who needed them? There were so many other people who could supply whatever you were missing.

"I want Aunt Loo," Orion whispered.

Aunt Loo was a big motherly woman who did all the commune baking, and hugged and bandaged the children when they came to her with splintery fingers, scraped knees, or nicked hearts.

"You can't have her." July felt another nick in her own heart. Didn't the kids think she could do anything right?

The commune was only a twenty-minute drive away. If Orion seriously needed Aunt Loo, maybe July should drive him up into the mountains. But she didn't want to set that precedent. What if he wanted to go there every day? Twice a day? They had to learn to live down here in the city sometime.

A great yearning for Aunt Loo's kitchen flooded

July's heart. Warm bread. Pale homemade butter. Fresh cookies. Clean dishes. Hot tea with clover honey, a wood-burning stove, and big warm hugs.

She wanted to go home, too.

Orion sniffled. "I'm going to my room." He left with dragging steps.

Someone pounded on the front door.

What now? July crossed the room and opened the door.

A very large man with a gun in his hand stood on the welcome mat.

July took two steps back, her breath trapped in her throat. Was there a spell for this? Of course she couldn't think of one when she really needed it. Craft had never been her strong point. Research, now . . . point her at any problem and she could look up solutions in a flash. But this?

"Who's being killed?" asked the man. "I heard screams." He peered past her into the living room.

"That's not death. It's a teenager."

His dark brows lowered over his eyes. "Mind if I come in?"

"As a matter of fact—" July remembered the instructions she had gotten from the oldest Aunt just before she left the commune. "You haven't lived out in the world for a long time," Aunt Grace had told her. "Think about every invitation. There are some things you don't want to invite into your life. It's all right to say no to them."

The man pushed past July, gun pointed at the

ground, his dark eyes shifting back and forth. "Where's the body?"

"There is no body." There was a man with a gun standing in her living room looking at all her boxes. He wasn't pointing the gun at her, though. She tried to check his aura. Another thing she had never been good at. She just wasn't a very good witch!

She saw a faint glow around the stranger. It looked kind of nice. Pleasant, friendly colors. No big scary splashes of violent intentions or anything.

Or would she know what that looked like?

Well, yes. She taught at the university. As part of her curricula in Alternate Cultures, she had her students try to see auras, and she practiced herself. Sometimes she thought she had finally found a magical skill she could master. She'd seen a few muddy auras in her time.

"I mean, there *is* a body, but she's still alive. Claire," July called. "Could you come out here a minute?"

"No!" screamed Claire. Her door slammed.

A faint yowl sounded in the backyard. July glanced at the French doors that led from the living room to the back patio, then focused on the problem again. "Young lady, you get out here right now!"

"No!"

Orion raced into the living room, saw the man, saw the gun, stopped, his eyes wide. "Mom?"

"He heard screams," July said.

She must be crazy, calling her kid into the same room as a stranger with a gun. Even if she could see the stranger's aura a little. What if he was some kind of maniac who knocked on doors and pushed his way into people's houses and did horrible things to them? Where, oh where, was her medicine bag? where was Orion's baseball bat? What if the guy pointed his gun at Orion? July stepped between the intruder and her son.

"Screams?" Orion whispered.

"Your sister screamed a couple minutes ago," July said over her shoulder to him.

"She did?"

"Kid, how could you not notice that colossal, bloodcurdling scream?" asked the stranger. His hand dropped all the way to his side. He made a gesture with the gun as though he were holstering it, but he wasn't wearing a holster. He glanced down in annoyance.

"She screams all the time," Orion said. "Are you going to shoot us?"

"No." He pressed a button on the gun and slipped it point-down into his pocket. "Hi. Sorry about the invasion. I'm your neighbor to the south, Ian Brewster." He stuck out his gun hand.

July hesitated, then shook hands. "I'm July Rhodes, and this is my son Orion. You always run around with a gun?"

Red brushed Ian's cheeks. "When I hear screams, yeah. Kinda my job. I'm in security."

"Oh." July bit her lip. "Well, chances are you'll hear screams from our house. Claire screams a lot. It just means she's frustrated."

"Rowrl." A cat dashed in through the open front door, crossed the living room, and jumped to the top of the bookshelf, where it settled on *The Magical Household.*

"Spanky! Bad cat!" said Ian.

The cat was large, almost monumental, with short white fur, a black tail, and some ink-blot splotches on its back. It sat with its tail curled around its front feet and stared at July with large orange eyes.

"Greetings," July said.

The cat blinked.

"Spanky, get down from there." Ian walked over and grabbed the cat, his hands around its rib cage. He held the cat out. It dangled from his hands like a fox fur.

"Sorry. He likes to get into things."

"He's yours?"

"Well, kinda, in a way. He's a neighborhood cat. He stops by my place, and sometimes he follows me around when I take my walks. I get the feeling lots of people are feeding him. Doesn't look like he ever misses a meal, does he?"

The cat submitted calmly to being held with its feet unsupported. July cringed inside. It looked all wrong.

But then, what did she know? Frizzis had always

been Martin's cat. Martin was the one who studied and practiced and really got going with the power plays. Martin was the one whose legs Frizzis stropped, whose lap Frizzis chose.

"Hey, Mister," Orion said. "That's no way to hold a cat."

"Say what?" Ian tilted the cat so he could stare into its face. The cat stared back. The cat's whole back half dangled.

"You gotta put your hands under his feet." Orion held out his arms.

Ian shrugged and draped the cat over Orion's arms. Orion maneuvered until he had the cat's back feet supported on one hand and the front feet over his shoulder, so that the cat rested comfortably. "Oof, he's heavy. You gotta give him a place to push off of, so he can get down when he wants to."

"Mrr," said the cat.

"But that means he can claw you."

"So?"

Ian shook his head and smiled. "I'm not going to let him claw me!"

"Yeah, but he's not."

"Mrr," said the cat. It tensed and jumped down.

"Ouch." Orion stared at his palm. Eight red pin-pricks broke the skin.

"I like my way better," Ian said. "He sure likes that book. What is it?"

The cat had jumped up onto *The Magical Household* again. As Ian headed for the bookshelf, the cat lay down and spread out so that the book was completely eclipsed by his body. He purred.

"I'll get him out of here for you," Ian said.

"That's all right. He's welcome to visit as long as he likes."

Ian shrugged. "Sorry about the scare, I mean, the gun and all. Just didn't know what kind of situation you had over here. Does your kid scream after ten at night?"

"Sometimes she does." Claire seemed to think that screaming was an effective mode for her. She had screamed at the commune all the time. She was always either screaming or singing, and she claimed both things helped each other. Everyone was used to it. July was pretty sure Claire didn't scream much at school. No teacher notes about it had come home. Nobody had called and said July had to come in and discuss her daughter's behavior.

Claire did sing solos a lot, both at school and at the commune. She loved to sing, and loved how people watched her when she did.

Ian said, "Could get you in trouble with the neighborhood association. They're mighty strict about the local covenants. Big anti-noise rules."

"I'll see what I can do," July said. She already knew what she could do. Exactly nothing. Claire never listened to her anymore.

Ian nodded twice. "Well . . . nice to meet you."

"Yes." July rubbed one hand across the other.

Ian stood there for an awkward moment, then turned and left.

July rushed to close and lock the door behind him. She glanced at Orion. Nobody at the commune had a gun. Was Orion traumatized? She'd heard a lot about trauma and kids, but she wasn't sure what to do about it.

"Maybe he'll teach me how to shoot," Orion said.

"Shoot what?" Where had this come from? The commune hadn't had television. But the kids were allowed to read anything they could find. Last thing July knew, Orion had been reading books about naturalists.

"Animals."

"Orion!"

He shrugged and stared at the floor.

"No son of mine is going to shoot animals," she said.

His lower lip jutted, and he stomped out of the room.

"Right?" July headed for the bookshelf and the cat. It stared down at her, its orange eyes full of fire.

She returned its gaze for a while, then lowered her eyes. "Wrong, I guess. He's going to do whatever he wants to, sooner or later. Everything's beyond my control."

"Mrr."

"Have you come to live with us, or are you just visiting?"

The cat stood up and stretched along the top of the bookshelf, its rear in the air, tail hooked, its front paws far out before it, its shoulders low to the shelf. It opened its mouth and curled its pink tongue. Then it jumped down and hopped into the open book box.

July went to look.

It patted the spine of one of the books, then hopped out of the box and headed for the front door. "Prrt?"

"Just a sec." She took the book out of the box. It was a slender red leather-bound volume she had never seen before. Embossed silver letters spelled the title on the front: *Star Song*.

She carried the book to the front door and let the cat out. "Thanks for coming," she said.

"Mrrp." It headed into the night.

July sank down on the couch, switched on the floor lamp, and fell into the book.

She woke in the middle of the night, startled out of dreams by an unfamiliar sound.

At the commune, there had been no traffic at night, no car horns blowing, no sound of music blaring from a park where somebody was having a party. Once in a while a confused rooster cut the night with a misplaced crow, and owls hooted from the eucalyptus trees some summer nights.

At the commune, if you heard someone moving around outside the house at night, it was someone you knew. You could turn over and go back to sleep.

There it was again. Something scraped at the house's foundation. What was it?

July grabbed her bathrobe and wrapped up in it, then went to her window. Her bedroom was on the second floor of the new house. She leaned forward just enough to peer through the sheer curtains down at the backyard.

Pale light from half a moon shone down. A weedy lawn, dark in the faint light, covered most of the yard except for the patio. A couple of scruffy, shadowy palms huddled near the back fence. Nothing moved.

Something flickered in the corner of her eye. She turned her head.

Ian stood on the back porch of the house next door, his big shaggy head cocked. He turned and stared toward July's house.

Another scratchy sound. Why hadn't July put those wards up right after Ian left? Then maybe they'd have protection against—whatever it was.

She was so tired since the move. It was hard for her to find the energy for anything.

"Spanky," Ian called, his voice quiet.

The big cat ran from her patio across the yard, eeled through an opening in the fence, and went to Ian. Ian stooped and stroked the cat's back.

Well, it wasn't the commune, but at least she had a couple of neighbors she had actually met.

Strangely comforted, July went back to bed.

The next day, Claire and Orion figured out how to get to school from their new house. They hadn't had to change schools; the commune children were bused to the school in July's new neighborhood, which was why she had looked for a house there. Orion and Claire spent the day with kids they had grown up with.

July spent the day unpacking and falling into bouts of despair. Could she even live like this after so many years in the mountains? She had no confidence in her life skills. She woke again and again to find herself curled up on the big couch in the living room, tasks yet undone around her. She forced herself up through the gloom and went on with her work. She had taken a week's vacation from her job to get moved in, and she was running out of time.

Claire came home from school and complained because the commune kids said everybody was planning a big working next weekend, and Claire wasn't there to learn the music and sing a part. Orion came home talking about the new rabbit his cousin Andy at the commune had got for a pet.

By that time, July had cleared most of the boxes out of the living room and put down a braided rag rug. The living room looked more like a place to live.

It was also to cast spells, if you lit incense and a bunch of candles, rolled up the rug, and drew cabalistic symbols, on the floor. Which July did, after supper. She gathered her ingredients and printed out lyric sheets and instructions for herself and the kids.

She had to do something strong to root her and the kids in the new place. Otherwise she was afraid she might end up back in the mountains, marginalized but trapped in the comfort of known life.

Star Song gave instructions for summoning a familiar.

"Let's do it," July said.

Claire hugged her knees and scowled. "What makes you think this'll work? We never did anything like this at home."

July wished Claire wouldn't talk. She had laid a big silver triangle in glitter on the floor, added geometric and curvy symbols inside and outside the triangle, put a small plate with tuna on it in the center, then asked Claire and Orion to sit at two of the points of the triangle while she sat at the third. Glitter! She'd never heard of anybody using glitter in a summoning. She'd searched *Star Song* for a copyright date and hadn't found one, or any sign of an author. The book design was nice, with a pleasant, legible font and clear illustrations, but she had very little faith in what was inside the book.

Faith. Another area where she needed work.

But how did you manufacture faith in something you'd never seen before? How had the book gotten into her box, anyway?

You had to start somewhere. She decided she had faith in the stray cat who had patted the book.

"I told Andy you were going to get me a dog," Orion said.

"Oh, sweetie." July stared at the glittering lines. Had she drawn the figures right? She checked the diagram in the little red book. They looked the same.

She had never cast a spell by herself before. Martin did all the witch planning and prep work, and told July what he needed her to do to make things work.

Martin was up in the mountains. With Belinda. Just before July left the commune, she had watched Martin and Belinda work together. They'd done an earth-moving spell for the new reservoir. July could never have managed something like that.

"We don't know what we'll get," July said. one last recheck. She glanced at the kids. Claire was at her snottiest, sulky and scowling.

"Breathe," July said to Claire.

"I don't feel like breathing."

"Don't breathe, then."

Claire glared.

July swallowed a giggle.

Oh, yeah. July also needed to learn how to be serious. She had been kicked out of the general ceremonies on the mountain after she laughed out loud during a serious moment.

"But don't you sometimes think we look incredibly silly?" she'd asked Aunt Grace afterward.

Aunt Grace had smiled. "It's always good to appreciate our own essential absurdity," she had said, "but it disrupts the others' concentration. Please stay home next time."

Stay home. Being barred from the big group ceremonies had been the start of the end. That, and the fact that Martin and Belinda had discovered how many things they had in common. July had known when she and Martin first moved to the commune, back when Tim was only a year old, that one of the principles of commune life was open marriages, but she hadn't been ready to actually live that way. For years and years, Martin had resisted, too.

Orion crossed his fingers. "Hope we get a dog," he whispered loudly.

"Okay, everybody got their lyric sheets?"

"This song is so lame!" Claire grumbled.

"Oh, come on, Claire, quit being such a mugwump. Just give it a shot."

"You know I hate it here, don't you?" Claire said.

"I am entirely aware of that fact."

Claire unfolded her lyric sheet with angry crackling noises. July wondered how Claire got paper to behave that way. Orion opened his paper, too. It only made half the noise Claire's had.

July pulled a pitch pipe out of her pocket, played a note. "Ready?"

One of her children glared at her, and the other

sat there with both hands in the air, crossed fingers held high.

"Spirit. Spirit. Spirit, come and see. We're here with our hopes. Send us our destiny. Spirit. Spirit. Spirit, come and see . . ." July started the song, and Orion sang with her. They both managed to find a key and stay on it. In a way.

Claire's lovely soprano voice rose up for a moment and joined theirs. She sang one chorus all the way through with them, and the song sounded great. Claire's voice beautified anything she sang, no matter how inane. Then she closed her eyes and sang, "Goddess. Goddess. Goddess, come and see. Grant me the wish that is mine, I pray thee!" She slipped into a harmony that bent and teased around the edges of July's and Orion's song.

July sang on. She beat on a coffee-can drum with a wooden spoon for rhythm, and sang, though she knew the spell wouldn't work. How silly they would look if someone, say, Ian, peering in through the French doors, happened to see them.

"Spirit, come and see—"

"Goddess, come and see—"

—*Just how silly we can be,* July thought.

Orion faltered, then started singing Claire's words.

July felt an uprush of giggles and almost succumbed. She placed her hands palm down on the floor instead, and felt calm flow into her. All the tensions that had coiled up in her during the day—

during the week—unknotted as she sang. She let go of goals. She let go of the viewpoint outside herself that kept saying she looked and sounded like an idiot and that her children hated and resented her. She let go of everything and just sang.

She felt movement, something rising up from the floor into her hands and legs where they touched down, something warm and cool at once, gentle and steady and present.

"Spirit, spirit, spirit—"

"Stars shine down, stars show us, stars shine down, stars show us. Stars shine down, stars be here now . . ." July realized she was singing new words that weren't on her lyric sheet, and that the tune she sang curled around what her children sang. She couldn't remember when everything had shifted.

Silver trails of glitter melted until they were liquid lines of light on the floor. Colored fire danced in the air above them.

July felt doubts rise. What was she doing? Was this really happening? Because she had started it? When had she ever started something that worked?

"Goddess. Goddess. Goddess, come and be—"

"Stars shine down, stars be here, stars take me, stars give me, stars lead me, stars be here now." Her voice sounded rougher now, not curly and beautiful. The light dimmed.

Faith.

A big white cat with Rorschach blots on his back had come into her house and given her a sign.

A little book had given her direction.

Whatever happened next was what should happen.

"Stars shine down, stars be here. I give you all I am. Stars be here, stars lead me now." She opened herself.

Faint chimes sounded. Colors flared through the air, danced across the faces of her children. Energy flowed through her.

Thump! Something dropped to the floor.

The air cleared.

A large animal squatted in the center of the triangle. It slurped the tuna.

"Spanky?" said Orion in a voice that squeaked.

The cat finished the tuna and glanced at Orion with narrow eyes, then turned to July. *That's not my name.*

"Pardon me?" July touched her ears. Had she actually heard the cat speak?

And I feel peculiar. It straightened from its feeding crouch. It didn't look the way it had the day before. It was bigger than it had been, broader, not so graceful. Its tail was short and stumpy, and its ears flopped over just a little. *What happened?*

"I don't know."

"Woof," said the cat. It leaped into the air. *Who said that?*

"You did! You did!" Orion yelled.

"Arf!" The cat jumped in the air again. The hair on its spine bushed, and its short tail puffed up to three times its original thickness. It growled and hissed.

Hey! The cat came to July and set its heavy paws on her knee, staring up into her eyes. *This wasn't what I had in mind!*

"I'm sorry. I think we had a wish collision." July had wished for a spirit guide. Orion wanted a dog. July didn't even know what Claire wanted. Had Claire's wish come true, too?

You want a home, the cat muttered. *You want some pet people. You want a regular source of tuna. Next thing you know, they dress you funny and call you names . . .*

"Are you our familiar?" July asked.

Its eyes were still wild with orange fire. It stared at her. She felt as though she were falling into its eyes, into some warm strange place where she didn't have to think.

The cat leaned closer, and July did, too.

It licked her nose.

She startled.

I'm something, anyway, the cat said. It moaned aloud. *Now that you three have summoned me, at least we can talk.*

"What's your name?"

The cat turned to check the children. Claire still looked sulky. Orion bounced up and down. The cat stared at Orion for a long time, until he settled and looked abashed.

You may call me Bavol.

"Bavol." July sighed and smiled. She had done her first spell! At least, the first one she had prepared for by herself. She had invited a new force into the home to help her. She wasn't sure what had happened, all in all, but something had answered her. She had left the commune and learned she had the power to make a new place her home, even without Martin's help. "May I pet you?"

Please do.

She stroked her hand down the cat's back. It closed its eyes and shaped its back to her hand. After a while, it climbed into her lap. It was big and heavy. It was warm and solid.

She skritched it under its chin.

It purred.

She hugged it, and it snuggled with her. Her heart opened.

"Hey, Mom. My turn," said Orion.

July opened her arms. Bavol stayed for a moment, then rose and stepped to the floor. He stared up at Orion. *Okay, kid. Let's get a couple things straight. I'm not a dog.*

Orion bit his lip. "Okay."

"Woof," said Bavol. He jumped again. *Damn!*

"So what are you?" Orion asked.

Bavol.

"That's what I tell them at school? I have a pet Bavol?"

Sure, why not?

Orion shrugged. "Okay."

I'm not a dog. I don't do dog things. I don't come when I'm called. I don't fetch. Don't you dare give me a bath.

Orion's eyes clouded.

But you can touch me.

Orion sniffed. He dropped to the floor and petted the cat.

Ouch! Not so hard!

Orion moderated his petting technique. Bavol put up with it for a while. Then he went to Claire.

"How are you the answer to my prayer?" Claire asked. "Or are you? Are you just another cheat?"

Bavol stared up into Claire's face and purred.

After a long moment, Claire gathered Bavol in her arms and buried her face in his fur. She sniffled. He purred so loudly July could almost feel it from across the room.

Your prayer will take a little longer, Bavol said at last. Claire nodded her head, her face still pressed against his fur, then set Bavol on the floor. She rubbed her eyes and looked away.

July studied Claire. What prayer? Claire used to tell July everything. That had stopped last year.

If only July knew what Claire wanted. She had let Claire decorate her new bedroom however she liked. Result: matte black walls, black lace curtains, black rug and bedspread and sheets. July felt cold just standing in the doorway. She had been hugely relieved when Claire stuck glow-in-the-dark stars to the ceiling. But even that didn't give July the clues to decode her new teenage daughter.

Claire dipped her fingernails in the silver lines on the floor. The silver transferred onto her nails, leaving them sparkling bright. Claire actually smiled.

"Claire, thanks for helping me with the spell," July said.

Claire's smile vanished. "You owe me."

For a moment, despair swamped July. Then she thought, *Wait, I'm the mother. I have tools. I have weapons.* "I owe you? Guess I'll pay you back in food and shelter and clothes and things like that, huh?"

Claire's eyes narrowed further.

"No, wait," July said. "I've been doing that for years! Maybe you owe me a thing or two. But you can keep the manicure anyway."

"Fine." Claire got up and stomped out of the room. She slammed her bedroom door.

At least she hadn't screamed.

"Bavol, what did she wish?" July whispered to the cat.

I can't tell you. I can tell you it won't hurt her.

Better than nothing, July guessed. She glanced toward the French doors to the backyard.

A tall, dark form stood there.

"Oh, God."

It's just Ian, Bavol thought. *He's been there since you started the spell. He has a peeping problem.*

"Is he dangerous?"

Only by mistake.

"What if he talks about what he saw?"

Bavol stared at the door. *I've been watching him for some time now. He doesn't have anyone to talk to.* A moment later, he said, *And now he won't talk, even if he finds somebody who'll listen. I may be under an enchantment, but I've still got chops,*

"You're under an enchantment?"

Did I think that? Damn! I've been waiting for you for a long time! I forgot what it's like when people can hear me. Never mind, huh?

"But—"

"Hey," said Orion. "Look at this stick, Bavol."

I'm looking.

"Watch this." Orion tossed the stick at the couch.

Bavol flew across the room after it. He pounced on the stick and picked it up in his mouth. He turned around and trotted toward Orion, then stopped two feet from the boy and spat the stick out. *Hey! That was evil! You're a bad boy! Cut that out!*

Orion laughed.

I mean it! I'm not a dog!

Orion grabbed the stick and tossed it again.

Bavol ran after it. This time he stopped before he pounced and turned to glare at Orion.

"Aw, come on," Orion said.

Bavol growled. He picked up the stick in his mouth. *I'm only doing this because it tastes good.* He brought the stick back and dropped it at Orion's feet.

Orion sat down and hugged Bavol. "Thanks," he whispered.

July went to the French doors and opened them. "Hi," she said to Ian. "You want some coffee?"

Ian's mouth dropped open. Too late, July remembered what Aunt Grace had said about inviting people in. Ian had been in the house before, but not by invitation.

"What—what was that—I—"

July sighed. "Come on in." She stepped aside. "But you—"

"Yes?"

"Was that—those colored lights, and then—the cat just—" He stared into July's face.

"The cat is our cat now."

"Yeah, but—"

Bavol approached, Orion right behind him. The cat gazed up at Ian's face.

"He says you have a peeping problem," July said.

Red blushed over Ian's cheeks. "I have a peeping problem? Oh, yeah, like he hasn't been there with me every time, looking in all the same windows like he's searching for something he can't find, same as me—"

I've found it. Bavol sat on July's foot.

July stooped and stroked a hand along the cat's back. "What are you looking for, Ian?" She should be afraid of this man who sometimes carried a gun, wandered into other people's backyards, and looked into their windows without asking. Somehow, he didn't scare her, though. She could see his aura clearly now. There was no harm in it.

Stars shine down. Bavol leaned against her leg. He was warm and solid.

"I don't know," Ian said.

"Maybe it's in the kitchen."

Ian's eyes twinkled.

"And even if it isn't, there's coffee," July said. "And cookies."

"Chocolate chip cookies," said Orion.

Ian hesitated, glanced from July to Orion to Bavol. At last he stepped over the threshold into the house. "So, I saw your daughter this time," he said as he followed July, Bavol, and Orion to the kitchen. "I *heard* your daughter. Wow. Not only is she a champion screamer, she can really sing!"

"She's good, isn't she?"

"Almost as good as Madam Vasari's students."

"Who's Madam Vasari?"

"She's the voice teacher who lives down the block. I can tell you what everybody does around here. Except I'm not sure about you guys. What was that you were doing again?"

"Summoning friends," said July.

ECLIPTIC

by Von Jocks

Von Jocks believes in the magic of stories. She has written since she was five, publishing her first short story at the age of twelve in a local paper. Under the name Evelyn Vaughn she sold her first romantic suspense novel, *Waiting for the Wolf Moon*, to Silhouette Shadows in 1992. Three more books completed her "Circle Series" before the Shadows line closed. Her short fiction most recently appeared in *Dangerous Magic*, from DAW Books. The book was selected as one of the top one hundred of the year by the New York City Public Library, and her story was nominated for a Sapphire Award. Von received her Master's Degree at the University of Texas in Arlington, writing her thesis on the history of the Romance Novel. An unapologetic TV addict, she resides in Texas with her cats and her imaginary friends and teaches junior-college English to support her writing habit . . . or vice versa.

WHEN she can no longer run, Magdeleine forces her bruised body to crawl. The forest grows thick here. Thorns cut her palms, tear her chemise. When she falls to her chest, her chin digs a furrow into the mulch. *Alors.* It matters not.

She has fled beyond pain, beyond fear, beyond

grief. Only one trouble haunts her still. When finally she crumples to the forest floor, she cannot see the stars.

She rolls wearily onto her back, searches the canopy above her for a hint of night sky, of starlight, of moon. But the forest is too deep.

She could see stars better from the dungeon.

The thought prompts a choked laugh. She closes her eyes, wills her soul to depart this ugly world. If they catch her again . . .

But life remains tenacious.

A warm body, fur soft as water, slides past her dirt-encrusted cheek. The cat bumps her forehead against Magdeleine's, chirps encouragement.

"Non," protests Magdeleine, her voice but a crackle. It is too much even for Cassiopeia to ask . . .

But Cassiopeia—her cat—curls into a glossy pillow against Magdeleine's shoulder, her neck, her ear and begins to purr.

A distant howl shivers past them. Magdeleine no longer fears the legends of this deepest of French forests, not for herself. Against the beast she's discovered in mankind, no wolf could compare.

But she fears for her four-footed companion. She must survive, must reach the Sacred Well, if only for the cat's sake.

The thrum of Cassiopeia's serenade, ebbing and flowing with her tiny breath, weaves a coarse kind of healing magic. *Magic*— the art of believing in possibilities, of acting on sheer hope. But hope equates with caring . . .

The grief surges back as well.

The price of living is to remember.

"Witch!"

'Twas a cruel blow, to recognize her accuser. Pointing, beside the self-proclaimed witch hunter, stood the very man she had nursed back to health but a week before.

"She bewitched me!"

Magdeleine shook her head, backed away. But villagers converged on her. *"Witch!"*

"I helped you," she cried as they grasped her.

"With your dark arts," insisted Monsieur Pryor, the witch hunter. The man she'd healed nodded confirmation. "With your *familiar!*"

Cassiopeia! Magdeleine searched the crowd for sight of her black-and-white cat caught up in greedy hands, like so many others had been, her neck wrung. She sank into the grip of the men who held her, relieved to see no sign of her pet. 'Twas an increasingly dangerous time for cat . . . and women.

"You *saw* how sick I was," the man accused, now addressing the villagers. "She fed me potions, anointed me with salves. And for payment?"

The crowd waited on his pronouncement so raptly, Magdeleine momentarily hung still.

"She said we must stop killing cats!"

They gasped. Magdeleine protested again. They did not understand—they held their own lives in the balance! But men she'd known since childhood tied her wrists and ankles. They dragged her to the castle, across its drawbridge and beneath its bladed portcullis. They crossed the yard with her, to stairs carved into the ground. Burly guardsmen wrestled her into the shadows, past men who hung from chains in the wall. Men who pressed their faces against bars. Men who shouted rude things and men who turned away. The guards shoved her into a separate cell with only one high, barred window, and shut the iron door behind her.

A dungeon.

On her knees where she'd fallen, Magdeleine stared at the rush-covered floor between her hands. She'd saved his life, she kept thinking. *She'd helped him!*

And if the stars and portents told true, these people must indeed stop killing the cats.

"My poor daughter," murmured a gentle voice, worn as old vellum. "'Tis a shock, *oui?*"

Slowly, Magdeleine looked to see who shared this undeserved cell. A white-haired old woman sat serenely to one side with a white cat on her lap, a dark blue mantle drawn around her.

Magdeleine recognized the cut and color of the cloak—and the secret symbol of a crescent moon which the crone signaled by cupping her hand.

"Grandmother!" The old woman—grandmother

by tradition rather than blood—opened her arms. Magdeleine fell into their comfort, knelt in the rushes beside her, laying her head in the grandmother's lap.

"I helped him," she moaned. "I healed him, and yet he accuses me! How could he do that, Grandmother? How could he?"

Grandmother held her, shushed her in a way that did not rebuke so much as reassure. But another voice said, "Because you are a woman."

Opening her eyes, Magdeleine saw a second woman standing in the shadows, where the window's light did not reach. "What?"

"He is a man. And you're a comely young woman. Likely he wanted you, but was prevented—by marriage, perhaps by status. Since you are a woman, born in sin, this must be your doing."

Magdeleine shook her head at the sarcasm thickening the woman's voice. "'Tis not *fair!*"

"No," said Grandmother. "My innocent child. It is not fair."

The woman in the corner said, "At least you did not marry him. Better this prison than that. Better *honest* torture."

Then a dark form slid between the bars on the high window, leaped to the floor with a tiny thud. It meowed annoyance.

"*Cassiopeia!*" Magdeleine caught the cat to her breast, buried her face, breathed water-soft fur. She knew too well what would happen to a suspected witch's familiar—what was happening to too many cats across the county, perhaps all of southern France. All because of this foolish witch scare.

Selfishly, her relief was for this particular cat rather than the future of humankind. She'd had Cassie since childhood, growing up in the apothecary shop her widowed mother inherited from her father. Since her mother's death—

How could cats *not* count as family? "Oh, Cassiopeia, how did you get here . . . ?"

Cassie squirmed from Magdeleine's too-tight grasp and leaped to the dungeon floor. She craned her neck around to dramatically lick all traces of Magdeleine's tears off of her black side, her white-marbled flank.

"'Tis too dangerous for you here," Magdeleine scolded, more afraid for her pet than herself. "You must hide."

But Grandmother patted her shoulder. "Here is as safe a place as any."

The other woman stepped from the shadows. Perhaps dark-haired Magdeleine was "comely," but this woman was stunning, with thick red hair and full lips and large eyes. The curves of her body broke the line of her dirtied chemise in several obvious places. "The guards tell me they've had less problem with rats since they began arresting witches."

Indeed, as her eyes adjusted to the shadows, Magdeleine saw at least four other cats lying or sit-

ting about the corners of the cell, seemingly con-
tented. Their eyes reflected the meager light like
green and yellow stars.

"Then you are accused of witchcraft as well?"
she asked.

And Grandmother smiled sadly. "Aren't we all?"

Magdeleine awakes to daylight trickling through
the high canopy of the woods. She reaches for her
cat.

Gone.

She pats the bare ground, levers herself agoniz-
ingly up. "Cassiopeia?"

Her voice cracks. Like her faith in mankind, it
has been broken. She cannot bear to lose the cat.
Not now . . .

"Cassie!"

The impatient yowl defies her growing panic.
She rises onto lacerated feet, lurches in that direction. "Cassie . . ."

The cat sits primly beneath a gooseberry bush
dotted with ripe berries. *"Mrowr!"*

Magdeleine drops to her bruised knees and begins to eat all she can pluck, clumsy and ravenous.
The juice bloodies her fingers.

She, too, has turned bestial . . .

Without the herbs hidden in Grandmother's
cloak, Magdeleine could not have stomached the

dungeon's gruel. Even so, she stopped eating at a guard's loud protest.

"*I—do—not—torture—women.*"

Grandmother touched her arm in a reminder to silence.

"They are not women," argued the witch hunter's voice. "They are servants of the devil!"

Silence argued back.

"You need this job, *mais non?*" The voice turned sly. "How much *do* you owe the doctor of physick?"

"I'll not torture women," repeated the guard, more quietly. "Witches or *non.*"

Monsieur Pryor said, "We begin when the comte returns. Perhaps fortune will favor you, Roussel. Perhaps your father will die before then, and your misplaced benevolence won't cost him his life."

"Fuck you," said the first voice—in the cell the redhead, Judyth, snorted.

"Beware that they do not bewitch *you,*" warned Pryor.

Magdeleine ached with stillness, wondering if the men had left. Cassiopeia and another cat, an orange tabby, ducked heads into her forgotten bowl. Cassie growled at the usurper, but neither stopped eating gruel.

"Torture?" Magdeleine whispered finally.

Judyth said, "What did you expect? They are *MEN.* Women have been little better than slaves since before memory, and—"

"Not all women's memory," cautioned Grandmother gently. "Magic comes from hope."

"—our strength threatens them."

"Surely not *all* men are so depraved," Magdeleine protested. "That one said—"

"He says it now," warned Judyth. "He will change. In any case, he still *imprisons* women. And he *does* torture, *n'est ce pas?*"

Magdeleine's healing hands ached. "My mother loved my father enough to forever leave the Sacred—"

"Hush," warned Grandmother, cautious. The Sacred Well of the Goddess, with its priestesses and its healing waters, was never be mentioned within earshot of men. Magdeleine's mother never spoke of it except to Magdeleine.

Had her father known he'd married a witch?

Magdeleine's mother had come from the ancient Well. As did many of its daughters, she'd left its sanctuary for the world of men. "'*Twas dangerous, oui,*" she'd once explained. "*But 'tis our only hope for change and healing. To work magic, one must trust in possibilities . . .*"

"She was foolish," stated Judyth now.

Her anger confused Magdeleine. "Have you—either of you," she added, looking to Grandmother, "have you ever been there yourself?"

Judyth shook her head. "'Tis only a myth, prattled to little girls at bedtime like fairy tales to keep despair at bay. But *nothing* keeps despair at bay, not in these dark times."

"I was born there," said Grandmother.

"Impossible," protested Judyth . . . but she sounded more envious than angry. "Men are forbidden."

"For generations, yes," agreed Grandmother, busying her hands by weaving rushes to create what looked like a small mat. "I never knew my own father. But some centuries, men join the priestesses. And women do return from the outside world, fat with babies."

Both Judyth and Magdeleine waited, silent—like little girls at bedtime.

"Many thousands of years ago," began Grandmother quietly, "as now, the world crept through different constellations, to different ends. During the Age of Leo, humankind learned to worship the sun. During the Age of Cancer, we worshiped the moon. And in the Age of Gemini, along with writing, humankind found balance."

Finished with Magdeleine's gruel, Cassiopeia began to clean her whiskers.

Judyth sank into a crouch and fingered a tabby cat's ears. "Balance cannot exist."

"Women told stories, bore children, healed. Men protected, hunted, provided. During the Age of Taurus, people learned to farm and build villages. The Earth was worshiped as our Mother, and women ruled."

Judyth shook her head.

"But nobody can stop the turning of the stars," warned Grandmother. "And next . . ."

"The Age of Aries," provided Magdeleine. Her mother had taught her enough of the zodiac to recognize the constellations' backward order.

Grandmother nodded. "The skills of the warrior surpassed even those of the healer and the storyteller. Men became leaders and, under Aries' influence, believed their power exclusive, adversarial. Women were silenced, enslaved, and denounced."

"I told you," noted Judyth. In the twilit shadows, her eyes seemed unusually bright.

"But never is there one aspect without its opposite," Grandmother assured them. "Men demonized the Goddess, destroyed Her places of worship. But women, who could whisper the old legends in the safety of their huts . . . women remembered. 'Twas during this time that descendants of the priestesses—with the help of their consorts—rediscovered a sacred place so deeply hidden, in the darkest of woods, they could remain safe."

She did not say, the Sacred Well. But Magdeleine and Judyth both knew.

"There they built a society to honor the Old Ways. They have remained e'er since."

"Thousands of years," repeated Judyth, marveling.

"Thousands of years," said Grandmother. "For

some time, the daughters kept wholly to themselves. They forbade men entry—for women, too, were susceptible to the adversarial influence of Aries. But of course they could not survive alone. They needed men to beget children, if naught else. And wiser mothers knew they could accomplish little by remaining wholly separate from the world. So they began to venture out again, to try rebuilding the ancient balance. They have not yet succeeded."

"The Age of Pisces," guessed Magdeleine.

"Yes. We live in the Age of Pisces now," agreed Grandmother. "Despite its dualism, and the efforts of its greatest prophet, differences overshadow symmetry. People believe themselves either leaders or followers, either blessed or damned."

"Evil or good," noted Judyth. "Male or female."

"It is never so simple as that," cautioned Grandmother. "Men are our sons. Our fathers. Our husbands and our lovers. They cannot help the stars they live under, anymore than can we. But we are barely two-thirds of the way through the Age of Pisces. I fear that, despite our efforts, the worst draws near."

Judyth stalked back to her shadows. Magdeleine watched Grandmother finish the mat. The older woman then propped it where the floor and wall met, sprinkled more rushes over it.

A cat promptly slid under its shelter, hidden from sight.

Grandmother shared Magdeleine's smile. Then she glanced toward the cell's iron door. Magdeleine looked—and felt fear. A man stared quietly back in through the grating, his pale gaze uncertain. Guard? Comte? *What had he heard?*

When he noticed their attention, he turned quickly away.

"He," said Grandmother softly, "is the one who does not torture women."

Magdeleine stumbles deeper into the oldest of forests, lost. *Follow the stars*, advised Grandmother. But she cannot see them. Instead, she sees cats, a baker's dozen, weaving in and out of the ferns, the underbrush, the trees. Cassiopeia brings a dead chipmunk, in the evening, but Magdeleine dares not build a cooking fire.

Beyond even exhaustion, she senses someone following. Must she lead the world's evil to the walls of the Sacred Well?

Better that she die. But not, she prays, like Grandmother or Judyth died. And then there is her cat . . .

Magdeleine treks on, beyond darkness, until she stumbles into trees. Finally, battered by her own mistakes, she sinks to the ground, cranes her face upward. When it gets dark enough, her mother taught her, one can sometimes see the stars.

Except in the deep woods.

Without the stars, Magdeleine is leading nothing.

She could barely sleep her first night in prison, except for Grandmother. Not since her mother's death had Magdeleine felt such refuge. Still she startled when, deep into the night, someone rapped twice on the door.

She began to sit up, but Grandmother's worn hand drew her back down into silence.

Judyth moved to the door and repeated the double knock, more softly.

The door cracked open, and Judyth slipped out. *Was she escaping?*

Then Magdeleine heard muffled conversation, Judyth's teasing, a guard's arrogant reply. A body thudded against the door, not once but twice. Then again. And a fourth time . . .

Rhythmical.

When she realized what Judyth was doing, Magdeleine covered her ears with her hands, arms crossed to hide her face. But when Grandmother's body shook beside hers, she peeked.

In the very faint light of the moon, through their one window, she saw Grandmother laughing at her.

"The joining of men and women can be many things," the old woman whispered. "Including a source of power. You may yet learn this."

It did not surprise Magdeleine that Grandmother knew she was a virgin. It relieved her that Grandmother believed they would yet escape to such things as marriage and . . .

And such.

But . . . "I thought Judyth hated men," she whispered.

"Judyth," clarified Grandmother, "hates feeling helpless."

When the door reopened and Judyth slipped back in, she showed no chagrin. "I won't live on that gruel," she said, and tossed something into Grandmother's lap.

'Twas a hunk of bread.

Then Judyth sank back into her corner to eat the portion she'd kept for herself. Grandmother offered a piece to Magdeleine, who shook her head.

"The difference of paths invalidates none of them," the older woman cautioned. "Either/or thinking, clinging to false rights or wrongs—that is the dark side of Pisces."

"'Tis the way *MEN* think," added Judyth, mouth full.

Magdeleine hesitated. Then Cassiopeia ducked her head under Magdeleine's hand, entreating.

Reluctantly, Magdeleine nodded. "If you have enough."

"It is a woman's prerogative to sacrifice for her children," warned Grandmother, watching her tear off a bite and feed it to the cat before trying some herself. "Remember this, child. Promise me."

Swallowing, Magdeleine felt fear again. It grew easier to recognize by the hour. "Why?"

Grandmother said, "Thank you for the bread, Judyth."

"Thibaud is a brute," admitted Judyth. "Strong enough. Good thighs. But stingy. The guard who watched Magdeleine today . . . perhaps he could get us cheese, if she asked him."

Then she laughed at the expression Magdeleine must have shown.

Grandmother did not laugh. "There will be no time for cheese. I must show you both some magic, while Thibaud is elsewhere."

Magdeleine knew that magic, instead of the demonic powers men like Pryor feared, came from hope—from belief, and the willingness to act on that belief. Magic was as natural as the stars, but no less wonderful for that. Whatever Grandmother would teach, she wanted to learn.

Or she thought she did.

The next morning, she awoke to a hissing by the door. At first, Magdeleine thought 'twas a cat—she knew not how many of them hid behind Grandmother's rush-woven blinds.

Squinting against the meager light, she saw the quiet eyes of a guard beyond the grille.

"Hssst," he called again.

Grandmother and Judyth slept on. They'd

stayed up very late the previous night, working the most horrible magic Magdeleine had ever known.

She rose and warily approached the door. Perhaps Judyth's path *was* valid . . . but so was Magdeleine's distaste for such a path.

The guard—Roussel, yes?—said, "Word has come. The comte will arrive by midday."

Magdeleine waited, alone by the door.

He widened his eyes, as if to better make her understand. "When the comte arrives, the questions will start. They want to know how many witches there are, what powers you have."

But . . . such knowledge did not even exist!

"I thought you should know." He turned away. He had brown hair, thick and unruly.

Magdeleine said, "Your father is sick?"

His eyes, sad like February, reappeared beyond the grating. "You know of him?"

Judyth might have let him think 'twas sorcery. But belief in a supernatural magic did little to ease people's fears about witches or cats.

"I overheard Monsieur Pryor yesterday," Magdeleine admitted.

He said, "I overheard you, too."

Men were not to know about the Sacred Well, not even her father.

"The bedtime story," she challenged.

He did not look convinced.

Cassiopeia wove about her feet, but Magdeleine continued to watch this man's gray eyes, his gentle brow. She wondered if, perhaps, she could trust him.

She'd thought she could trust the last man she'd healed. And yet . . . "What ails your father? What sickness has him?"

"He burns, night and day. He coughs, but little comes of it, and his breath rasps, weak. The doctor of physick has bled him, twice, but refuses to come again until we have more money." Roussel's eyes watched her, suspicious and hopeful.

Magdeleine surrendered to the hope.

"Find some stinking rose," she suggested. "Mash it, and steep it in honey. Feed it to your father, spoonfuls a day. Understand?"

"*Are* you a witch?" he asked, and she wondered just how terrible a mistake she had made. He was, after all, a man. He *did* torture. . . .

"Does it matter?" she challenged.

His eyes scowled. He left without answering.

Magdeleine feared she'd just lost points in some contest she could not comprehend. Did she want to win any game that required old people to die unnecessarily, when she could ease their suffering?

"He will testify against you," predicted Judyth from her corner, awake now.

"The man I healed last week will testify against me." Magdeleine touched the iron grating on the door's small window. She wondered what the rest of Roussel's face looked like—cruel, or kind?

Judyth snorted, "You could at least have asked for cheese."

But Grandmother had been right.

They had no time for cheese.

A cat's scream grates the darkness. Magdeleine gasps awake, aching. Did she sleep? Sleep can no longer heal her oozing wrists, her throbbing ribs— her broken heart.

She tries to call to her pet, but can no longer make sound. Hunger gnaws at her. She has lost Grandmother's cloak, perhaps a day ago, perhaps two. Lost it to the grasping, thorny woods.

She still cannot see stars—or hope. But faint, on the night breeze, she smells woodsmoke and roasting meat.

Hunger bites as deeply as the fear. *She has been followed.*

Animals—cats—race past her, farther into the wood, fleeing someone. Magdeleine pulls herself up on trembling legs, then swollen feet. She can no longer think past anything but the need to run.

So she runs.

She had never before seen the comte. Despite his fine clothes he did not impress her, standing in the middle of their little cell. But the stocky guard, Roussel, fascinated her. He was a solid man with broad shoulders, thick arms, hair-roughened cheeks. If not for his sad eyes, she would fear such blatant strength. Perhaps she should.

But the way both comte and guard looked to the witch hunter indicated which man was truly in charge of this meeting.

"I ask in the name of God," announced the chisel-faced Pryor, although he wore no cleric's robes. "For the sake of your immortal souls, I advise you to answer truthfully. *Be you witches?*"

Grandmother, the respected elder, answered for them all. "You have no right to ask us this question."

"I have every right! God made woman subject to man, and *you will answer!"*

"You have no right to ask us this question," repeated Grandmother. Her calm, in the face of his shouts, showed which *person* was truly in charge of this meeting.

From the flush on Pryor's face, he knew it—and hated it.

"Roussel!" he hissed. "Take her!"

Magdeleine wanted to say or do something. But in planning their magic, Grandmother had warned her. . . .

"No." Roussel turned quiet eyes to the comte. "You are my liege, '*Sieur.* I would die for you. But I will not torture women."

"They are *witches*," corrected Pryor. Roussel ignored him.

Magdeleine looked toward Grandmother. The

older woman stood in a shift as white as her long, braided hair. Her eyes had gone peaceful, drowsy—an effect of herbs she'd taken for hours now, from the lining of her discarded mantle.

The comte shook his head in disgust, but turned toward the open doorway. "Thibaud!"

A different guard appeared. "Couldna' stomach it, eh?" he laughed at Roussel. When Pryor pointed at Grandmother, Thibaud grasped her vein-etched hands and wrenched her toward the door. Grandmother stumbled.

Magdeleine cried out. "Stop hurting her!"

Both Judyth and the quiet-eyed Roussel stared, even as the others ignored her for their own grisly intentions.

But of course. Compared to the torture that awaited them . . .

"Remember," called Grandmother as she vanished. She meant, *Remember our magic.* But Magdeleine did not want this magic.

"I am sorry," said Roussel, finally, and turned away.

Judyth spat at his words, and his back stiffened. But he still left, still obediently barred the door with a thud.

Magdeleine stared at the iron grating, suffocating on her helplessness.

Could hope or magic exist in such a world as Monsieur Pryor controlled?

Throughout the afternoon she heard muffled

shouts, but not Grandmother's. When Thibaud dragged the broken old body back to the cell, in the darkness, Grandmother said nothing. She only sighed after Magdeleine fed her some gruel—heavy with pain-killing herbs—between her chattering teeth.

Judyth growled, swore, pulled herself up the wall by the bars of the window. "Tell them what they want to know!" she insisted, when finally she could speak. "Make something up. But do not let them do this sacrilege!"

Grandmother shook her head. By the next morning, her face bloated and her blotched, broken hands misshapen, she did not even look human.

And that day, they did worse.

And the day after . . .

Each day, Magdeleine waited and tried not to think. With trembling, useless hands, she wove mats from the rushes for cats who sought sanctuary in their cell.

At one point, Roussel said through the grating, "My father is improving."

Magdeleine ignored him.

She lies facedown, ghosts of misery haunting her spent body. When she inhales, dead leaves and sticks touch her mouth, only to be blown away on her exhale. Debris clings to her face—somehow, she has managed a few final tears for her failure. Her useless feet throb with her heartbeat. Blood dries on her chemise from scrapes on her elbows, her knees.

Life loses its tenacity, after all. To die in the deep woods . . . 'tis not so bad. Better than dying in a dungeon, or at the stake. Grandmother's and Judyth's magic has bought her this much, at least. And perhaps in her next life . . .

But a prickling against her cheek will not let her give in to kindly defeat. 'Tis Cassiopeia, patting her with a barely sheathed claw. Her cat has not yet left with the others.

Something smashes toward them through the brush—a human beast. How can she have lived to adulthood without knowing such beasts exist?

Magdeleine's voice will not catch; she cannot urge the cat on without her. Must even Cassiopeia sacrifice herself? She reaches a weak arm out, digs her fingers into the mulch as if to drag herself, one-handed, onward. Fingernails tear, futile. No use. No hope.

No more magic.

The beast crashes closer, stops. She hears breath rasping above her. She closes her eyes, wills her soul to depart. But the fear has returned to prolong life and suffering. . . .

What remained of Grandmother died in Magdeleine's arms, at least four cats purring comfort against her abused and mutilated body. Only in that did Magdeleine take meager comfort. Grandmother's spirit remained unbroken. She'd died overnight, instead of during her tortures.

And she'd answered them not.

Such abuse was not her choice. But her reaction to such atrocities, she'd controlled to the last.

Her private death, unconfessed, infuriated Pryor. He had Thibaud drag the body away for burning, on the conviction of her silence. Later that day, the stench and shouts from the courtyard confirmed his success in putting the old woman to the fire.

For the first time in days, Magdeleine spoke. "Are you certain, Judyth? Perhaps there is a way . . . ?"

Judyth scowled, proud eyes already glassy from the herbs—almost the last from Grandmother's cloak. "Do not waste this, little sister."

"But the magic . . ." How could she believe in, hope for *anything*?

And Judyth said, "Magic or not."

They came for her that evening, as they'd come for Grandmother. Roussel stood awkwardly inside the open door, Pryor, the comte, and Thibaud crowding the middle of the cell, blind to the cats. But when Pryor asked if they be witches—

Judyth said, "But of course I am."

All three men stepped back from her.

"Why else would you have arrested me?" Judyth challenged. "Your only mistake was in wasting time on the old woman. You see . . . my curse upon you has increased with every hour I live."

Now Magdeleine could see the whites of Pryor's and Thibaud's eyes. Perhaps Judyth's path had validity, indeed.

"You cannot curse me," proclaimed Monsieur Pryor. "I am protected by God."

And Judyth laughed her most ugly laugh. "God was looking elsewhere when you fucked me, *'sieurs.*"

The men blanched. Even Roussel, eyes widening at her revelation, stiffened. Had *he . . . ?*

"Take her," rasped Pryor.

"But . . ." Thibaud had begun to sweat.

"She has confessed. We will burn her now, before more of her evil takes root. *Now!*"

The guard approached Judyth with small, wary steps. She extended her wrists with an evil smile.

He stepped back.

"Shall I just follow you?" she suggested.

The comte stepped forward, tied her hands, pushed her toward the open doorway, and Judyth looked over her shoulder. Grandmother had claimed herself too old to bother escaping. Judyth had declared no desire to continue in such a world as this; she would try another lifetime. They'd both given Magdeleine their magic . . . for what good it would do.

Roussel loomed larger, once Magdeleine stood alone with him. He seemed a different and more dangerous creature than herself, as surely as the panthers in the woods differed from her Cassiopeia. His big, callused hands could do unimaginable damage, should he choose. : . .

But even as Magdeleine considered abandoning the magic, she saw the cats reappearing. Two peeked from Judyth's corner. An orange tabby waited outside the barred window. A white, furry head appeared, staring at her from beneath a straw blind. Then a soft gray cat, with darker points. A big-eared patchwork cat.

And Cassiopeia, the clever white markings on her black face familiar as ever, looked upward from Magdeleine's feet. Perhaps humankind deserved their grisly fate, cats or no cats. But her pet, Magdeleine could not deny.

"Roussel," she said softly, before he could leave.

His back stiffened. She had not spoken to him since the tortures began, had accepted neither gruel nor bread.

She clenched her fist, careful not to let any of Grandmother's powder spill.

"How is your father today?" she asked, her voice uneven.

He turned, squinting suspicion at her sudden interest. "My father . . ."

When she stepped closer, he shadowed her. What large creatures men were. No wonder they could so easily beat and maim and tear . . .

And yet, she could as easily torture cats, and did not. Size excused nothing.

She swallowed her fear. "Do you believe in magic now?"

He frowned in confusion. "If aught of you had magic, you would have escaped."

Opening her hand, she blew sleeping powder into his face.

His eyes widened as he choked, staggered back from her. *No!*

But Grandmother had been a skilled herbalist. Roussel dropped quickly to his knees in the rushes. When he tried to turn back to her, his eyes bright with accusation, he lost balance and fell to his side.

"When one has nine-times-nine lives," she told him, repeating Grandmother's words, "one understands more important things than simple escape."

His eyes fluttered shut.

Cat after cat appeared from their hiding spots then, streaking out of the cell. Magdeleine draped Grandmother's dark blue cloak over her body and stepped through the still-open door, into the dungeon's shadows. Not even the other prisoners—men behind bars, men hanging from chains—seemed to see her. While the rest of the castle's occupants thronged cheering into the courtyard to see Judyth burned, Magdeleine simply . . . left. She climbed the stone stairs from the dungeon, ran beneath the portcullis, and silently crossed the drawbridge behind a parade of over a dozen cats.

This, she thought grimly, was how magic worked.

She faltered when she heard high-pitched screams behind her. They did not sound like Judyth. A roar of spectators drowned them. Ugly.

She ran, circling the village to reach the woods, then the forest proper. She ran past breath, past balance.

When she could no longer run, she forced her bruised body to crawl . . .

Large, hard hands roll her onto her back—and she sees the quiet-eyed guard, Roussel, kneeling over her. "Mother of God," he murmurs, touching her face. "When did you last eat?"

She has no strength to answer. He slings a sack from his shoulder and upends it.

Two small bodies, sleek and furry, slide to the ground. Magdeleine finds voice at last.

The guard looks up at her cry, confused. Then he lifts one of the corpses by the ears. "Rabbits," he tells her.

Rabbits. Not cats . . .

She watches as he builds a fire, skins the rabbits, sets their lean bodies on a spit to roast. He carries a waterskin, from which he pours liquid across her cracked lips. She coughs on it, but swallows some. He rips a piece off her chemise—she flinches at how easily—and dampens it.

He wipes her chin, her cheeks with gentle, callused hands. He bathes her hands, her feet. Then he covers her with something heavy and soft.

Grandmother's cloak. He must have reclaimed it from the thorns.

Roussel talks, as he turns the rabbits. "Thibaud found me, accused me of treason. I . . . I think I killed him."

Should she lament endangering him? Her reasons for escape outweigh his for imprisonment.

The roasting meat makes her so hungry, she cries. Finally, Roussel props her up against his broad arm and shoulder and feeds her tiny pieces with his fingers. She eats very little—but enough to root her back into life. Juices soothe her throat, and the edges of her voice return.

"You're not taking me back?"

He shakes his head. "I cannot go back myself."

"The fire," she manages. "Someone could see. . . ."

"Nobody followed me."

"But Monsieur Pryor?"

"He's dead."

She stares up at his unshaven face, amazed. "You . . . ?"

Roussel shakes his head. "Thibaud told me, before . . . He said the other witch made as if to speak, even as the flames took her. When Pryor leaned nearer, to hear her confession, she grasped him with her legs and pulled him into the pyre. I . . ." His quiet eyes hold hers, confused. "Magic?"

Remembering the screams, Magdeleine wonders

how many women Judyth has saved. A familiar voice howls for attention, and she sees Cassiopeia, still safe, sliding past Roussel's braced knee. Several of the other dungeon cats wait, sitting or lying in the firelight, all watching the man who holds the meat.

"Feed them some?" she asks.

Roussel squints at her.

"Please."

So he gives a piece of rabbit to Cassiopeia. "Why cats?" he asks. "I have never seen so many."

He already knows her as a witch. What harm can there be to tell him?

"Women who can see portents and read the stars—they predict a great sickness coming. 'Twill be a plague such as we have ne'er seen. Our only hope is the cats."

He shakes his head, bewildered.

"It has something to do with the rats," she explains, knowing little more herself.

He considers that, then feeds the other cats pieces of meat as well. Lying wrapped in Grandmother's mantle, Magdeleine notices something *beyond* how gracefully he moves. She notices something about all the cats—large cats and small. Bony cats and supple. Their eyes reflect the campfire in an almost supernatural glow.

Like stars.

And they all sit to one side of him, in one direction.

A trickle of hope threads into Magdeleine's aching heart. *Follow the stars . . .*

The hope taunts and exhausts her; she closes her eyes. When she opens them again 'tis daytime, and the guard sleeps beside her, shaggy head pillowed on his thick arms. She watches him, notices his eyelashes against his unshaven cheeks, the softness of his mouth in sleep.

Men imprison women. They accuse and torture them, beat and rape them . . . *because* they are women. Even if they *are* sisters, mothers, daughters.

Lovers.

Very carefully, Magdeleine skims free of the mantle. She pushes herself up slowly.

Cats watch her, alert.

Magdeleine tries to stand—and, with a cry, collapses atop her companion.

"What?" His sleepy surprise becomes unforeseen humor as she crawls back off him, as he sits up. "What do you need?"

"I . . . just to go. Let me go."

He scowls. He is not holding her.

She stands. Her feet throb, her legs tremble. A few bites of rabbit and a night's sleep can only heal so much.

"You journey to the place the old woman spoke of," realizes Roussel. "Your sacred place."

She says, "Perhaps."

"Let me help you."

"I cannot."

"I have no place else to go."

She says nothing, wishes away the guilt.

"You do not trust me."

"How can I?" Roussel worked for the comte and, through him, the witch hunter. He kept her locked away, merely because other men told him to.

He is a man.

"I helped you," he protests, and his words pierce her. When she spoke them, nobody listened because she was different. Because she was a woman. 'Twas not fair . . .

"It is forbidden," she says, torn.

He says, "So is witchcraft."

And she has no answer.

To be carried through the woods in Roussel's arms disorients Magdeleine in unexpected ways. He cradles her to his broad chest, her head pillowed against his shoulders, her swollen feet dangling. He does not complain.

The cats travel near them, appearing and disappearing through the underbrush, pausing to watch songbirds or chase squirrels.

Magdeleine's doubts assail her worse than wounds. Is she betraying Judyth and Grandmother, her own mother, thousands of years of women? If Roussel betrays *her* . . .

Such a fear burns too badly to hold.

He cannot know the last, secret route to the Goddess sanctuary. At least she knows the legends.

Roussel feeds her water, nuts which he has found. But they speak very little.

'Tis dusk, by the time they reach the Sacred Well of the Goddess.

"Is this it?" the guard asks. He bounces her slightly, to keep her from drooping too low in his arms.

A rivulet runs down a cliffside across the clear pool from them, splashing into the water's surface. It harmonizes with the birdcalls and insect buzz, the chitter of squirrels and the rustle of leaves, soothing Magdeleine as no music ever has. She can *feel* the magic here, can *feel* the hope that waits, a mere breath or two away.

"This is it." A sense of loss closes her throat. Its grip only tightens as the guard wades unhesitating into the pool with her. He sets her carefully in the shallows—and lets her go. The healing water accepts her, flows over her aching body like a caress . . . and yet she feels hollow.

She already misses the warmth of Roussel's body, the regularity of his breath and heartbeat. She hates to betray him, or to leave him to the plague that looms, mere months ahead. And yet . . .

He could so easily betray *her*. Her, and generations of women.

When he says, "I'll find us dinner, while there's

still light," she nods. Then she reaches quickly up to grab his wet hand before he goes.

"Thank you, Roussel." she says when, startled, he looks down at her.

She may not get another chance.

"It is not enough," he says finally, and wades out of the water. "Magdeleine."

After he leaves, the music of the water and the forest surges, soothing, back around her. She sees that the cats have vanished to their own secret routes.

'Tis time.

Magdeleine leans back into the water's embrace, then lifts her feet from the bottom and floats. Twilit shadows dust over her eyelids as she rests in the water's embrace. Her face, knees, and hands bob to its surface, rocking from the cataract. The rest of her sinks lower, supported by unseen forces.

Thus cradled, Magdeleine rests. Heals. Only when she feels strong enough does she open her eyes to a star-dotted, darkening sky . . .

Take a deep breath . . .

And dive.

Just as her mother and Grandmother predicted, the cliff's face vanishes beneath the waterfall, becoming a small cave. The forest's music vanishes under the beat of water slapping the surface. The beat becomes a roar as Magdeleine kicks her feet, scoops water back with her hands, swims through Mother Nature's portal—

And surfaces, reborn, into a similar pool in another world.

"There she is!" calls a female voice, delighted. Women stand on the bank with torches, while others wade into the water to greet Magdeleine. She allows them to draw her into their welcoming arms.

"Isabeau's daughter," some of them say. Her mother's name was, indeed, Isabeau. "She brought the cats."

Several of the dungeon cats throng the water's edge. Others are held and caressed by the women.

"The cats brought me," counters Magdeleine, dizzy, trying to reconcile such kindness with her imprisonment, with a world of torture . . .

One stately woman, handsome with her gray hair cut short, says, "Perhaps both are true."

"You must be hungry," exclaims a blonde woman, her mother's age.

"You must tell us what you know," adds a dark-complected girl, younger than herself.

"*Enough*," calls the stately one. "You overwhelm the child. Go tell the village she is here."

The women reluctantly turn away, some giving Magdeleine hugs or kisses, many of them waving. Some of them say, "Yes, Melusine."

Magdeleine's eyes widen, for Melusine is a legendary fairy.

"'Tis a family name," assures the older woman—but her eyes laugh, as a fairy's might. "You are Magdeleine?"

She nods, still overwhelmed.

"Thank the Lady you are safe. And that you brought the cats! Or let them bring you," she concedes, before Magdeleine can protest again.

And yet . . . "Someone else brought me," she admits. Now she must confess her own betrayal of the sanctuary that has so welcomed her.

But Melusine only nods knowingly and asks, "Do you trust him, child?"

"I am one woman! How can I risk—"

"This," insists the priestess, "is a place of magic."

She need not add, *and hope*.

Magdeleine stands straighter in the water. She speaks the words even as she finally, truly believes them. "I trust him."

"Then go fetch him," says Melusine. "Our circle has already agreed. We may not survive the plagues, much less the Age of Pisces, without allowing men back in. Select men, of course. Those who have earned our trust. It is only . . . fair."

Magdeleine smiles, backs up in the thick, sloshing water—then dives.

When she surfaces, she sees Roussel. He sits forlornly at the water's edge, his forearms braced on his knees, scratching Cassiopeia behind the ears.

Both he and the cat look up at the same time.

"Magdeleine," he says, emotions warring in his quiet eyes. As she struggles slowly, dripping, from the water, he wades in to offer a hand. His own is dry, large. But gentle. He steadies her past the slippery rocks at the edge and then, following her out, wraps Grandmother's mantle about her. "Then you are a witch," he admits.

"Are you afraid of witches, *'sieur?*" she asks, picking up her cat. Cassiopeia tolerates Magdeleine's kisses only a moment before rejecting the wet embrace, leaping back to the ground. She has her own way in.

Roussel asks, "Are they all like you, *'demoiselle?*"

"Come find out."

This time, *he* takes *her* hand. It occurs to her how brave this is, considering what he has been told all his life about witches. Yes, he merits her trust.

When she turns back to the pond, the Sacred Well of the Goddess, she gasps in delight.

The water is alight with the reflection of dancing stars.

GAYLE GREENO

GHATTEN'S GAMBIT
In THE FARTHEST SEEKING, a new generation of human Seekers and their catlike Ghatti companions journey into a dangerous wilderness, while in the tunnels beneath Marchmont's Capital a deadly piece of long-forgotten technology is about to be rediscovered. . . .

☐ **SUNDERLIES SEEKING Book 1**   0-88677-805-0—$6.99

☐ **THE FARTHEST SEEKING Book 2**

0-88677-897-2—$6.99

And don't miss:

THE GHATTI'S TALE

☐ **FINDERS, SEEKERS Book 1**   0-88677-550-7—$6.99

☐ **MINDSPEAKER'S CALL Book 2**   0-88677-579-5—$6.99

☐ **EXILES' RETURN Book 3**   0-88677-655-4—$6.99

Prices slightly higher in Canada   **DAW: 147**

Payable in U.S. funds only. No cash/COD accepted. Postage & handling: U.S./CAN. $2.75 for one book, $1.00 for each additional, not to exceed $6.75; Int'l $5.00 for one book, $1.00 each additional. We accept Visa, Amex, MC ($10.00 min.), checks ($15.00 fee for returned checks) and money orders. Call 800-788-6262 or 201-933-9292, fax 201-896-8569; refer to ad #300.

Penguin Putnam Inc. **P.O. Box 12289, Dept. B** **Newark, NJ 07101-5289**	**Bill my:** ☐Visa ☐MasterCard ☐Amex_____(expires) Card#_____

Please allow 4-6 weeks for delivery.   Signature_____
Foreign and Canadian delivery 6-8 weeks.

Bill to:

Name_____

Address_____City_____

State/ZIP_____

Daytime Phone #_____

Ship to:

Name_____ Book Total $_____

Address_____ Applicable Sales Tax $_____

City_____ Postage & Handling $_____

State/Zip_____ Total Amount Due $_____

This offer subject to change without notice.

Lisanne Norman
THE SHOLAN ALLIANCE SERIES

"will hold you spellbound"—*Romantic Times*

☐ **TURNING POINT**   0-88677-575-2—$6.99

☐ **FORTUNE'S WHEEL**   0-88677-675-9—$6.99

☐ **FIRE MARGINS**   0-88677-718-6—$6.99

☐ **RAZOR'S EDGE**   0-88677-766-6—$6.99

☐ **DARK NADIR**   0-88677-829-6—$6.99

☐ **STRONGHOLD RISING** 0-88677-898-0—$6.99

Delicate negotiations are underway with the Primes, a preciously unknown faction of the hated Valtegan race. But the Sholans and Humans must first avert a full-fledged rebellion—one begun in a laboratory engaged in illegal breeding experiments. . . .

Prices slightly higher in Canada   **DAW: 180**

IRENE RADFORD

THE DRAGON NIMBUS HISTORY

☐ **THE DRAGON'S TOUCHSTONE (Book One)**
0-88677-744-5—$6.99

☐ **THE LAST BATTLEMAGE (Book Two)** 0-88677-774-7—$6.99

☐ **THE RENEGADE DRAGON (Book Three)** 0-88677-855-7—$6.99

The great magical wars have come to an end. But in bringing peace, Nimbulan, the last Battlemage, has lost his powers. Dragon magic is the only magic legal to practice. And the kingdom's only hope against dangerous technology lies in the one place to which no dragon will fly . . .

THE DRAGON NIMBUS TRILOGY

☐ **THE GLASS DRAGON (Book One)**   0-88677-634-1—$6.99

☐ **THE PERFECT PRINCESS (Book Two)**   0-88677-678-3—$6.99

☐ **THE LONELIEST MAGICIAN (Book Three)**
0-88677-709-7—$6.99

Eluki bes Shahar

THE HELLFLOWER SERIES

☐ **HELLFLOWER (Book 1)**   UE2475—$3.99

Butterfly St. Cyr had a well-deserved reputation as an honest and dependable smuggler. But when she and her partner, a highly illegal artificial intelligence, rescued Tiggy, the son and heir to one of the most powerful of the hellflower mercenary leaders, it looked like they'd finally taken on more than they could handle. For his father's enemies had sworn to see that Tiggy and Butterfly never reached his home planet alive. . . .

☐ **DARKTRADERS (Book 2)**   UE2507—$4.50

With her former partner Paladin—the death-to-possess Old Federation artificial intelligence—gone off on a private mission, Butterfly didn't have anybody to back her up when Tiggy's enemies decided to give the word "ambush" a whole new and all-too-final meaning.

☐ **ARCHANGEL BLUES (Book 3)**   UE2543—$4.50

Darktrader Butterfly St. Cyr and her partner Tiggy seek to complete the mission they started in DARKTRADERS, to find and destroy the real Archangel, Governor-General of the Empire, the being who is determined to wield A.I. powers to become the master of the entire universe.